I0654491

ICE AND FIRE

A Suspenseful Thriller Set in Hawaiʻi

THE CURIOUS CELLIST
BOOK 2

PAT DUNLAP EVANS

PUBLISHER'S NOTES

This is a work of fiction. Names, characters, businesses, organizations, and incidents are used fictitiously or are the products of the author's imagination. Any resemblance to actual persons, living or dead, business establishments, organizations, events, or locales is used solely for literary purposes and is entirely coincidental to any factual occurrences, past, present, or future.

Style Note: Fictitious news articles in this book employ the Associated Press (AP) style, which does not include diacritical marks.

This novel has been digitally produced. Despite our best efforts, errors may appear. To submit a correction, please e-mail AMChaiLiterary@gmail.com. Include the chapter number, error, and correction.

Copyright © April 11, 2025, by Pat Dunlap Evans

Text revisions and corrections, July 16, 2025. Audiobook published, July 16, 2025. Note: Audiobook pronunciations are best possible using Amazon's Virtual Voice Beta.

Book Two of the Curious Cellist Series

Cover design: Pam Boyd Roberts

Cover Photo: © DesignPics / Shutterstock

Published in the United States of America by A.M. Chai Literary, a business registered in Texas. All rights reserved, including the right to reproduce this book or portions thereof in any form whatsoever, without prior written permission.

For permissions or rights, please contact AMChaiLiterary@gmail.com.

ISBN: 979-8-9927090-2-5 (Print Paperback)

ISBN: 979-8-9927090-0-1 (Kindle)

ISBN: 979-8-9927090-1-8 (E-Pub)

❀ Formatted with Vellum

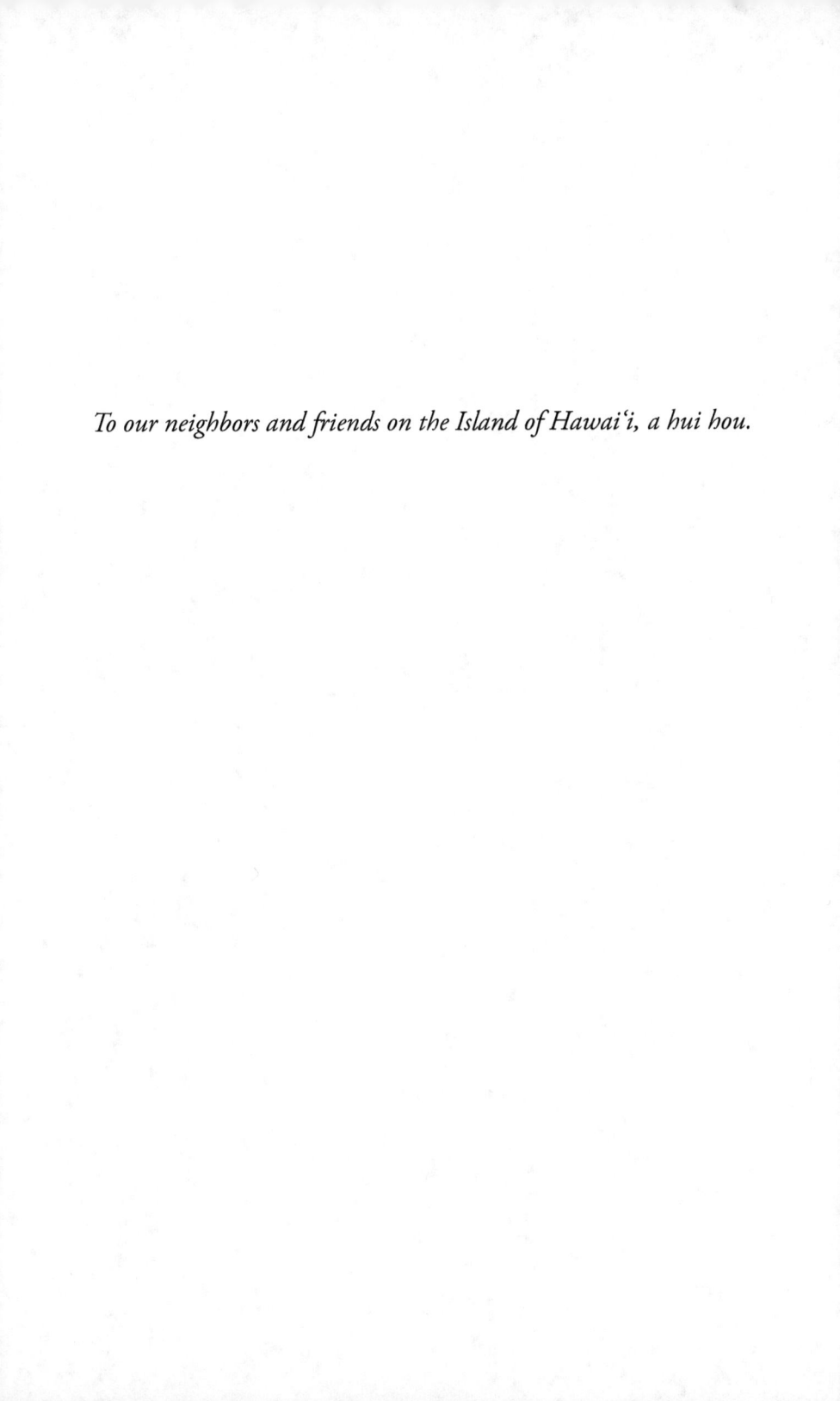

To our neighbors and friends on the Island of Hawai‘i, a hui hou.

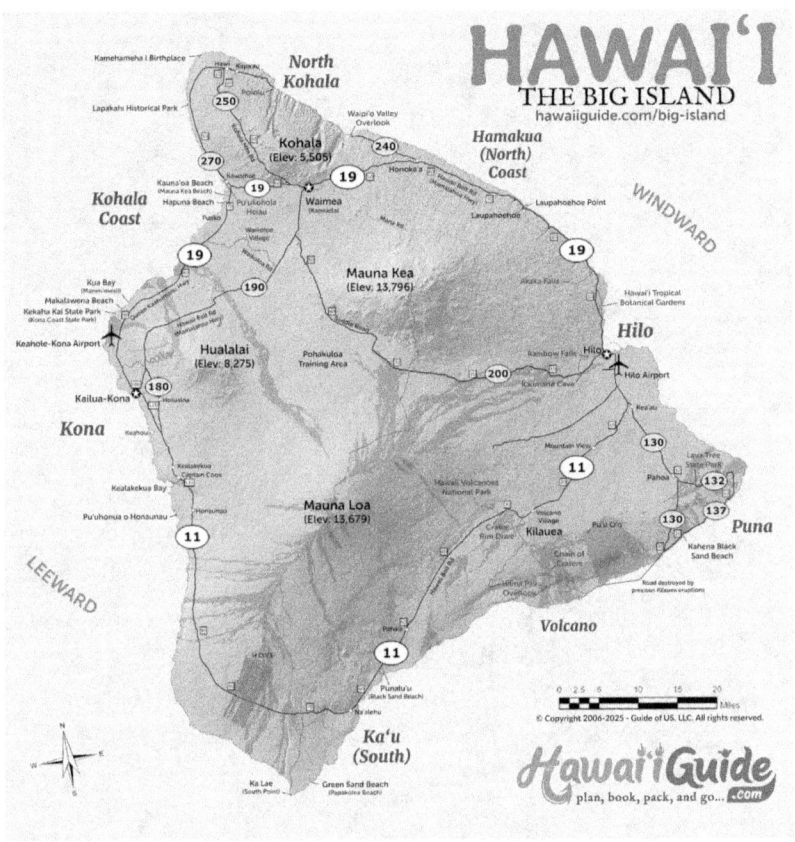

Map of the Big Island courtesy of
Hawai'i Guide Travel Resources
John and Tori Derrick
HawaiiGuide.com

Chapter One

KANAKA ADVOCATE DAILY

Renowned Japanese Astronomer Dies

HILO, Hawaii (AP) — A resident astronomer with Japan's Pleiades Observatory died yesterday in what appears to be a hunting accident at Maunakea Puuhonua Holoholona — locally known as MPH — a federally leased wildlife management area on the slopes of Maunakea.

Fellow hunters stumbled across the astronomer's body in a section where only bow-and-arrow hunting is allowed.

Emergency responders could not revive the man, who was shot in the neck by what authorities initially surmised was a stray arrow.

An autopsy is pending. The victim's name will not be released until his family is notified.

Representatives at Pleiades Observatory offices did not respond to requests for comment.

According to Haruto Yamamura, president of a visiting astronomy club from Japan, the well-known researcher had been scheduled to host a star gazing event later that evening for club members at The Onizuka Center for International

Astronomy Visitor Information Station on Maunakea, commonly called the VIS.

Yamamura said through an interpreter, "The Japanese nation has lost a leader in planetary research. His planned topic was, 'The Legacy of NASA's Kepler Space Telescope in the Discovery of Earth-Like Exoplanets.'"

Monty Harris, R.P. Knight Observatory communications director, remarked, "Hawaii's close-knit astronomy community is stunned by this loss. Among astronomy's many goals, planetary researchers hope to find Earth's twin someday. The Japanese researcher's work centered on confirming if recently discovered exoplanets beyond our solar system had habitable atmospheres and surfaces."

After being pronounced dead at the scene, the Japanese researcher's body was taken to the medical examiner's office in Hilo.

Details will be provided as they become available.

For information, contact reporter Wallace Huppenthall at (808) 765-1212.

Chapter Two

FROM YOUR BEST FRIEND

Marie Ingles

As I scrolled through a local news article about a Japanese astronomer who was killed in a hunting accident, my laptop dinged with a new email. The sender's name was "Your Best Friend."

Normally, I would have deleted this as spam, except for the subject line. It read, "Urgent Update from Dubai."

Dubai. Paranoia set in. Was this from my former bestie, Lena Verano? Was she still in Dubai? Does Lena know Ryan and I moved to Hawai'i?

✿

A MONTH AGO, RYAN AND I DID THE NUTTIEST THING AND flew one way from Dallas to Hawai'i Island, where we rented a spacious condo in the Hōkele Kilohana area for six months. The condo is completely furnished and has two expansive patios—called *lanai*. Every morning, we take our coffees out to view the resort's tall swaying palms; red, yellow, and white flowering hibiscus; the pink blooms of Hong Kong orchid trees; and the far-distant summits of Maunakea, Kohala, and Hualālai mountains across a placid golf course lake.

This dream-like move was not what we had in mind when Ryan and I married last year. But Ryan experienced a career crisis and sold the controlling interest in his Dallas-based criminal defense firm to his partner, Colleen Ballard.

That didn't mean he retired completely. Colleen video-called us this morning.

From our lanai, Ryan and I peered at my laptop's image of Colleen's pasty skin and matching beige linen suit, while beyond our heads, she could see palm branches fluttering and golf carts zipping by.

Colleen's envious smile brightened. "Oh, my, you two have escaped to golf paradise. But thanks to human greed, crime is up here. Let me know if you have time to work on any cases."

I nervously glanced at Ryan, only to see his ocean-blue eyes ignite. But before he could say yes, I interrupted him a bit too sweetly. "Ryan, with nine-hour flights between here and Dallas, don't you think you and I need more time to settle in?"

His disheartened sigh was loud enough for Colleen to hear.

She laughed sardonically. "Ryan, let me know when Marie decides you are ready. I realize you needed a break from the frenzy, but we are so overloaded, I could use both of you, especially Marie, as our ever-efficient 'Nancy-D.'"

After Colleen signed off, Ryan huffed and gave me an ironic glare. "Sounds like she wants my wife more than me."

"She can't bill your fees for simply investigating."

"But my lovely wife won't let me take a case. So, how can I bill anything at all?" He half-chuckled, then went inside.

I understood his disappointment since I also felt the pull to play sleuth. Over the past month, we had re-explored most everything to see on the island, save for a sunset tour to the summit of Maunakea, the state's highest peak. That's where many of the world's top astronomical observatories are located.

But after a month of living here, I think Ryan and I both wonder, is this all there is? The beach. The glorious views. The ideal weather. Yes, those are amazing things, but we need a life too. That means hobbies, cultural pursuits, and friends. People.

The people we meet around the resort are polite, charming, and helpful, but they are either tourists, the resort's managers, or the maintenance workers. That means we'll have to become joiners. Maybe join the small orchestra in Waimea. Or see what the West Hawai'i Astronomy Group is about. Ryan could join Rotary in Kona. Or the men's golf group at the resort.

Admittedly, we needed a break from *some* people in Dallas, but the main reasons we left were to end the marathon our lives became after we married, one year to the day after I was acquitted of killing Luca Scarlatti. By that time, I'd been working full-time at Ryan's firm, alongside his private investigator, Billy Bob Hughes, and Billy Bob's computer analyst (and girlfriend), Natalie Sherman. So, instead of being a newlywed, my days were quickly consumed by investigations, and my nights were gobbled by the Metroplex Opera, where Ryan served as board chair, and I continued as first-chair cello.

All of this activity was not long after Lena Verano judo'd my first husband Cole Donovan over a penthouse balcony rail, not long after a white limo rumbled over his athletic body that had landed on the street below, and not long after Lena framed me for killing Luca Scarlatti, a crime she and her bisexual boy-toy Terrance Nichols had committed.

Oh, dear. There my mind went with another Memory Lane. I try to resist these flashbacks, yet nothing stops the anger and pain.

When Billy Bob later received transcripts that proved Lena

and Terry had killed Luca, and Lena admitted to killing Cole too, I thought, "My God, what kind of psycho could kill my twins' father and then rush over to my house to take care of us?"

At least Lena and Terry are on the FBI's Ten Most Wanted Fugitives list. Still, we've had no news of them since Billy Bob tracked the pair to Dubai. The FBI requested extradition, but the United Arab Emirates is biding its time. It's likely the two are still there since I don't think either could leave without an alarm going off somewhere.

I live for the day when Lena Verano will be captured.

That's why this email intrigued me. "Urgent Update from Dubai." During my time at Ryan's firm, I learned a lot as an unpaid sleuth. Number one: Never let a gut hunch pass you by. That intuition frequently chimed in when a witness was lying.

My nickname "Nancy-D" came from an insult I'd overheard one day when Billy Bob, Natalie, and I strolled past the staff break room. Out an ajar door, we heard a gossipy voice.

"I wonder how much the boss's wife gets paid. That Marie Ingles is nothing more than a menopausal Nancy Drew. You know, that girl detective."

Everybody in the break room laughed.

So did Billy Bob and Natalie, who silently snickered behind their doubled hands.

I issued a loud "Ahem" to let the staff know I'd heard their insults. From inside, I heard someone whisper, "Hush, it's *her!*" Then I peeked in the door long enough for them to see me, and I gave the receptionist a look that could melt her Tupperware.

She gasped and turned her back as if she could disappear.

But her nickname for me stuck. Wisely, Billy Bob and Natalie shortened it to Nancy-D and did not include the term "menopausal."

For investigative purposes, Natalie even set up a fake Facebook profile for a lovely redhead named "Nancy D. Drew, although Ryan hated the idea. With his ever-so-blue eyes squinting at me across my desk, he asked, "Marie, I thought you gave up MakeFriends after that harem of snobs from the Metroplex Opera Guild attacked you. What did they call themselves…D'Posse, right?"

"Don't worry. I've blocked all D'Posse members from my 'Nancy D. Drew' and 'Marie Ingles' pages. And I only use the Marie page to stay in touch with my brother and his kids."

"Please keep it that way. For all I know, Doreen is trying to peer into our living room," he huffed.

He didn't realize, but using the Nancy D. Drew account, our investigative team could locate witnesses who helped solve cases of whodunit (the crime) or who had it (the money).

Being Nancy-D was fun, and I grew to relish my day job almost as much as my cello concerts at night, although Ryan and I were exhausted by the long hours. Three nights a week, we would grab a quick bite after work, then head to Claridge Performance Hall, so named after the opera's founder, Rebecca Claridge. While I rehearsed with the orchestra and cast, Ryan pored over opera finances.

On performance nights, we carted our hanging bags into the law firm's restrooms where we wriggled into glitzy formal gear, then raced to the elaborate, pre-concert socials for major donors in the Green Room.

After performances, I met Ryan at glittering cast parties, where donors mingled with the vocal stars. Ryan's role at these events was to glad-hand the largest donors, while mine was to plaster on a smile and ignore the glares of D'Posse members who *loved* to think I had killed Luca.

After a while, this intense schedule took its toll. Each of us knew something had to give, but Ryan's reasons for wanting to sell his firm surprised me.

"I don't want you to quit the orchestra. Or stop your

investigative work, unless you want to. But the other day I blew up at Colleen — earnest, brilliant, beige-suited Colleen. When I apologized later, I told her I was burned out. And darn if she didn't offer to buy the firm. I'll have to finance her deal, but if you're okay with this, she will become the managing partner of the re-branded Ballard / Ingles while I move to 'of counsel' status. That means I can take cases when I want, but I can spend more time with you. That is, when you're ready to take time off too."

I didn't tell him then, but his decision made me fearful. We'd had many upheavals over the past two years. Cole's death. My murder trial. Finding Cole's hidden money. Falling in love. Getting married. Working two jobs. And now, Ryan's sudden desire to spend more time with me meant I'd have to stop playing Nancy-D.

I certainly didn't want to quit the orchestra. I'd worked too hard to get the first-chair role. Still, something had to give. And since Ryan wouldn't be at the firm daily, it was better for me not to stay on, since the staffers clearly resented me, even though I didn't even get paid.

And so, after Ryan became of-counsel, our weekday schedule suddenly became sleeping late, brunches out, midday fitness jaunts, lounging by our backyard pool, afternoon cello practice, my evening rehearsals or concerts, and Ryan's board meetings.

We had just settled into Ryan's "of counsel" lifestyle, when Ryan peered at me over a Scotch, one Sunday by the pool. "Marie, why in the hell are we still in Dallas? We've got money to live anywhere. Europe and California are way too crowded, but you can't beat the climate in Hawai'i."

I peered at him over my sunglasses. "Hawai'i? Where did that come from?"

"Our honeymoon, remember? We both fell in love with the

expanse of the Big Island. Those massive volcanic mountains. The miraculous rainbows and wide beaches. Heck, even taking a drive made us happy, bouncing along the Kohala Coast, or winding over Kohala Mountain and then barreling downhill into Waimea for lunch. And we still need to see a sunset atop Maunakea. That's a bucket list to-do. What do you think? I'm game for an adventure."

"But what about my first-chair position?"

"Maybe you can get some solo performances. Or maybe there's a chamber group."

"What about your opera board duties?"

"Leave the B-O-R-E-D duties to the geezers. I'm forty-three, we've got money, and I'm weary of squeezing funds from donors' wallets. Sure, I can take a legal case to stay busy, but before I get entangled, let's go on a quest. The Big Island could be our dream come true."

Because Ryan was two Scotches into this fantasy, I murmured a dismissive, "Let's talk this over tomorrow when you are, well, not drinking Scotch."

He gave me a sidelong frown, displeased with my sarcasm. "As you wish," he said in a snarky imitation of Westley, the farm boy in *The Princess Bride*, who meant "I love you" each time he said, "As you wish."

The next day, I didn't mention Hawai'i. Neither did Ryan. Several weeks went by with no discussion of his boozy Hawaiian dream.

But at the third weekend's cast party, after I'd played a solo in Mozart's *Don Giovanni*, I again smiled and nodded at the glaring opera Guild D'Posse ladies who were fawning over Ryan to the point I walked over and put my arm around him to remind the ladies (and my naïve husband) that he was very definitely remarried.

My handsome guy did not know how to fend off admiring

women. For decades, he'd hidden behind massive, thick-lens horn rims, only to have laser correction a few years ago and discover he was suddenly attractive. Especially to the D'Posse snobs who loved to glower at me after my cello solos, then murmur shallow praise with a hint of a sneer.

"Isn't it embarrassing to spread your legs so wide around your instrument?"

"Don't you orchestra people hate playing under the stage in that dank pit?"

"Do you get calluses from playing that thing?"

That's when Ryan's escape plan appealed. Why *did* we grip, grin, and pretend to enjoy the people who so unfairly blamed me for crimes I did not commit?

Dallas media headlines had vindicated me months before, after police found Luca Scarlatti's amputated penis in a cooler at Lena's Verano Highland Park Funeral Home. But these women still doubted me, even after tests proved that Lena's DNA was found on the baggie that held the gruesome tidbit.

Over and above that, the many millions my late husband Cole had pilfered from investors and Metroplex Opera in his Ponzi scheme were recovered and returned, albeit at only one for every five dollars. But why keep blaming me for those things too?

On our ride home, Ryan answered my question with a sweet smile. "Because you are so beautiful and talented."

He said that with such adoration, I melted his way and put my head on his chest. As he drove with one hand, he pulled my cherry blossom hairpins out with the other and gently stroked my hair. Then he caressed my cheek and lips as my hand found its way to him. We both became so aroused, we barely made it inside before shucking our clothes in the utility room and launching our bodies onto the massive kitchen island.

The quartz was cold on my back, but I didn't care. I simply needed Ryan the same way he needed me. And when we both collapsed in relief, we lay there listening to the other breathe. Ryan even rolled on his side and slept for a bit. Right there on the kitchen island.

The next morning over coffee, I revived the topic. "That was an interesting island experience last night, but have you thought more about moving to the island of Hawai'i?"

"No. You were right to spoil that silliness. In sober light, Hawai'i seems a bit extreme."

"But it also sounds sexy, even 'in your face,' especially after last night's cast party. Too many in our social circle would rather believe lies than the truth. And flirt with my husband. Or sneer at me for my calloused fingertips and knees spread wide. As Tina LeBlanc and your dear ex Doreen sniggered at me, I realized that a change, even as extreme as your Hawai'i fantasy, might be good for both of us. A wild, crazy, romantic change with glorious views."

He studied me over his readers. "Are you serious?"

"Stone-sober. Why *are* we in Dallas? Our collective children are out of the nest. With the internet, you can be a lawyer anywhere. And maybe I could do guest solos with the Oahu orchestra. But after last night, I refuse to do things that make me angry, jealous, or sad. Why not explore the meaning of 'aloha'? For how long, we can decide."

Ryan's eyes positively twinkled as he toasted me with his coffee. "Let's rent a condo at Hōkele Kilohana for six months. That should tell us if the Big Island is truly the dream."

Before either of us could change our minds, we jumped on a rental site and chose a spacious end unit at the Royal Palms, a lovely development with a golf course, beach club, fitness center, business center, lap pool, and path to the wide, arched beach. Over the next two weeks, we boxed and shipped our important papers to a retail mailbox center in Waikoloa Village. Then we packed my cello, our laptops, two suitcases of clothes, swimsuits, and flip-flops — rather, "slippahs" — and giddily locked our Highland Park home. We left the keys with a realtor to manage or sell the property if the move becomes permanent.

After our almost nine-hour nonstop flight landed at the "Ellison Onizuka Kona International Airport at Keahole," or KOA, we walked down the curving airport ramp, heads held high, trying to feel we were "home."

We grabbed our luggage at what must be the friendliest baggage claim area on the planet, then drove our SUV rental northwest to a small grocery near the Hōkele Kilohana. There, we bought some ridiculously expensive basics and wearily drove off in search of our condo. Once in the garage, an exhausted Ryan dragged in the bags, while I found enough cookware to scramble eggs and make toast for dinner. After that, we quickly showered and went to bed.

We slept nine straight hours, but the sun still wasn't up as we staggered out on our lanai for our first cups of Kona coffee. As daylight filtered over the resort's golf course lake, we oohed and ahhed at our peekaboo views of Kohala, Maunakea, and Hualālai mountains. And in the far distance, we could just make out the low silhouette of mighty Mauna Loa, the world's largest land mass, a good sixty miles away.

BUT NOW, EVEN AFTER WE ESCAPED TO AN ISLAND paradise, I could not ignore the mysterious email from "Your Best Friend." I knew better than to click it open.

The preview revealed the message's first line. "I'm sorry."

I murmured to the sender, "I've learned a lot since you left."

I clicked "show the original" and then forwarded all tracking data to Billy Bob and Natalie's encrypted email accounts at Ballard / Ingles.

Next, I turned my laptop toward Ryan. "Take a look. I bet Lena Verano sent me this. We need to schedule a Zoom call with Billy Bob and Natalie."

Chapter Three

HERE WE GO AGAIN

Marie Ingles

D ays before our scheduled Zoom video call with Billy Bob and Natalie, Colleen Ballad surprised us with a 5:00 a.m. phone call.

Dead-dog asleep, Ryan did not hear his mobile vibrating, so I grabbed it and tiptoed outside to our bedroom's lanai. I whispered, "Colleen, Ryan's still asleep. We love you, but it's 5:00 a.m. here. May I call you back about noon, your time?"

"This is urgent, Marie. The firm got a jail-cell call from an astronomer with UT's Big Bend Observatory. He was on vacation, visiting some buddies on Hawai'i Island, but was arrested for killing a Japanese researcher."

"I read about that. The article said it was a hunting accident, wasn't it?"

"Police say it's murder. The Japanese fellow was killed by the same type of arrow the Texas astronomer used that day for hunting. He swears he didn't do it and is crazy-scared."

"I know how that feels."

"Of course you do. And Ryan got you out of that jam, thankfully. But here's the deal. A wealthy bigwig on the board of Big Bend Observatory wants to hire Ryan to defend the Texan. But, since the murder victim was killed on land that is leased by the federal government, this will be a federal case. I'll have to find a Hawai'i attorney to sponsor Ryan *pro hac vice.*"

"Good gosh. What did you call that?"

"*Pro hac vice.* That means, 'for this instance only.' Ryan can serve as lead counsel if a Hawai'i attorney sponsors him. They'll handle court filings and so forth. These relationships happen all the time. There are a few applications and fees —"

I opened the bedroom's sliding door and went back inside. "*Pro hac vice,* huh? Ryan? Wake up. It's Colleen. You've got your wish. A case."

Chapter Four

NEW CLIENT, NEW PARTNERS

Marie Ingles

This past Monday, Ryan and I flew to Honolulu. In a brightly lit interview room at the Federal Detention Center in Honolulu, we met our local council. The managing partner, Mike Iona, looked to be in his mid-fifties. A muscular man, lushly dark-skinned, with a wide mouth and broad nose, likely of Polynesian descent, although he didn't volunteer his ancestry. But as I double-checked his business card, it listed his first name as Makoa, not Mike, and that sounded Pacific Islander to me.

I made a note to ask about its meaning later.

The female half of our local counsel was an aging Britney Spears look-alike who received a double-take from me and Ryan, but for different reasons. Ryan's double-take was likely because she was sexually attractive in a trashy way, but I had one of those immediate chemical reactions that told me she was going to be trouble.

I'm guessing she was thirty-five, tanned, and shapely. Her hair was surf-blown blonde, swept up in a messy do that revealed untouched brown roots. When she zealously presented her card to Ryan, it read, "Sonya Pruitt, Esquire," while at the bottom in teeny type, it said, "Diamond Client Champion."

She crooned, "I cannot tell you how thrilled I am to meet the renowned Ryan Ingles. Big Mike was ecstatic to be involved with such a high-profile mainland firm."

I made another note to ask Ryan about Sonya's Diamond Client Champion rating. I also wondered if we should call Mike Iona, "Big Mike," like Sonya did.

Mike was the one to introduce us to our new client, Nocona Parker, a quirky fellow with an angular face, hair parted in the center, two long brown braids, and a soft tenor twang.

He quickly volunteered that he was descended from Quanah Parker, the last chief of the Comanches who once pillaged the northwestern regions of Texas. "I'm his ninth-generation grandson, born from one of Quanah Parker's eight wives. Her name was ToPay. Quanah Parker's father's name was Peta Nocona, so that's where my first name comes from," Nocona recited with pride.

Mike Iona, the male of our new co-counsel partners, asked, "So, I guess there's no connection to the Parker Ranch?"

As Nocona shook his head no, I scanned his face for signs of Native American heritage. He had high cheekbones, deep-set and energetic hazel eyes, and a downturned mouth, although his skin color was the same beige as Colleen Ballard's.

Ryan interrupted with a probing voice. "I find it intriguing that you describe your Native American pedigree before protesting your innocence."

"I thought that was obvious. I'm tellin' you, this entire deal is a nightmare. I just got here a week ago. Came to visit some college buddies. They're R.A.s at Knight — that's resident astronomers. I'm staying at a buddy's apartment. All I did was go hunting at that wildlife refuge. I can't pronounce it, but everybody calls it MPH."

"Maunakea Puʻuhonua Holoholona. It's a federal wildlife management area that holds recreational hunts to help control wild animal populations," Mike Iona said.

Nocona nodded. "Right, that's how to say it." Then he tried to pronounce the name again but bumbled it, laughed, and shook his head. "I'll have to practice."

Ryan smiled. "We all need to practice. Now, tell us all that happened."

"Well, later that night, I was in the shower when cops bashed in the bathroom door. Seemed like six of them dragged me buck-naked to my bed. They slammed me down, cuffed me, and hustled me to a van, wrapped in nothing but a fuckin' towel. Oh, pardon me, ladies."

"Not to worry, Nocona, Ryan will —" I said.

Mike jumped in. "We've filed a complaint. Some county-level cops get fanatical when they've got a murder case."

I couldn't tell if Mike was defending the local cops or trying to take charge.

Ryan interrupted my musings with an assured voice that reminded me of the day he came to my rescue at the Dallas police station, what seemed like eons ago.

"Nocona, I'm sorry you've experienced such abusive treatment. You can be sure your Oahu-based counsel, as well as Ballard / Ingles of Dallas, will represent your interests to the max. I will serve as lead attorney, while our island partners will steer us through the state's legal requirements and procedures. Now, please describe each detail leading to your arrest."

For the next hour, Nocona recited details about his hunting trip at MPH.

"My buddies helped me get the licenses and permits to hunt. The Big Island has a huge problem with overpopulation of wild animals that have no natural predators. I'm sure you've seen 'em — goats and sheep roaming the highways, along with babies after babies, dodging cars, becoming roadkill."

He was spot on. Much of the island's "dry side," the northwestern portion, remains denuded by scattered herds.

Mike appeared dismayed. "Oh, and don't forget invasive plants like fountain grass and *kiawe* trees. You Texans call them Mesquite. And then there are feral pigs and mongoose that eat anything that attempts to live, from Wiliwili or Koa tree sprouts to the eggs and chicks of Nēnē — that's our state bird."

"People come from all over the world to hunt here. But I have no clue how one of my arrows wound up in this guy's neck. It sure didn't come off my bowstring. Police said the serial numbers on the arrow that killed him were in line with other arrows in my quiver."

Sonya interrupted. "Clue me in. Why not use a gun?"

"MPH allows only archery in certain areas, like for hunting game mammals. You can use shotguns for birds and turkeys," Mike said.

Nocona's eyes turned golden with delight. "Getting to hunt with bow and arrow on such expansive grounds was a kick. I mean, it's another world up there. I'd planned to donate my harvest to a food bank that preps the meat so locals can buy it. My buddy set this all up."

"What's his name?" Mike asked.

"Marlin Fischer."

We each did double-takes.

"Yeah, I know, 'Marlin Fischer' is a goofy name for a Hispanic guy who hunts and fishes. His dad — Mr. Fischer — hosts fishing tours in Cabo San Lucas, so that's how Marlin got his first name. We were roommates at Caltech."

I asked, "Why did you mail your archery gear to the Knight Observatory offices? Why not to your buddy's apartment?"

"Marlin warned me that package delivery at his apartments was iffy. Porch pirates."

Ryan paused, as if gathering courage to deliver a rather blunt question. "Do you think your buddy killed the Japanese astronomer and blamed it on you?"

"No way. He wasn't even at the hunt."

"Did he have a grudge against this Japanese researcher?"

"I wouldn't call it a grudge. I mean, astronomers want to be the first to discover this or that, so we keep our data hush-hush until we publish. After that, most data become public. Especially if our work was financed by government grants. So, yes, astronomy is competitive, but it's also collaborative. Otherwise, we'd have to reinvent the wheel with every project."

Mike Iona perked up. "You got arrested because your arrows have the same color feathers and serial numbers?"

"My arrows are custom-made, with fletching to match Caltech colors — orange and white."

"The feds are reaching. The arrow similarities seem to be the only evidence. There's no motive and no witnesses. I can almost guarantee Ryan can get these charges dropped," Mike said.

Sonya fiddled with a frizzy strand and licked her lips as if auditioning for a movie role. "How many arrows were missing from your…what do you call the thing-ee?"

"Quiver. My quiver holds six. All of them are still there. But I mailed extra arrows, not sure how many. I should've counted, but I wanted to be ready in case I got to hunt a second day. Sometimes when your arrow misses, you can't find it, no matter how long you look. But I found all six that day. So, this other arrow, well, I don't know where that came from."

Ryan asked, "Where are your extras?"

"The feds probably have them."

"Well, someone got his hands on at least one. Does your apartment have security video?"

"I don't think so. Marlin's place is kinda Banana Republic."

"We'll interview him to find out more. Ballard / Ingles not only represents you, but we also conduct extensive investigations to gather rebutting evidence. My law firm has two private investigators at your disposal. I should say three, as my brilliant wife works as an investigative administrative assistant."

I think I blushed.

Sonya interrupted Ryan's compliment. "Nocona, when you have out-of-state council, our firm handles the red tape and initial court appearances, like bail hearings. We're also supposed to monitor Ballard / Ingles' activities to make sure they follow the Hawai'i Rules of Professional Conduct." She paused, waiting for I don't know what, then giggled, "But I'm sure we won't have any ethical issues. After all, you've got one hell of a courtroom champ in Mr. Ryan Ingles."

As Sonya's green eyes flashed Ryan's way, I thought to myself, "Here's another one, a woman on the make for my hunky husband." Even worse, I hated feeling that same old jealousy creep in. During my marriage to Cole, I doubted his fidelity for good reasons. And I'd recently escaped the flirtatious Guild D'Posse in Dallas. Now I felt insecure about this sleazy Miss Diamond Client Champion, whatever that meant.

Who was I these days but a forty-year-old woman with a cello in my upstairs closet?

As Ryan grinned back at Sonya, I reminded myself that every man enjoys flattery, even good ol' "Diver" Ingles, the all-American linebacker we shallow collegiate cheerleaders dismissed as too homely to date, since we couldn't even see his eyes behind his goggle-like eyeglasses. But after laser surgery, oh, they surfaced so pacifically blue. That's not the only reason I fell in love with him. Ryan was there for me when I needed him most, so why would I doubt him now?

WHILE WAITING FOR OUR RETURN FLIGHT TO KONA, A text dinged on both of our phones. Billy Bob said he had forwarded the mysterious email message to his contacts at the FBI.

"Since it's FBI business, we won't hear anything for a while," he texted.

I texted back, "I cannot wait to see Lena escorted off a plane in handcuffs. And I hope she'll get what she gave me. Pure hell."

Chapter Five

MY SIDE OF THE STORY

Lena Verano

D amn it! Marie didn't open my email, or so says this app Terry installed on my iPad. The app's on a private network, a "VPN." I think that means a Very Private Network. Or maybe it's Virtual. Oh, who cares? Terry is the nerd in our family. He says this app encrypts data so the UAE's online censors can't read it.

He also says using a VPN is not illegal unless we use it to commit a crime. Sending an apology isn't a crime, is it? After all, I truly am sorry for framing poor, needy, but gorgeous Marie. Except I'm not sorry for killing her husband, Cole. I thought that would make her happy. She'd be free at last!

Maybe I shouldn't have emailed her. I bet her new hubby Ryan will forward it to that hulk of a PI in Dallas. What's his name? Bobbie, Buddy, something. No, Billy Bob. That's it. Perfect name for a rusted-out tank of football player. Trouble for me, he had more ammo than I realized. Somehow, he hired a team of Arab investigators to record me and Terry having a heart-to-heart in the Ritz-Carlton hot tub.

Recording private conversations is illegal in the UAE, so I

don't know how Billy Bob got away with it. Unless he bribed somebody. Guess I answered my question. In this town, *dirhams* get you anything. But you'd think every human — even murderers — would be entitled to privacy in a hotel hot tub.

Still, Dubai operates under *Sharia* law, so watchful eyes try to catch you sinning in this glitzy, sand-blown port. The place literally sizzles with astounding skyscrapers, swanky shops, luxury spas, and probably a few more escaped murderers like me and Terry, avoiding extradition.

Terry tells me the only agreement the UAE has with the American feds is a "mutual legal assistance treaty." As he mansplained, "That means they'll cooperate, but they won't turn anybody over unless the USA offers a valuable trade. A pair of run-of-the-mill murderers like us are not important enough. I think we're safe for a year or two. But eventually, we'll need to make a move. Maybe we should have picked Vietnam. I've always liked the food."

I don't know how Terry finds out stuff like he does, but he gets around. Still, there has been a lot to learn. The first thing we discovered was that one of us needed to have a job to get a visa, so we could stay longer than thirty days.

Because I can't whip out my Texas funeral director's license to find work here, Terry got a reporter gig at an English-language weekly.

Since I'm his partner, that meant I could also have a visa.

But now, I'm feeling trapped. And tied to Terry. He's the only one with a job, while I've got the money we live on. Terry's salary only pays for his partying.

Don't get me wrong. He and I remain close. We talk, laugh, sleep in the same bed, and go out together. But even after we married officially, the man cannot get it up (with me). After too many failed attempts, he finally admitted he's not the bisexual person he desperately tried to be for our marriage's sake.

So, for us to screw the gender we prefer, he and I agreed to an open marriage. After all, we only got married because we had to. The apartment complex where we live requires males and females living together to be married, even though the UAE's weird and ever-changing laws now say it's okay for unmarried couples to live together.

I mean, talk about mixed messages when governing.

I didn't want to go to an Arab singles bar to hustle dates, but my hormone therapy eventually compelled me to put away the vibrator and seek my first adventure.

At first, I struck up one-nighters with European travelers at hotel bars. But quickies in hotel rooms with guys named Sven, Nigel, or Antonio left me without the passion I had for Luca Scarlatti, who unfortunately was also screwing Terry.

Marie was right. I shouldn't have dated Terry.

After a few too many loveless encounters, I gave up on hotel bars and began hanging around wine stores. That's because you can now buy alcohol in Dubai. Evidently, tourists complained about being arrested for doing the same things you can do in almost every country in the world, like having a cocktail or buying a bottle of wine. So now, all you need is to be over twenty-one and have a valid ID.

The trick is, alcohol can only be consumed in licensed venues or private homes.

I guess *Sharia* law means you can do everything privately, whether you're screwing or drinking. So, I was discreet. A few months ago, I spotted a tall, bearded Arab at the wine store. He was quite handsome, so I made sure to bump into him and start a conversation.

Because I have dark hair and eyes, he seemed attracted when I flirted. We exchanged cards and later had a few dinners.

He didn't push immediately for the dirty, and I kind of liked that.

At least he's not an extremist. His name is Vahid, and he studied in America at UCLA. He collects fine wines and even has sex. That's now okay for a single guy in Dubai. But I'm legally married. You see, *Sharia* law gets fussier about adultery, for Muslims, anyway. Since I'm an American and not Muslim, the UAE probably wouldn't put me in jail for adultery, but they would deport me into the arms of the FBI.

But Vahid is a UAE citizen and a Muslim to boot, so he might be punished. Again, the UAE is all over the place in terms of inconsistencies.

Terry circulates freely in Dubai's gay underground and always finds a way to get laid. He comes home and buoyantly confides graphic details I don't want to know. Being homosexual isn't explicitly outlawed in the UAE, but some of its laws criminalize same-sex activity. Depending on what you're caught doing, and I don't want to visualize that either, Terry could get one to ten years if caught in the illegal act.

This worries me greatly. Without my husband's valid visa, what would happen to me?

Back to Marie: I emailed her that apology because I truly did not intend to kill Cole. Pitching the fucker over the balcony was a total impulse. I'd had a judo class that morning. That night, after the opera, I'd had a few, and Cole was going on in that self-absorbed, arrogant way of his. Mansplaining how he'd lost all my money. Looking to me for sympathy. The more he talked, the angrier I got until my judo training kicked in. Afterward, I hoped his apparent "suicide" would free Marie from his abuse and help the Metroplex Opera too, since Cole was milking funds to float his Ponzi scheme.

Hell, his Odyssey Investments cost me a bundle I could use right now. It's pricey in Dubai, but my repaid funds are stuck in my Dallas bank. Since I don't want to raise red flags, I can't access the account. Or sell anything I own in Dallas, like my funeral home, my three-freaking-million-dollar house, or my town car. So all I've got are diminishing offshore investments that pay our expenses.

As for leaving this elaborate sand bucket, I can't simply hop on an American Airlines flight. But I do want to leave. So, I casually asked my new beau Vahid about charter jets. You see, he's an operations manager at Dubai Airport. Still, I must be cautious. I wouldn't want him or Terry to know I'm the only one who would take the flight.

Terry and his limp dick can head to Vietnam.

Oh, I realize I'm not a good person. Something in my psyche always goaded me to eliminate people who piss me off. My first husband was *numero uno*. Cole Donovan was *il secondo*. And the great Luca Scarlatti was *il terzo*. He got what he deserved for screwing Terry while also fucking me.

But I'm not all bad. I truly am sorry for the ordeals Marie and her sons went through. She was the first female friend I cared about. And I do hope she is happy.

I checked Ryan's bio on the Ballard / Ingles website and saw the two had moved to Hawai'i. I can't believe the Ava Gardner of Cellists is living on a gigantic lava hump in the Pacific with no orchestra to star in.

She'll never forgive me for framing her. But hell, her arrest was supposed to be a mere distraction while I sold my assets and left town. I never thought the police would move forward and charge her. How could I know that the lying detective had a grudge? As for the DA, why did he let an obvious frame job go to trial? But the jerk indicted her, which meant I had to come to Marie's aid. See? I really was a friend. But I got so confused with my roles, sometimes I couldn't remember if I was the good friend or the bad murderer.

And when Rebecca Claridge's son Barry went nutty-delusional during Marie's trial, I was flabbergasted. What a fucking gift! Barry blathered on as if he or his mother had killed Luca. None of us could tell where in the fuck this story came from. Did he think his seventy-year-old mom could manage to kill Luca Scarlatti and cut off his dick?

I still don't know what Barry was up to, but I figured he would eventually recant. So, Terry and I ran. If not Barry, if not Rebecca, the police would start looking at everybody Luca had ever screwed. And that was both of us.

Dubai was the first city that came to mind. Its soaring skyscrapers made the place seem sophisticated and exciting, but I didn't know there were these friggin' *Sharia* laws.

What is life without sex? Maybe I am what one hack called me in a *Dallas Morning News* op-ed — a sociopathic sex addict.

If so, it doesn't matter what I do. I can't help it, right?

The next question is how long Terry and I can last in a nation that punishes our sexual pursuits. Homosexuality and adultery for him. Heterosexual adultery for me. But with the FBI demanding extradition, we remain stuck until I can find a way to flee the traps set for us.

Chapter Six

HAWAII PU HERALD

"Not Guilty," says Texas Astronomer

HONOLULU (AP) — A Texas astronomer pleaded not guilty in federal court yesterday to the charge of capital murder in the bow-and-arrow murder of astrophysicist Shin Watanabe, a Japanese national who was researching projects for the Pleiades Observatory on Hawaii Island.

Watanabe was killed last week while hunting at Maunakea Puuhonua Holoholona, locally known as MPH, a federally leased wildlife management area on the slopes of Maunakea.

The Texan, Nocona Parker, is employed by the Big Bend Observatory in West Texas. Parker, who wears his long brown hair woven into braids, claims to be a descendant of the Native American Cherokee Chief Quanah Parker.

However, Parker is not affiliated with the Parker Ranch on the Big Island.

After Senior Judge Noel Peterson asked how he would plead, Parker vehemently shouted, "Not guilty, your Honor. I did not do this."

According to sources, Parker arrived on the Big Island ten days ago to visit college friends who work for R.P. Knight

Observatory, based in Waimea. FBI officers arrested Parker at his friend's Waimea apartment after Parker returned from hunting wild game.

An FBI spokesperson said, "The arrow that killed Mr. Watanabe was identical to the custom-made arrows Parker had shipped to Hawaii Island and later used to hunt game the day Watanabe died."

Texas defense attorney Ryan Ingles, a former star linebacker for the University of Texas football team, represents Parker as lead counsel. Local counsel is provided by Makoa "Big Mike" Iona and his associate attorney, Sonya Pruitt, both of Honolulu.

After the proceedings, Ingles and his entourage made a statement in front of the Prince Kuhio Federal Building.

"Our hearts go out in sympathy to the Watanabe family. But someone else murdered Shin Watanabe, not Nocona Parker. Federal authorities have only one piece of evidence, an arrow similar to the arrows our client used for hunting. However, arrows are not bullets that can be traced and identified. These same arrows can be ordered online by anyone. Our firm's investigative team will arrive on the Big Island tomorrow to provide added resources to what should continue as an active investigation by federal, state, and county authorities. Until then, our client has been released on bail, thanks to Judge Noel Peterson's fair ruling. Although we are eager to punish whoever killed Mr. Watanabe, it's important to ensure we've got the right guy," Ingles said.

Bail was set at $150,000. Parker agreed to remain on the Big Island.

According to Big Bend Observatory's website, Parker's specialty is spectrographic planetary research, hoping to find unmistakable signs of current life on exoplanets. These are planets beyond our solar system.

Pleiades Observatory Director Hiroshi Urata remarked,

"Shin Watanabe was working on a similar project before his death. Police should take a look at Nocona Parker's research."

Urata explained, "An amazing number of recent discoveries have been made in this field. The closest exoplanet, Proxima Centauri B, is over 20 trillion miles away. Using today's technology, it would take a spacecraft 75,000 years to arrive there. Still, we humans remain hopeful that we are not alone in the universe."

Watanabe was married and the father of three teenagers who live in Yokohama, Japan.

"Shin's family sometimes visited him on the Big Island. I feel a deep sense of shame that such a fine scientist and family man would be killed so brutally after coming here to study the stars," Urata said.

Released on bail, Nocona Parker left the federal building escorted by Ingles, his wife Marie, Iona, and Pruitt. The Ingles and Parker returned to the Big Island later that same day.

Contact our crime reporter Ikaika Kelekolio at Ikaika.Kelekolio@hawaiipuherald.com.

Chapter Seven

MY SIDE OF THE MIRRORS

Jürgen Bergen / Zeno Kühn

Shin Watanabe was a *glücklicher umstand*. As we were leaving the Knight offices one day after work, he bragged to me about having permits to hunt at MPH. Naive man even gave me the dates.

He had no clue I was not Jürgen Bergen, the olive-skinned, dark-haired Israeli-Swiss project manager for the Hawai'i Island Large Telescope, or HILT, as it is called. You can do a lot with skin bronzers, hair dye, and colored contact lenses these days. In actuality, I am the very blond and green-eyed Zeno Kühn of Berlin, who will become the world's foremost researcher at the Astrophysical Wide European Telescope in Chile, or AWE-T as it is known.

The Americans snidely call it "Haughty," but they are simply jealous. Europe is years ahead of HILT due to the delays here from activist protests.

I fantasize about my return to AWE-T. I hate living on this giant rock. And it's been maddening to spend so much time overseeing what are essentially construction sites, first for AWE-T in Chile, and now at HILT. Unknown to Americans, Jürgen

Bergen landed the HILT job because of Zeno Kühn's expertise at AWE-T. I invented a wonderful resume for Jürgen, stating he was my assistant project manager at AWE-T, but ready for a leadership role. Several colleagues were happy to sign rec letters too, especially since I wrote them.

Despite my ultimate plans, Jürgen has taken pride in his efforts at HILT. The artistically designed outer building and the interior main support are complete. But well, let's just say HILT will not see first-light on Maunakea. As project managers, Jürgen and I know which parts to target. The expensive, irreplaceable parts. The mirrors, the mounts, the electronics. If a pair of goobers like Timothy McVeigh and Terry Nichols can blow up a federal building in Oklahoma, an astrophysicist like Jürgen can surely disembowel HILT.

After I heard Shin Watanabe boast about his hunt, I spent a week researching who might be the first target for law enforcement to chase instead of Jürgen. It didn't take long to discover this pseudo-Indian astronomer, Nocona Parker. All you need to do on this island is listen.

One afternoon at the FORC Restaurant's bar in Waimea, I chatted with one of Nocona's buddies, a fellow oddly named Marlin Fischer. As we hoisted Kona craft beers, Marlin mentioned that his Native American pal was coming to hunt at MPH.

"He's mailing his archery equipment to me at Knight," Marlin volunteered.

Aha. I had my first fish, thanks to a man named Fischer.

My next step was to identify a local activist to frame and get the anti-astronomy groups stirred up. He had to be an archery hunter. And he had to be about my size and weight.

After researching news articles and websites, I chose Kekoa Palakiko, a sovereignty activist whose father was a famous activist too. Because Kekoa was more muscular than I am, I bought weights to help pump up my arms. And I purchased darker skin bronzers to add to my costume arsenal.

My next steps were to follow Kekoa around. I got his home address in Keauhou from a snoop site. On my weekends off, I parked my SUV down a block from his house, ensuring I could see him come and go but not appear obvious.

Whenever Kekoa came out and jumped into his Jeep, I followed. Sometimes, he went to work as a tour guide for Hawai'i Trail Explorers. Or sometimes he'd go to activist meetings all the way to Hilo or even up north to Hāwī. The man drove all over this island. But eventually, he led me to one of his remote fishing spots near South Point, which locals like to brag is the most southern tip in the United States. It took us more than an hour to get there from Keauhou on the winding road around the base of Huālalai and onto the flows of the massive Mauna Loa.

At first, I thought Kekoa was headed to South Point Road, where you drive a narrow, bumpy street for many kilometers. But no, being a naturalist, Kekoa would not go where tourists go. Instead, his black Jeep turned south on Kahuku Ranch Road, then took an immediate right on a primitive gravel trail.

For fear he would notice me, I didn't follow but kept driving for several blocks. Then I did a U-turn and drove back to where Kekoa had turned off.

With my running lights off, I followed what was left of the dusty cloud Kekoa's Jeep had stirred on an off-road trail. A half-kilometer apart, our two vehicles bumbled and bounced over the hardscrabble black rock and ash until eventually, I saw Kekoa's brake lights ignite. He stopped near an unexpected cluster of trees rising from the lava terrain. Uphill from his vision, I slammed my brakes, turned off my engine, and awaited my chance.

He got out, walked back to the Jeep's boot, and then pulled

open the tailgate, naively unaware as I watched him strip to a swim Speedo. He donned a wetsuit over it and gathered his spear-fishing gear, but left his clothes inside the back tailgate. Then he headed barefoot over the huge lava rocks that locals vault freely, with no fear of discomfort to their feet.

Must be genetic.

I waited until Kekoa was likely in the water fishing. Then I pocketed my phone, put on latex gloves, grabbed the bag of clues to plant, and got out of my car. From there, I walked tentatively downhill to his Jeep.

I'm no local, so I stepped lightly for fear of falling.

When I got to Kekoa's Jeep, I glanced uphill to see if other vehicles were coming, but there were none to see.

Kekoa hadn't even locked his Jeep.

I took photos of his license plates, lifted his wallet from his jeans, and left my clues inside the tailgate, beneath assorted junk. There, I tucked a piece of the custom-logo tape I had used to reseal the archery package delivered to Nocona. And I hid a broken shaft from one of Nocona's arrows, with orange-and-white fletching and an orange "nock."

Clues hidden, I closed the tailgate, glanced around, and then hurried back to my car. From there, I drove for two-and-a-half hours back to my apartment in Waimea.

Although I was exhausted from the drive and stress, various security cameras would be my alibi. I made sure Jürgen Bergen was seen shopping at ACE Hardware and Foodland Grocery. Then I used his ATM card to get cash, and "we" later ate at Jade Palace Chinese Restaurant.

That night, I was so elated, I could not sleep.

With Kekoa's IDs now in hand, I searched online and found a black Jeep Wrangler for sale in Hilo, the same model and year as his.

There are many bronzers at Long's Drugs these days, so

turning Jürgen's bronzed olive skin even darker was easy. I've been dyeing my blond hair to dark brown for months. Luckily, Kekoa keeps his dark hair short, or I'd have had to grow one of those ponytails that local males wear.

Fully bronzed and dressed in camo fatigues, I filled out the dealer's form, presented my stolen IDs, signed "Kekoa Palakiko," and then drove the new/old Jeep home. I parked it behind the apartment building, hidden by an oleander hedge.

The next weekend, I bought a whiz-bang archery set from a local guy on Craigslist. Practicing archery took some time, but with these new high-tech bows, an idiot can kill anything if you get near enough.

I used publishing software to duplicate Kekoa's license plates and laminated them between sheets of plastic.

With all plans and gear in place the morning of Shin Watanabe's hunt, I dressed in my Kekoa camouflage disguise and drove to MPH a good two hours before the hunt. At the front gate, I told the guard I wasn't hunting but wanted to buy supplies at the mini-market.

"I'm camping up the *mauna*," I said in my best Hawaiian-accented English.

As the young guard scanned my documents, he shook his head. "Unless you've got a federal ID, you can't shop at the store. Way out here, it's only for our employees."

"You shittin' me, Brah?"

"Sorry. They're not my rules. And if you don't have other business here, I'll have to ask you to turn around," the *Schweineschnitzel* said.

He did his job.

I scowled in fake anger, grabbed my IDs in a huff, and then turned around, showing off my Kekoa license plates. From there, I drove east on Saddle Road to a restroom and picnic park at the base of Maunakea. For any security cameras that might be there, I made a big deal out of going into the restroom. And I talked "Braddah" to several tourists I met along the way. Such fools, fawning over a man they thought was a genuine Native Hawaiian.

When I got back in my Jeep, I drove west past the MPH entrance, then pulled off Saddle Road and parked at one of several gates that lead to trails or facilities dotting Maunakea's slope.

From there, anyone could see the black Jeep. And I wanted them to.

I still had a long hike to the MPH Unit 1 area where Shin Watanabe had told me he'd be, but as I said, I've been working out. From the back of the black Jeep, I grabbed a duffle that held a compound bow and, most importantly, the arrows I'd stolen from Nocona Parker's package.

Gear in hand, I trekked uphill until I could scale a tall chain-link fence dividing the hunting areas. This was the part I feared wouldn't work, but it was easier than expected. The area is so remote, I assumed the security crew covered it with drones, but I didn't want them to spot me until it was time for my Kekoa Palakiko persona to drive away.

Once inside the fenced area of MPH Unit 1, I found a bushy, grassy clump to curl inside until the hunters arrived.

At the appointed hour, Shin Watanabe arrived in a van with several buddies and got out. Each wore the mandatory flame-orange cap and hunting vest. His buddies were in full camouflage, like me, but Shin was wearing a camouflage shirt over blue jeans. That bit of blue denim made him easier to track.

Using a scope to watch, I stayed hidden as the group spread out. Each hunter was supposed to give the other at least fifty yards of space.

Eventually, Shin trailed away by himself, so I decided to

follow. My major challenge was to keep adequate coverage. The terrain is speckled with scrubby bushes, tall dry grasses, and mounds of ancient rock. The best places to hide were bushes, although painful to crawl inside because of the thorns. So, I often ducked behind a rock or small *pu'u*.

Killing Shin Watanabe was a Viennese *Waltzer*. He would move in one direction. I would silently move the same, then crouch in a hiding place. It took most of the morning. But eventually, he spotted a big-horned black sheep.

Shin slowed and crouched. Then he knelt, grabbed an arrow, and loaded his bow.

I quickly surveyed the surroundings to see if anyone was in sight, but the other hunters had scrambled quite a distance. I could still see them, but I had enough cover, I was able to nestle low, set one of Nocona's Caltech arrows, pull back, and fire.

My aim was off. I was going for Shin's chest, but the arrow hit his neck. He grabbed at it, squirmed, and writhed, then collapsed in a wriggling pile. I loaded a second arrow to take him out of his misery. But by the time I was able to sneak nearer, he collapsed dead still. My first arrow must have severed his jugular.

Thankfully, the black sheep bolted toward Shin's hunting buddies. A perfect distraction! I watched them awkwardly run toward it, trying to get near enough to shoot. Then I turned and strode toward the fence line.

Not much later, I heard a voice shouting behind me, "Shin, Shin, are you okay? Oh, my God, I didn't hit you, did I? Shin?"

I kept walking in a normal stride as if I were a hunter.

Then another voice shouted, "Call range patrol. We need an ambulance out here."

Knowing I had a good ten-minute lead on security, I crouched low until I got to the high fence, scrambled over, then scooted in a low shuffle across Saddle Road to my Jeep.

This was the turning point. Now, I wanted the hunters, rangers, and security drones to see me, that is, see Kekoa Palakiko driving away. Sweating with nerves, I started the Jeep's engine and drove like a wild man west on Old Saddle Road toward Waiki'i, a small ranching village. There, I pulled into a private lane and switched license plates. Back in my Jeep, I made my way to Mamalahoa Highway and sped to my apartment in Waimea.

Once there, I returned the Jeep to its hiding spot behind the oleander hedge.

Exhausted but relieved, the first stage of my plan was complete. Now I only had to wait for law enforcement to unravel my clues and arrest Kekoa Palakiko. Protests and chaos would erupt soon on the Big Island. Like the rumbling volcanoes some worship, America's astronomy efforts will dissolve in the flow of pagan fire.

My amazing AWE-T will prevail, no matter that it's one meter narrower?

After I destroy HILT, that meter won't matter.

Chapter Eight

808 INSIDERS

Da Real Scoop

Today at 8:25 a.m.

D id you see the latest news? We at 808 Insiders were *Casablanca* "shocked" when we read our morning daily and saw who makes up the legal team for Texas astronomer Nocona Parker. In case you missed it, Mr. Parker — who every media outlet reminds us has no connection to John Palmer Parker of Parker Ranch fame — was arraigned yesterday in Honolulu for (oh dear, we must add "allegedly") murdering a prominent Japanese astronomer. Both were hunting at MPH on the Big Island.

Leading the defense is none other than Ryan Ingles of Dallas, Texas.

Dallas, you ask? Why not some local *braddah*?

Dat's what we wanna know!

Another point: Ingles once represented his admittedly stunning wife, at that time known as Marie Donovan. She is a trained classical cellist, of all things, who stood trial a while back for killing a Dallas-area opera maestro named Luca

Scarlatti. Mrs. Donovan was the widow of famed Super Bowl-star quarterback Cole Donovan.

Intrigued?

Well, Ryan Ingles got his future wife off — uh-oh, an embarrassing malapropism. Rather, we should say the case was dismissed after a key witness, Barry Claridge, son of Metroplex Opera founder Rebecca Claridge, buckled under cross-examination and insinuated that either he or his mother had killed Maestro Scarlatti.

There was such confusion, the judge had no option but to dismiss the case against Mrs. Donovan, but without prejudice, meaning, yes, she could be charged again.

This Dallas-based story may not seem of interest to you, dear 808 Insiders, but we're sure the Big Island's reputation as the site for astronomical research matters a boatload to the state's coffers. After all, astronomy is the state's second-largest "industry," if you can call a bunch of scientists industrious.

Still, we wonder why Ryan Ingles was chosen to defend Nocona Parker, rather than a Hawaii-based firm. Granted, Parker is from West Texas, where his ancestor, Comanche Chief Quanah Parker, lived as a warrior among the Plains Indians. Somewhat like Kamehameha I, he was a pragmatic leader who sought a place for his people in a rapidly changing land.

Talk about a tale of two nations. 808 Insiders bets Quanah Parker and King Kamehameha could share some stories.

From *Da Real Scoop*, Nocona Parker's legal fees are being paid by a bigwig on the board of the Big Bend Observatory, who also happens to be Parker's godfather. But why can't that bigwig spread some poi-joy to a local defense firm?

As they say, grow local, buy local. We know several island lawyers who could provide more knowledgeable representation, especially since Ryan Ingles is pure *malihini*.

Local counsel representative "Big Mike" Iona was unavailable when we called his Honolulu office for comment.

Hey, Big Mike, if you see this, did you know the questionable history of Marie (Donovan) Ingles? How about your associate, the ever-sassy Sonya Pruitt? Did she know she's working with a former jailbird?

Rest assured, 808 Insiders will take top position on this one.

Most Relevant:

Heather's Hilo Haven — Top position? What you mean by dat?

Hilo Rain Man — Go home, Jailbird Haole!

Heather's Hilo Haven — Who, me?

Kona Wave Rider — Just what we need. More transplants taking local jobs.

Grant's South Point Acres — I say the Leg should ban all mainland transplants. Put up a wall!

Waikoloa Night Skies — We saw how that worked a few years ago. This island has probs only imports can solve.

Grant's South Point Acres — You must be imported, asshole.

Heather's Hilo Haven — Who, me?

808 Insiders — Comments have been discontinued.

Chapter Nine

TEAM MEETING ONE

Marie Ingles

R yan and I were absolutely giddy as we awaited the arrival of Billy Bob and Natalie at the Kona airport. It's a small, open-air facility, so we parked across from the baggage area. When our FlightAware app alerted us they had arrived, we walked across the street and waited until eventually we saw the rectangular block of a human named Billy Bob Hughes rolling two bags.

He appeared to have gotten wider and balder over the past year, while Natalie Sherman remained her tall, slim self.

As the two caught our eye and waved, I noticed that Billy Bob's light blue and white seersucker suit jacket was drenched with sweat, and he was huffing and puffing in exhaustion from the journey.

Ryan laughed. "Good gosh, Nasty Man. Take your jacket off. You'll pass out in this humidity."

As I hugged Natalie, Billy Bob shucked his coat, undid his shirt buttons, and attempted to tug his pants above his bulging tummy. He murmured gruffly. "Natalie feeds me too well."

She punched him playfully. "You just eat too much."

Ryan chuckled, grabbed one of the rolling bags, and pointed toward the parking lot. "Car is across the street."

When we got to the crosswalk, Natalie asked us to stop while she unzipped the outer pocket of her travel bag. She took out a wispy white cotton t-shirt, stripped off her flowing, long-sleeved top — right there on the sidewalk — and pulled the t-shirt on over her black bra. On the front of the t-shirt was a palm tree, plus the phrase "Truly Native" in huge letters.

Several waiting cars honked madly, and some local guys hooted through their open windows and gave an energetic thumbs-up *shaka* to Natalie.

Ryan snickered. "That ought to impress the gentry."

"Boss, Nat did all kinds of research about the demographics here. She figured she'd go on the offensive before anybody gives her shit about being Black."

As we made our way to our SUV, Ryan whispered, "Nasty, I'll tell you more about that once we're in the car."

Billy Bob picked up on Ryan's cue. "Gheesh. Always this hot here, Boss?"

"Kona gets humid after the afternoon clouds roll in. Where we are is a resort area called Hōkele Kilohana. It's still plenty warm but a few degrees cooler. The humidity is hell because we're near the shore. Best thing to do is get that suit off after we get you to your condo."

"T-shirts, shorts, and flip-flops, rather, *slippahs* are the daily uniform," I joked.

Once we were inside the SUV, Ryan pushed the max button on the AC, and we headed north toward our condo.

Ryan angled his voice toward the back seat. "Natalie, I didn't want to say anything at the airport, but us white guys are the ones who get the stink-eye from locals. We are called *malihini* to our faces, which means 'newcomer,' but we're called *haole* behind our backs. That means 'foreign,' and not nicely."

I scoffed, "On the Nextdoor social media page, *malihini* and tourists get the blame for everything from speeding to traffic and burglary. You wouldn't believe it, but one day, I was walking from my car to a grocery store in Waimea, and a local guy in a pickup roared by, shouting, 'Get outa da road!' This was in a shopping center!"

Billy Bob shook his head in dismay. "They'd better not give me any shit, 'cause this redneck will not put up with it."

Ryan said, "They won't bother you, Nasty. You're too effing big!"

"Why are you still calling him 'Nasty'?" I asked.

"Old habits, my darling. I've told you the stories."

Natalie was quiet during all this. When I glanced back to see why, she was looking up stuff on her laptop.

"Like Billy Bob said, I've been researching. Maybe because I'm African-American, I was curious about the locals' resentment. I'll read you some stuff I found."

"Come on, Nat. Don't bore us to death with your factoids. You'll put Ryan to sleep with this stuff. And he's driving!"

"But this history is important to know when we interview islanders. This stuff happened, and that's why there's a lot of resentment."

She read to us from the back seat. "'With guns aimed at him, Hawaiian King David Kalākaua signed a new constitution on July 6, 1887, which was nicknamed the 'Bayonet Constitution.' The guns were pointed by a militia group called the Honolulu Rifles, made up mostly of white settlers affiliated with a group called the Hawaiian League. The latter group demanded a transfer of power from the Hawaiian monarchy to the settler-friendly legislature. The new constitution also granted voting rights to foreigners by linking the right to vote with property ownership. In 1893, Kalākaua's successor, his sister Queen Lili'uokalani, attempted to restore some autocracy to the Hawaiian throne. She had opposed the 1887 treaty her brother signed that ceded the port of Pearl Harbor. Because of this, American and European entrepreneurs tried to abrogate her authority. Led by Sanford Dole, the Missionary Party demanded her abdication in 1893 and declared the queen deposed. They also announced the establishment of a provisional government, pending USA annexation."

"Nat, com'on —" Billy Bob groaned.

"Hush. And let me finish. 'To avoid bloodshed, Lili'uokalani surrendered, but she appealed to President Cleveland to reinstate her. He ordered the queen restored and rejected the treaty of annexation that his predecessor, President Benjamin Harrison, had sent to Congress. Dole defied the order, saying President Cleveland did not have the authority to intervene. Two years later, Dole's group suppressed an insurrection in the queen's name, and Lili'uokalani was kept under house arrest on charges of treason. On January 24, 1895, to win pardons for her supporters and to avoid potential bloodshed, she agreed to sign a formal abdication.

"However, she fought bitterly against the 1898 annexation by the United States. In that year, she published *Hawai'i's Story by Hawai'i's Queen* and composed "Aloha Oe," the islands' beloved song. Thereafter, she withdrew from public life.'"

Billy Bob sighed loudly.

"Luckily, I'm done, or else I'd give you a piece of my mind. All of this was to educate you on why there's a Hawaiian sovereignty movement to secede from the United States and reestablish the autonomous kingdom of Hawai'i."

Billy Bob chimed in. "Okay, okay. But that happened long ago. That's no reason for some dude to shout at Marie in a parking lot. And what the hell would happen if the state seceded now?"

"That would leave the islands open to other takeovers. No telling which nation would be here in a heartbeat," Ryan said.

"From what I've read, the Hawaiian Kingdom would seek treaties with the U.S. for protection, but they'd surely end the cheapskate leases the military has had for decades. It's a complex issue," Natalie said.

We shook our heads at that philosophical point and continued north on Queen Ka'ahumanu Highway, or "Queen K" as everybody calls it. As we drove along, Ryan and I gave tour-guide descriptions of which volcanoes were the oldest, active, or extinct, and especially how to pronounce Hualālai, which towers above Kona and follows you as you curve your way northwest, where we live. Luckily, the weather gave us clear skies, so our friends had glorious views of Maui across the ocean channel to the northwest, and they could see the summit of the mighty Maunakea to the east.

Ryan pointed out the silver and white domes of the astronomical observatories glimmering atop Maunakea's summit. "There are twelve observatories up there now, and a giant telescope is soon to be completed. It's called HILT, short for Hawai'i Island Large Telescope. Lots of controversy over that one. Activists have tried to stop its construction."

"But why?"

"Long story about the sacredness of the mauna. We still haven't gone up to the summit for a sunset tour, but it's on our bucket list."

As we rounded a curve, I pointed back toward the east. "It's clear enough, you can see Maunakea's sister, Mauna Loa. In Hawaiian folklore, she is the 'fire' while Maunakea is the 'ice.'"

Ryan nodded. "Mauna Loa erupted in 2022. I wish we'd gotten to see that."

"She can erupt again. And from what I've read, her sister Maunakea could still erupt. You never know which way

Madame Pele will send her fire. She is the goddess of volcanoes and lives on Mauna Loa and Kīlauea. Pele's powers are fire and lava, while her sister, Poli'ahu, provides the snow and ice," Natalie said.

I should have known Natalie would research the fables of the Big Island, but before she could start reading more to us from her laptop, Billy Bob grumbled, "Nat, you read me that goddess stuff on the plane."

Natalie scoffed. "And you slept through most of it."

"Billy Bob, you and I may not believe in volcanic goddesses, but I think it's good to step lightly here and show respect for Hawaiian history and local beliefs."

"I agree, Ryan. This is *their* island home." Natalie paused for a moment, perhaps wondering whether to say more, but she probably couldn't help herself. "Even though it's sinking much faster than the so-called experts first thought," Natalie said.

"Sinking? Ryan and I moved to an island that's sinking?"

"Yes, but only the lowest shorelines will be underwater, and not for several decades."

"Gads. Sinking islands. Fairy goddesses that spew fire from mountain to mountain. For sure, I'm not buying —" Billy Bob trailed off, shaking his head.

LUCKILY, THE RENTAL CONDO NEXT TO OURS HAD BEEN available, so Natalie leased it. After getting the bags in, the two came over to our condo. Ryan whipped up his latest recipe for Mai Tai cocktails, and a bit later, we grilled ahi tuna and local veggies, followed by Tropical Dreams chocolate-fudge ice cream for dessert.

Everybody helped clean up, but Natalie suddenly stopped short beside the sink. "Oh, I forgot to mention. Guess we're jet-lagged. Before we came here, I signed up for every Hawai'i social media group I could find on MakeFriends and Nextdoor. One post I read before our flight was on a MakeFriends group page called '808 Insiders.' Are you on this site? Today's post was ranting about Ryan representing Nocona Parker. It even listed snarky details about Marie's trial back in Dallas."

Hands full of dishes, Ryan set them down with a bang. "What's this?"

"A MakeFriends page called '808 Insiders' posted this morning about you representing Nocona. It was spiteful, asking why a local firm wasn't on the case. And it mentioned Marie's court battle over Luca Scarlatti's murder."

Ryan sighed heavily. "Natalie, I don't have the right temperament for it tonight, but first thing tomorrow, please show it to me."

I understood his frustration. "Who on Hawai'i Island knows about my trial? We moved here to get away from these unfair accusations."

Natalie shrugged. "I'll see what I can find about the administrator of this page, although it might be a fake account."

"Can you hack MakeFriends?" Ryan asked.

"They've got all sorts of firewalls. I'll have to see."

"Boss, should we dispute the post?"

"Billy Bob, social media is just that. Not genuine news."

Natalie shook her head. "A lot of people believe what they read on social media, even when it's a blatant lie. This 808 Insiders group has thirty thousand members. Its slant is gossipy, cynical, or angry, especially about government and county issues. From what I could tell, it gives the local populace a platform for rants."

I murmured, "This reminds me of Terry Nichols's column, 'Out and In.' That made me look like the murderer everybody hoped I was."

Ryan patted my shoulder protectively. "We'll look into this tomorrow. For now, Billy Bob and Natalie, eight o'clock is midnight to your bodies. Marie and I will finish the dishes."

As we hugged them goodnight, I figured the two would wake up before dawn. And they did. At 7:00 a.m. the next morning, as Ryan and I stumbled out to the lanai with coffees, Billy Bob and Natalie were well into their third cups, laptops open, plotting, and taking notes.

Despite the early hours, it felt good to be a team again. I told everybody, "Just tell me what you need. Shall I handle calls and interviews like I used to?"

Natalie smiled with glee. "Nancy-D is back! I'm so glad you will help."

I noticed how contented Natalie looked, compared to the aloof nerd she seemed to be when we first met. From what she later shared with me, she and Billy Bob started going out casually as friends, but as she put it, "Something happened one night in the Seychelles."

That same "something" happened to me and Ryan. And like us, the pair have been together ever since. Billy Bob is the firm's gruff, tough, muscle man with an amazing way of ferreting information from nervous witnesses, while Natalie is the fashionista who explores technology trails.

"Natalie, you're not the only one who missed Nancy-D," I said.

Ryan gave me a cautionary smile. "Even if you call yourself Nancy D. and add the 'Drew,' please do not get involved in this 808 Insiders stuff. Natalie should handle all posts for our team."

Natalie handed us printouts of the 808 Insiders page. "I've tried since 6:00 a.m., but I can't get deep enough to see who's behind this. So, I created a fake profile and replied with facts about Marie being exonerated. I also named the alleged killers and how they're on the FBI's Most Wanted Fugitives list. My

MakeFriends profile is Nalani Kawena. I thought 'Nalani' was near enough to Natalie. But for my last name, there wasn't an S."

We all chuckled about that one.

"The early Hawaiians didn't have a written language until missionaries arrived in the 1820s. Instead, the Hawaiians passed down their history orally and with dance," Natalie recited.

Billy Bob snarled, "What could they have written on, lava?"

Natalie thought for a moment. "Well, they did make pictographs. There are some in Hōkele Kilohana that you can see. But they also had sheep, goats, and so forth. You know, animal skin, as in parchment? It was only when —"

Ryan interrupted. "Okay, okay, all this is interesting stuff, but let's get back to this 808 Insiders thing. When you comment on it, please go ahead and defend Marie all you want, but do not make a big deal out of our not being a local firm. Let's stress that Honolulu's Iona Law Firm is overseeing us on the case, and we were hired only because a Texas bigwig is Nocona Parker's godfather."

"Right, Boss, the more facts the better."

"I'll write all posts as strictly factual," Natalie said.

Billy Bob barked into his "boss" mode. "Nancy-D's and my first step is to visit this MPH place I cannot pronounce. Marie, how about you get an appointment with whatever muckety-muck we need to interview?"

Chapter Ten

MPH

Marie Ingles

The next morning, Billy Bob and I headed out in the rental SUV to meet the manager of Maunakea Puʻuhonua Holoholona. Along the way at Waikoloa Road, I pointed out the blue tour helicopters parked on one corner, and the "fish mama" truck on the other corner, then drove *mauka*, which I'd learned on the evening news means "inland, or toward the mountain." The opposite is *makai*. That means toward the sea.

It was difficult to avoid the many goat families grazing along the roadway's edge. They seem to like the tender grass that sprouts after the off-shoulder areas are mowed.

Past the residential area of Waikoloa Village, we drove on a winding road to Mamalahoa Highway, also called the High Road, where we turned south a bit, then turned *mauka* again onto Saddle Road, officially known as Daniel K. Inouye Highway, or DKI.

The same morning, Ryan ordered another rental car delivered, so he and Natalie took that car to drive north to Waimea, where the R.P. Knight Observatory offices are. Ryan said that he planned to interview Nocona again and interview his host buddy, Marlin Fischer.

"Hopefully, one of them will have a new clue," he said as he kissed me goodbye.

His drive was much shorter than mine, as I drove through an otherworldly terrain. In areas of the most recent lava flows, little vegetation grows. On older flows, the vegetation can be grasses, ferns, lichen, and short trees. The higher you climb, the cooler the outside temperature gets. But on clear days, you have glorious views of Maunakea and Mauna Loa, which are the delights of this trip.

Even the crusty Billy Bob was amazed by the unique geology. "Look, there's even snow on the summits!"

"I may sound like Natalie, but I've read that winter temperatures at the summit on Maunakea can drop to twenty-five degrees. And blizzard winds sometimes roar more than a hundred miles per hour."

"Makes you wonder why there's a wildlife refuge way the heck out here."

Luckily, MPH wasn't at the summit but at about 6,500 feet. At this elevation, the terrain looked like parts of Texas's Big Bend country, with scrubby brush, rocky terrain, and a huge, brown mountain rising across the road from the refuge.

When I lowered my window at the MPH front gate, the jacket-chilly air blew inside. I showed our IDs to a friendly female security guard who checked us in and then directed us to the refuge manager's office.

As we made our way, I noticed the preserve was neatly arranged with rows of metal buildings on perfectly paved streets with names like "Wildlife Loop," "Silversword Avenue," and "Archery Road."

Billy Bob made one of his sarcastic comments. "The color of these buildings looks a bit like those suits Colleen wears."

That made me laugh. "I thought Ryan and I were the only ones who noticed Colleen's beige theme."

"Matches her personality," he scoffed.

"Aw, not fair. Colleen was such fun in the Seychelles. And she helped us get out of jail."

Just then, we pulled in front of the refuge manager's office.

Billy Bob snarled, "Being a manager at this post is either a punishment or a starter job."

"Hush. We've got to be solicitous, not cynical."

He grinned. "Aw, you're no fun either."

Inside, we met the uniformed refuge manager, Adam Beacher, a squatty, freckled redhead who seemed quite full of himself. I even wondered if I should salute.

He shook our hands and boomed, "Welcome to the largest wildlife refuge in Hawai'i."

Billy Bob grinned. "I'm from Texas, and this terrain reminds me of the Big Bend region."

"We've heard that from Texans who come through. I'm from Maine, myself."

"Maine! Wow, this must be a change of environment."

"Join the feds, see the world." He motioned for us to take a seat, then sat behind his imposing wooden desk. "As you can probably tell, this is not a glamorous post. But it's an interesting one, and I'm proud to manage it. Now, what can I do for you two today?"

"We're investigating the death of the Japanese astronomer."

"Not sure what you mean. I've already been interviewed by law enforcement."

"I imagine so, but we represent the man who was arrested, Nocona Parker."

"I don't know if I should say much more beyond what I've told the FBI investigator."

Billy Bob answered in his guy-to-guy collegial tone, "Mr.

Beacher, we're simply after the truth. Any facts you can share would be helpful. For example, do you have a roster of the hunters who were here that day?"

He fished in his Rolodex and pulled out a business card. "I gave it to, what's her title? Long-winded thing. FBI Supervisory Special Agent Pua Akana."

I wrote that down.

Billy Bob went full charmer as he pressed for more. "Sir, you could save us a lot of time if we could have a copy of that roster too. As the defense team, we're entitled to what's called 'discovery.' The prosecution is required by law to hand over any evidence they plan to use against our client."

"I'm aware of those rules, but I think the FBI should provide the roster, not me. Although this is a federal refuge, we hold public hunts during state hunting seasons to control wildlife populations. Because our hunts are public, there are names on the list who may not want it known they were here. Along with tourists, we host military top brass, Hollywood stars, tech millionaires, and local residents, of course. We try to provide as much privacy as possible."

"I understand that, but —"

"Look, this tragedy hurt our image a great deal. We had to cancel all public hunts and assess how MPH could've prevented this from happening. That means revising security protocols and adding costly technology. By canceling our hunts, we've angered a lot of folks who counted on coming here. And now our staff will have to keep our animal populations in check, but they really don't like eliminating animals they see every day. Heck, they even name some of them."

Billy Bob took in a breath but silenced a sigh.

Since his good ol' boy charm had failed, I leaned forward and casually batted my dark lashes. "But if we're going to get the list eventually, couldn't you save us several weeks?"

That seemed to work. Mr. Beacher sighed in submission and pressed his intercom button. "Miss McElroy, please bring a copy of the roster for bow-and-arrow hunters on the unfortunate day the astronomer was killed. I hope you have that date marked in red on your calendar, right?"

Billy Bob squinted. "Could you please add *all* hunters, not just bow and arrow?"

Mr. Beacher seemed exasperated but got the lists for us. We thanked him profusely, and Billy Bob promised to send him a case of Bar Harbor New England Clam Chowder.

Mr. Beacher joked, "In Waikoloa Village, one can costs me well over six dollars, and our mini-mart won't even carry it. Any help you can provide would be welcome."

After we got back in the car, I asked Billy Bob, "Where in the world did you dream up clam chowder?"

"He told us he's a Mainer. I may be getting older, but I don't always need our fact-fueled Natalie Sherman to come up with an idea or two."

The poor guy seemed defensive. Maybe he needed some praise too. "Billy Bob, Ryan speaks highly of all you do, and I'm thrilled you and Natalie came to help us with this case. Your clam chowder idea is the perfect example of how you get people to talk."

That seemed to work. "Thanks, Marie. Guess I overreacted. Things have not been the same since Ryan left town. Coleen's a tough boss. Praise isn't in her vocabulary, so I find myself on the defensive a lot. Natalie did a downright happy dance in our kitchen when I told her we were coming to see you two."

"Which reminds me, why is it you and Natalie have not tied the knot?"

He grimaced. "How did you get from clam chowder to my getting married?"

"Nancy-D at work."

We both grinned and headed *makai*, still marveling at the ever-changing views at 6,000 feet. But suddenly, thick low-lying clouds surrounded us, and it was dark as dusk. I turned on my wipers and headlights, but could not see ten feet. Some cars even pulled over and stopped on the shoulder, but Billy Bob and I inched along, our noses practically touching the front windshield, until the fog thinned at last. As the angle of our decline grew steep, the sun started peeking through the remaining mist to create the most magnificent double rainbow far beyond us.

"Holy moly, that's the biggest f-in' rainbow I've ever seen," Billy Bob said.

I pulled over and stopped so he could get out and take a pic. "This is why the University of Hawai'i mascots are the Rainbow Warriors, or 'Bows' for short."

As he snapped photos, he murmured, "This place amazes me. You go from beach to desert, mountains, cold, snow, fog, sunshine, and rainbows."

I proudly recited, "And there's a rainy tropical zone on the Hilo side. Eight independent climate zones, all within minutes."

"You sound like Nat with her research," he laughed.

⁕

BACK AT THE CONDO, BILLY BOB AND I LUNCHED ON SPAM *musubi* and *poke̅* from our local Foodland. Billy Bob didn't realize the *poke̅* was made from raw fish until he asked later, "What was that pokey stuff called?"

"*Poke̅*," I said. "It means chopped fish. The one we had was fresh ahi tuna marinated in a sauce. The container says *shoyu*, sesame oil, garlic, green onion, and red peppers."

"Marinated. You mean like *ceviche*?"

"Sort of. Different fish. Different sauces."

"So that was raw tuna, you're telling me?"

"Not cooked but marinated."

"But it was still raw." He grimaced as if he might throw up.

"You must have liked it. You ate it."

"But I didn't know it was raw-raw. The only *ceviche* I eat is the shrimp kind, where they've boiled the darn things before letting them sit in the lime juice and spices."

"Hawaiians eat a lot of raw fish. It's very popular."

"Gads. Well, if I mess up your toilets, it'll be your fault."

I glared. "Billy Bob, as I used to tell the twins, you'd better aim well, 'cause you're cleaning it up."

He shuddered and went back to his laptop searches.

After lunch, I used the law firm's accounts on several legal databases to research each name on the roster of hunters. The refuge manager was right. The hunters' names ranged from local residents to the famous, including a member of the U.S. Joint Chiefs of Staff, a Hollywood film star, two Silicon Valley kingpins, four Hawai'i state legislators, and one U.S. senator from Montana.

"Nocona Parker didn't realize he was hunting among the elite. Even so, I don't see anyone of interest on this list. But I did notice that Nocona and Mr. Watanabe were assigned to different hunting units. I don't know if that matters —"

Abruptly, the front door opened, and Ryan and Natalie strode in from their travels.

"Boss, Nat, did you two learn something up at Knight?"

"I hate to say this, but our day was spent spinning wheels. We met the director and interviewed Marlin Fischer, along with as many of Nocona's workmates as time allowed. His story and theirs did not vary beyond Nocona saying he's applying for a contract job at Knight since he can't leave the island. He also said he's fallen in love with Waimea."

Natalie nodded. "I don't blame him. It's quaint up there."

"Don't feel bad, Boss. Marie and I kind of struck out too, except we got the roster of all hunters on that day. Nobody of interest, but Marie noticed something. What was that you said?"

"Nocona was assigned to the MPH Unit 1, but Shin Watanabe was assigned to MPH Unit 2. I don't know if that matters, but it's something you need to look at."

"Definitely," Billy Bob said. "We also got a name from the refuge manager."

I fumbled through my notes. "FBI Supervisory Special Agent Pua Akana."

"Good work. Marie, please set up an appointment for us. Maybe we can find out if the FBI only sees Nocona for this crime, or if they would like to find the actual killer."

Just as I started dialing, Ryan got a call. He whispered, "Mike Iona." Then Ryan pressed "speaker" so we could all hear.

"Hey, Big Mike. I've got you and the team on speaker. What's cooking?"

"Not as much as I would like, Ryan. And to tell you the truth, the pot's been stirred by this *hammajang* on the 808 Insiders page. Have you seen it yet?"

"Just got wind of it."

"This morning, Sonya pointed me to a post about Marie. 'Said she was tried for murder, some time ago in Dallas. You got any details?"

Ryan blew out in frustrated dismay. "Yes sir, I can give you details. A lot, but in a nutshell, a woman named Lena Verano — she was Marie's best friend at the time — turned out to be a sociopathic killer who framed Marie for the murder of Dallas opera maestro Luca Scarlatti."

"No kidding. This sounds like something you might see on, what's that show, *Dateline*?"

"It's even worse. In Dallas, Marie did a lot of fundraising on behalf of Metroplex Opera. Her late husband was the Super Bowl star, Cole Donovan. After he retired, he got into finance and chaired the opera's finance committee."

"*Chee*, Cole Donovan, I didn't know —"

Ryan scowled, likely pained to be talking about my ex.

"Right, well, turns out Cole got into trouble running a Ponzi scheme. He embezzled opera funds and used investors' money to keep things afloat. This Lena Verano got pissed because Cole was about to run off with a pile of her cash. So, she pushed Cole off a high-rise balcony, although everybody thought he had committed suicide."

"'*Dis* true?"

"Yes. We have her admission on tape. And several months after she killed Cole, Lena and her boy-toy gossip columnist murdered the maestro because he'd rejected them both."

Mike laughed. "Oh my, so the maestro waved his baton *mauka* and *makai*."

Ryan chuckled. "Three-sixty at anything that moved. Lena and her beau set up Marie with planted evidence. The prosecution's case was ridiculous from the get-go, but a Dallas detective had an ax to grind. Turns out, he also lost a chunk in Cole's Ponzi scheme. So, he refused to investigate beyond the evidence Lena had planted. With no other suspects, the case went to trial. But after some bizarre witness testimony, the judge dismissed the charges."

Mike whispered out a whistle. "I'm speechless."

"Several months later, Marie and my team flew halfway around the world to the Seychelles Islands to recover the bulk of funds Cole had embezzled from Metroplex Opera, as well as from his investors. But Marie was not aware of any facets of Cole's Ponzi scheme."

Mike sighed a doubtful, "Hmmmm."

Ryan came back a bit harder. "Mike, you know humans live

and die by gossip. Honestly, that's one reason we left Dallas. A lot of people Marie and I socialized with preferred lies to the truth. The experience took a lot out of us, so we moved here to start fresh. But now these accusations are resurfacing. I've got my investigators looking into whoever posted that comment. We'll see what we can find."

"Good to know, Ryan. Please do me a favor and alert county officials. I guess the FBI already knows this stuff, but I don't wanna have our firm tainted by rumors and lies."

"I hear ya, Mike. We will straighten out any misconceptions."

"Good. The more details I have, the better job we can do defending allegations."

Ryan gave us another tense grimace. "Yes, sir."

Mike's voice paused for a moment, then asked, "I realize it's still early, but any progress on the Nocona Parker case?"

"Billy Bob's team drove to MPH today and interviewed the refuge manager. He gave them a roster of hunters on the day of the murder. Turns out our client was in a different hunting area from the victim, so that might be something. We'll see if the FBI agent will talk to us."

"That sounds promising."

"Better than my day of wheel spinning. My computer analyst and I drove to the Knight offices and interviewed staff there. I can't say we found a smoking gun, but you of all people know it takes a lot of questions and a lot of miles to arrive at the truth."

"*Rajah*. Just keep me posted. And I'll ask my PR firm to post more stuff about Marie's innocence. Also, we'll get the word out to local firms that this Texas *kahuna* hired you because he didn't know anyone here. But a Hawai'i firm *is* on the job. Iona Law. That ought'a give 'em *chee-hoo*."

"I appreciate your help, Big Mike. As you know, we are

malihini — is that how you say it? Having an islander like you on our team gives us a better sense of security."

"*Mahalo*. And keep me posted."

As Ryan pressed the stop button, he heaved a worried sigh. "Wow. We've got to watch our steps. Seems we've already pissed off local attorneys."

"Boss, we'll keep everything on the up and up. So, Nat, just keep an eye on the 808 Insiders site, but let Big Mike's PR firm do the legwork."

"I can still try to see who's behind it, right?"

"As long as nobody catches you."

As we sat around the table, the four of us silently stared at our laptops, realizing that even though we were in the United States, we were in foreign territory.

Chapter Eleven

MY SIDE OF THE MIRRORS

Jürgen Bergen / Zeno Kühn

Some nights after my workday at the top, I stay overnight at the Maunakea dorms. Called "*Hale Pōhaku*" or "Stone House," the dorms house about seventy people who work at the summit. This helps prevent problems from oxygen deprivation since oxygen at the summit is about forty percent less than at sea level.

This morning at breakfast, a telescope engineer told me that the Native American Texan, Nocona Parker, had hired an expensive lawyer and private investigator. "I heard some Big Bend Observatory bigwig is paying the tab," he said.

This was unexpected. If lawyers or investigators question me, I don't know how well I might do. Although I've studied English since childhood and attended university in England, I might need to feign "poor English" to mask any fluster on my part.

Intercepting Nocona's hunting gear was far more trouble than I expected. Since HILT isn't fully complete, I've rented office space at Knight's base operations in Waimea. That way, I don't have to go to the summit so often. But to intercept

Nocona's package, I had to check the mailroom every day. Logistically, that was a nightmare. If I was working up at HILT, I had to drive up and down jarring roads from 2,000 to 13,000 feet in elevation each day. That is not a good thing to do to your body or vehicle.

As I nervously filtered through arriving packages, pretending to check my mail, I almost wept with relief when I saw one addressed to Nocona's buddy, Marlin Fischer. The return address was to Texas, so I quickly took the parcel outside to my SUV, carefully unwrapped it, and kept what I needed: three of Nocona's fletched arrows.

Before I returned the package to the mailroom, I re-taped it with the custom-logo tape.

With this step complete, I felt such relief. I was on my way to confirming Europe's AWE-T as the world's superior land-based telescope, despite the altitude differential on Maunakea that Hawai'i tour guides love to tout.

"Maunakea is the world's tallest mountain," they boast. But then they add the qualifier, "when measured from its base on the sea floor."

Granted, Maunakea has 3,000 feet more altitude than Cerro Armazones in Chile, where the AWE-T site now rests below 10,000 feet. However, this elevation can sometimes be shrouded in clouds. Even so, AWE-T administrators never considered Maunakea because of the cultural and political issues here. The anti-astronomy activists don't want anybody atop Maunakea unless they pay up.

Regrettably for me, the activists' efforts did not stop HILT. Mine will. And once I seal HILT's fate, I will leave this lava giant forever. Let my hair return to blond. Stop bronzing in dual shades, darker for Kekoa, a lighter olive for my *doppelrolle*, Jürgen Bergen.

Oh, but it will be a relief to be Zeno Kühn again, future

resident astronomer at AWE-T, where I will be the first to discover evidence of life on Earth's twin. Not just the suggestion of life. Not mere theories that a planet beyond our solar system has a breathable atmosphere, tolerable temperature, and consistent orbit around a nurturing sun. *Nein*! I yearn to discover what man has sought since humans first searched the night sky. With the world's most powerful telescope, I will find verifiable proof of oxygen and methane in the atmosphere of that planet. Proof that life exists!

And then — oh, I dream of having the world's largest and most amazing telescope renamed after me.

Chapter Twelve

ALOHA, AUTHORITIES

Marie Ingles

Two days after our team's trips to MPH and Knight, the four of us drove south to Kailua-Kona, or "Kailua Town," as I've heard some locals call it.

Most everybody calls it "Kona," but what it means is "leeward or dry side." And "Kailua" stems from the word "kai," which means "sea," and "lua," which may mean twin or two. So Kailua-Kona may mean "twin seas or bays on the leeward side." It's directional, or that's what one article said.

The origin of words fascinates me. A chatty lady at the Waikoloa Village Book Mobile recommended an online dictionary called wehewehe.org. It helps translate words from 'ōlelo Hawai'i to English and back again. I even looked up "wehewehe." It comes from the phrase, *puke wehewehe 'ōlelo*, which means "book to explain words, or dictionary."

Maybe I am turning into Natalie. Each time Ryan and I hear a new term on the news, I look it up.

Our brilliant Natalie was on her souped-up laptop during the drive, pointing out this or that, much to Billy Bob's chagrined sighs. "Did you know Maunakea means White

Mountain? But it's also called *Mauna a Wākea*, or Mountain of the Sky Father, named after Wākea, the Polynesian god of the sky. Legend says Wākea married Papahānaumoku, the Earth Mother, and all ruling chiefs descended from them. Some Hawaiians believe the mountain is the origin of life, a place of great spiritual power that bridges the two realms between heaven and earth. In ancient times, only chiefs and priests of the highest status could visit the summit. When snow falls on the mountain, Poliʻahu, the snow goddess of Maunakea, descends to the cliffs overlooking the Hamakua Coast."

"Nat, you're gonna drive us nuts with this stuff."

"But we're in Hawaiʻi, and this is Hawaiian cultural lore."

"Boss, you don't buy the fairy tales, do you?"

Ryan grinned. "Nasty, I can't prove they're not true."

Billy Bob scoffed. "Typical lawyer."

"To me, these stories sound like Greek mythology," I said.

"Some Hawaiian people believe them verbatim. I suspect the term 'cultural practices' used around here to describe Hawaiian rituals may be a way to avoid legal issues related to religion," Ryan said.

"But, Boss, according to census reports, it's rare to find anyone in these islands who is one hundred percent 'Native Hawaiian.' And when you consider that the islands' first immigrants were from the Marquesas and Society Islands, to say you are 'Native Hawaiian' actually means your ancestors arrived from one of those island groups," Natalie said.

"It's like an American saying they're 'Scotch Irish,'" I said.

About halfway there, Natalie pointed to the Four Seasons Hualālai Resort, a gorgeous complex with private homes and a public beach. "Kukio Beach is another one I want to try. I read online that it has shade. The sun gets so intense here."

Billy Bob laughed. "I like shade too. No matter how much of that spray I put on, I turn into a gigantic strawberry."

"I looked up the word '*kukio.*' It means something like 'a small pool of water.' It's got a fringe of sand, but it's rocky. The water is clear, though, and there are lots of *honu.* Sea turtles."

"Oh, now I really want to go," Natalie said.

"Team, I promise. We'll have beach time this weekend. But for now, we've got a client who needs to get out of jail."

"Right, Boss. Did you hear anything more from Big Mike?"

"Marie told me their PR firm posted twice on the 808 Insiders site."

Natalie chimed in. "Sort of posted, but they replied to another user's comment, not to the original post."

"So?" Ryan asked.

"That means most users won't see it. It's a MakeFriends thing. If you reply to another user's comment, your reply will go under their comment and somewhat disappear, because it wasn't a comment to the original post."

Ryan shook his head in confusion. "This is why I don't do MakeFriends."

"That's why you have me. I'm monitoring the thread as we speak. They're still ranting about the FBI not using a local firm, and they're still going on about Marie's murder trial. Should I message Big Mike's PR firm to move their comment to the primary thread?"

"How about this, Boss? Nat writes up something for Big Mike or even Sonya to post, like a link to a news article when Marie's charges were dropped. That would be okay, right?"

I heard myself blurt, "Since Sonya was the dear who called this to Big Mike's attention, I'd rather he does it, not Sonya."

Ryan flinched. "I don't want to bother Mike any further."

"But someone is posting lies about me, your loving wife. And it's making your firm look bad."

"Mike and Sonya are our local counsel. Paper pushers, yes, but ethical supervisors."

"Right, Boss. I keep thinking 'co-counsel' means they're working the case like we are."

"Nope. We are Nocona's defense team. All on us."

"But when I get maligned on social media, shouldn't you stand up for me?"

Ryan tensed, both hands taut on the steering wheel. "I already defended you once, as I recall, and I did it for free."

"Whoa," Billy Bob murmured from the back seat.

Guess I wasn't the only one who found that snarky. I scowled at Ryan, hoping for an apology.

But he silently gripped the wheel and stared ahead.

Despite the SUV's air conditioning, the atmosphere inside was stifling. I wondered if Ryan's remark stemmed from frustration or regret.

Regardless, I felt blamed. "Now I'm guilty by association?"

Ryan puffed out a quiet sigh, something a wife would notice as regret.

I gently patted his taut right arm. "It's stressful for all of us to jump on a high-profile case when we're so new here."

Ryan exhaled regretfully again.

His football player side can be an asset when he's in court, but not a wonderful trait when he's worried or overstressed. To him, I probably seemed "Marie Needy," the hapless victim of circumstances, although I had nothing to do with 808 Insiders, nor did I have anything to do with killing Luca Scarlatti, or with my late husband's Ponzi scheme. Was I supposed to sit quietly and take these constant assaults?

From the back seat, Billy Bob ventured, "We'll take 'em, Marie. Whoever 'em is."

I chuckled to lighten the air, then peeked over to see if Ryan had loosened up. His grip remained tense. So, I stole a look back at Billy Bob and Natalie, who had a pair of "uh-oh" grimaces on their faces.

Natalie gave me a silent *shaka*. She'd even learned that.

"It's the official state hand gesture, ever since 2024," she said.

Thankfully, we were almost at the address we'd been given.

Ryan turned left up a road called Hale Makai, and then we turned into the lot and parked. The sign said, "Hawai'i County Police Department."

"Are we in the right spot, Boss?"

"It's the address Colleen sent, anyway."

Inside the modern offices, we timidly asked for FBI Supervisory Special Agent Pua Akana, who thankfully was there. Her dark eyes, bronze complexion, and welcoming approach made me wonder about her Hawaiian heritage. But like so many people on the Big Island, her almond-shaped eyes, high cheekbones, and long black hair also could show she was of Asian, Filipino, or Hispanic origin. Either way, she was a charming mix.

After Ryan introduced the team and we exchanged business cards, Agent Akana gestured us toward a conference room, where we sat around a wide table.

Ryan nervously began, "Supervisory Special Agent Akana, as you know, we represent Nocona Parker —"

"Mr. Ingles, before you say more, I must be clear. This is an ongoing investigation. The federal prosecutor's office provides all discovery."

"I understand, Supervisory Special —" Ryan began.

She held up a hand to interrupt again. "Pua. Just call me Pua. That's easier than all these syllables, don't you think?"

Turning on his courtroom charm, Ryan grinned and gave her a shot of his Pacific blue eyes. "And I'm Ryan. That cuts the syllables even more. And our investigative team members are Marie, Natalie, and Billy Bob."

As Ryan pointed to each of us, we three nodded and smiled, which seemed to loosen things up.

Ryan continued, "Now that we are on a first-name basis, our goal in visiting today is to establish a transparent relationship. Like you, we want to know who killed Shin Watanabe, especially since we are one hundred percent sure Nocona Parker did not."

Pua rolled her eyes and gave Ryan a sympathetic look. "I wish you luck with your firm's inquiries, but it's imperative not to interfere with FBI or local officers' investigations."

"Yes, ma'am, we understand that, but as a law firm, we have a duty to our client."

"Fine, and if your firm uncovers evidence that implicates other suspects, please notify me immediately. Although the FBI has several agents and analysts in Honolulu to assist me, the crime was committed in Hawai'i County. So, county police have an interest in this case, as do state police officers."

"State police?" Billy Bob asked.

"The state has centralized certain enforcement activities, but until they assign investigators to this case, I'm basically *it* on this island. The FBI leases space here, and I collaborate with county police on some cases, including this one."

Ryan nodded seriously. "Staffing seems to be a problem island-wide."

She shook her head in dismay. "Hawai'i County's population has exploded, but this is a big island in other ways. After all, half of it is the world's largest active volcano, and you've got to drive around that. That's why I welcome support, but I don't want to argue case points. What I need are facts."

Ryan nodded. "We will help all we can. In fact, our team noticed from the hunting roster that Nocona Parker was *not* assigned to hunt in the same archery area as Shin Watanabe. What was that you said, Marie?"

"Nocona was assigned to MPH Unit 1, while Mr. Watanabe was assigned to Unit 2."

Ryan glanced coyly at his folded hands, then grinned again. "That alone tells me our client should be released."

She chuckled. "Oh, you're a charmer. We also noticed the unit assignments, but your client could have made his way downslope to get near enough to shoot."

"But why would Nocona kill a fellow astronomer? He came here on vacation. His buddies helped him get hunting permits. He mailed his archery gear to one of them at the Knight offices. If he came here to kill a colleague, why would he make his hunting plans known?"

"That's what I mean about arguing case points. Tell these things to the FBI trial team."

Ryan tsked and whispered a sigh.

Billy Bob stepped in. "I've heard astronomers are gung-ho to find something amazing and new. 'Cause the ones who do might get a TV show like 'Nova.' But as talented as Nocona Parker probably is, he doesn't seem the type who would kill a guy to get ahead in his career."

Pua looked dubious. "I've had cases that surprised me. Last year, a local guy, who was so sweet I thought he couldn't kill a gecko, walked in and admitted he'd just killed his mother."

Ryan looked aghast. "That happen often?"

"Killing their mother? Or admitting it?" Pua said with a sardonic smile.

Ryan chuckled. "Pua, what else can you share? We are in unfamiliar territory."

Pua took a moment, then said with all seriousness. "You sound like a humuhumunukunukuāpua'a out of water."

We four looked at each other, eyes wide.

"Sorry. Another joke. That's Hawai'i's state fish. I like to say it so locals think I can speak the lingo." She grinned again.

"Gosh, my apologies. That's one word my wife has not yet looked up in her … what do you call that, Marie?"

"Wehewehe.org."

"A good resource for sure." Pua took a moment, looked through some papers, and then added, "Well, I do have something. If I have your word you will not share this with the media or public —"

She paused, and we four nodded sincerely.

"To be transparent, this morning we learned that a local activist was spotted at MPH's front gate the day Mr. Watanabe was killed. This guy flashed his ID and tried to get to the store there. Later on, his vehicle was spotted driving erratically on Saddle Road."

"Did he have an MPH hunting permit?"

"Not for this hunt, but he has hunted at MPH, so he would know the lay of the land."

"Will you share his name?"

"As soon as our field office has results on some physical evidence we are examining, we will notify you."

Ryan gave her a curious smile. "Physical evidence. Results. This sounds promising."

Pua grew serious. "Bottom line: With the island's cultural tensions, I don't dare arrest this activist without a ton of proof. He's the son of a hero. His father helped stop the sale of Parker Ranch to a billionaire vegetarian who opposed cattle ranching. That would cost locals a lot of jobs. Following in his footsteps, the son was part of the protests to stop the construction of HILT some years ago."

Our brilliant Natalie blurted, "I can understand stopping the vegan, but I don't understand trying to stop the construction of HILT."

"It's controversial. Some — but not all — Hawaiians believe Maunakea is the sacred point of contact between heaven and

Earth. Only the chiefs and priests were allowed to ascend the summit — again, according to the ancient tales. The activists want to sweep the mauna clean and limit who can go there."

"From what I've read, some activists even want to secede," Natalie said.

"Some think Native Hawaiians should seek at least partial sovereignty, similar to Native American reservations on the mainland. I hope you've read our history," Pua said.

"Oh, Natalie has read reams of history," Billy Bob grinned.

"Good. Too many *malihini* don't understand the Hawaiian view of our *'āina* or land. In the Hawaiian culture, if you take care of the land, it will take care of you."

Natalie nodded. "I read about that. Before Captain Cook arrived, land wasn't seen as something to be owned, but as a resource for the care of the people, right?"

"Yes. The *ali'i nui*, or high chiefs, held ultimate authority and managed the land for the benefit of the society."

Natalie smiled. "I've read about *aloha 'āina* and certainly respect its concepts. But to attack the beneficial science of astronomy as a way to regain control of what *some* believe is a sacred mountain—."

Pua interrupted with a sardonic glare. "Everyone around here says the same thing. 'It's a complex issue.' This is off the record, totally, but my grandparents' ancestors go way back and have Native Hawaiian blood. They tell me Maunakea wasn't all that 'sacred' when they were growing up. My *tūtū pā* tells stories about how he and his boyhood pals went up there to sled and loved to pee in the snow."

We all giggled at that image.

"Sorry, I hope that didn't offend. But now, well, Hawaiians know a lot more about how their ancestors got screwed. Some get worked up and want to secede. Or stop mainlanders from moving here. Stop tourism. Stop astronomy. Go back to fishing and farming. Ever since the protests over HILT went viral, you know, with video of movie stars in native garb, telling the world, 'We won't let you defy this sacred *mauna*,' well, people take one side or another."

"Humans will always find ways to argue," Ryan said.

"Especially lawyers," I laughed.

"Well, unlike some, I'm pleased to have astronomy and talented *malihini* like you on this island. My grandparents were island-born, but my parents went to L.A. for college and to make a living. So, I grew up a mainland girl. I guess that's why I prefer science to some rather impossible myths. I consider them fairy tales, like Santa Claus, Peter Pan, and so forth. But I don't think Hawai'i should be governed by fairy tales."

Ryan nodded. "We certainly don't have a say in the matter, but I'm glad to hear a common-sense local view."

Pursing her lips, Pua glanced at a printout she'd brought to our meeting. "Oh, I forgot. Before you leave, this screenshot landed in my email this morning. The county police PR person in Hilo sent me a MakeFriends post from the 808 Insiders page. It says that Marie Ingles, formerly Marie Donovan, was involved in the murder of an opera maestro. Are you the same Marie, and is this post accurate?"

Taken aback, my voice trembled. "I am the same Marie, but the post is not accurate."

Ryan jumped in. "Pua, all charges were dismissed. The whole thing was a frame job. And months later, our legal team uncovered evidence that the true killers had escaped to Dubai. They are on the FBI's Ten Most Wanted Fugitives list."

"Oh, my, I'm truly a special FBI agent, aren't I? I'm embarrassed I didn't look that up."

"Nor did 808 Insiders," Natalie said wryly.

Pua shook her head. "That group has mushroomed over the last month or two. But many posts are untrue. Sheila Huber —

that's the county police PR person — tells me she spends a good part of her day refuting lies."

"Being slightly paranoid, I wondered if this post might have come from a local law firm that did not get the Nocona Parker case," Ryan said.

"A possibility. But here's what Sheila said you should do." Pua read from her email printout. "Report the post to the MakeFriends admin as false news. Comment on the original post that the statements are libelous. And include links to reputable news sources."

"Will do."

"Shelia added, "Tell them that you've brought this to the attention of county police, and you are welcome to use her name. That's Sheila Huber, director of public information for Hawai'i County Police," Pua said.

I wrote that down as Ryan nodded toward Natalie. "That's great news. Our computer analyst will take care of it today."

Natalie nervously started to say something, but Billy Bob gave her the eye.

Pua noticed, but let it pass. "There are enough lies these days, from government to news and social media. We certainly don't need more. But I should get off my soapbox and return to the point of our meeting. Yes, I'm willing to look at other suspects. But I need evidence to release your client. Frankly, I've got a lot of political pressure."

✻

AFTER WE THANKED PUA FOR HER TIME, WE WENT OUT TO the SUV, got in, and buckled up.

Ryan seemed relieved. "Phew, we got over that hump." He paused for a bit, gathering courage, then patted my knee. "And, to my loving wife and all pals within earshot, I apologize for my short-circuit to Marie earlier. I'm pissed that these attacks on her continue, but I shouldn't take it out on Marie. I thought we'd left these accusations back in Dallas."

Suddenly overwhelmed, I choked out, "Me too." Admittedly, I teared up a bit, although I stared out the passenger window to hide it from everybody. I didn't want to reappear as "Marie Needy." We've had enough of her.

In the outside rearview mirror, I could see Billy Bob wink sympathetically at me from his side in the back seat. Then he gave me a silent thumbs up.

"Boss, Agent Akana said she's being pressured to convict Nocona. I think she shared that recent evidence with us for a reason. Maybe she wants us to do what she can't," Billy Bob said.

"I can research the hero activist's father ... find out who his son is and where he lives," Natalie said.

"Yeah, then I can follow him around and see what he's up to. I promise, Boss. He'll never see me."

"Billy Bob, Nat, I'm with you in spirit, but I don't know if we should go that far until we hear more about the physical evidence the FBI is pursuing."

"I wanted to tell Pua I've been trying to hack into 808 Insiders but getting nowhere. I guess Billy Bob was wise to stop me from saying more."

"Natalie, Pua doesn't need to know you are a hacker. We need to earn her trust by helping her do her job, but not illegally. You and Billy Bob can do some research, but as far as following the guy, well, I feel like we are on a rock with an island of enemies."

Everybody got quiet for a while as we drove along, but at a stoplight, Billy Bob's stomach growled so loudly, we could hear it from the front.

We all laughed.

"Billy Bob, that's an inventive way to tell me it's time for lunch. I hear Don the Beachcomber is a good spot. Anybody have a clue where it is?"

Natalie fired up her GPS, and off we drove toward the Royal Kona Resort on Ali'i Drive, a short walk from the shoreline. At the entrance, lava rock pillars supported a wooden *porte cochere* with a thatched roof.

After Ryan handed the SUV key fob to a young local valet, we walked inside. To the right, massive columns supported the resort's lobby, which was decorated with island-style wicker furniture and tropical plants. I could see an enormous fireplace in the center. And to the left was the resort's restaurant, a tiki bar with huge tiki-god statues, lots of bamboo, thatch, and nautical decor.

At the restaurant's front desk, Ryan gave his name.

I glanced past the hostess and noticed the place was full of islanders for lunch. I hoped they wouldn't glare at us "white guys," as Ryan calls us. Natalie fares much better with locals than we do. Sometimes, I want to put a sign around my neck that says, "Aloha, yes, I am white, and I live here, and I'm doing my best to be respectful of your island and culture." But then, that probably would make them resent me, too.

Chapter Thirteen

KANAKA ADVOCATE DAILY
Murder Charges Dropped

HONOLULU — This morning, FBI officials dropped capital murder charges against Texas astronomer Nocona Parker in the death of Japanese astrophysicist Shin Watanabe, who died while game hunting on the Big Island.

By phone interview, FBI Supervisory Special Agent (SSA) Pua Akana remarked that Maunakea Puʻuhonua Holoholona (MPH) records showed Parker was assigned to hunt in a different wildlife area from Watanabe the day of the murder.

"More importantly, several witnesses affirmed that Mr. Parker remained within his assigned hunting unit throughout the scheduled period. Because of this additional detail, prosecutors took a closer look at even more evidence the FBI has examined," SSA Akana said.

Replying to a barrage of reporters' questions, SSA Akana replied that the FBI examined a package containing Parker's archery equipment and found the wrapper had been tampered with. She added, "I cannot say more at this time."

Contacted by phone, Parker expressed relief. As for the

package containing his archery equipment, he said, "The package I mailed to my buddy at Knight was scuffed up in transit. I didn't think much about that, since it had come such a long way, and my archery equipment arrived in good shape. That's all I cared about. Luckily, I saved the packaging to reuse when I mailed my equipment back to Texas. The FBI examined it and found evidence that proved I didn't kill Mr. Watanabe. That's all I know."

Parker's defense attorney, Ryan Ingles, formerly of Dallas and now a Big Island resident, remarked by phone that he was grateful to the FBI for their efforts. "I've been in the defense field for many years and can tell almost immediately if a client has committed a crime. Nocona is a hunter, yes. Not a murderer."

Pleiades Observatory Director Hiroshi Urata pressed for more investigation. "The question remains, who killed Shin Watanabe? This is an international concern. If renowned international astrophysicists come to Hawaii Island to study the universe, how can they know they will be safe?"

By telephone, SSA Akana replied, "All murder cases are treated with the same diligence. But for this particular case, we have established a special task force that includes county police Deputy Chief Harold Koizumi in a lead role, several analysts from our FBI field office on Oahu, and state police Deputy Sheriff Buckner Urima, who may assign even more state investigators. I agree, there's more to this case than meets the eye. Someone tampered with the package containing Nocona Parker's archery equipment. What that means, our task force hopes to find out."

Asked whether members of the astronomy community, or even local island residents should fear for their lives, SSA Akana remarked, "I would ask everyone to be on the lookout for anything unusual, something or someone that seems out of place. Citizens with information that relates to this case should contact the FBI Hawaii Task Force tip line at (808) 999-1111."

For information, contact reporter Wallace Huppenthall at (808) 765-1212.

Chapter Fourteen

MY SIDE OF THE MIRRORS

Jürgen Bergen / Zeno Kühn

W*undervoll!* The FBI caught even more of my clues. The Oahu forensics team figured out Nocona's package had been resealed with tape that had a Hawai'i Trail Explorers logo. They didn't mention that in the media, probably to save them for a future trial. But surely this new FBI Hawai'i Task Force will look at Kekoa Palakiko since he works for that tour group.

Nocona Parker was merely bait, never a target. He's only a grunt scope aimer, a button pusher, not a dedicated astrophysicist like me. He works for the machine that pays his salary. On the contrary, I command the machine to perform for me. Directors from the world's most prestigious observatories look forward to my research proposals because that gives their observatory prestige. And new discoveries provide ammunition for fundraising.

Observatories must always go begging. More funds. Bigger scopes. Higher salaries.

Surely the task force will now question Kekoa Palakiko. His separatist *Freunde* on social media rant about their sovereignty over Maunakea and rail against the completion of HILT. They seem to think astronomers make millions. But the opposite is true. All observatories beg and borrow government grants to build these amazing instruments.

Even so, Europe's AWE-T and its lasers will surpass all land-based telescopes in visual acuity.

What these activists don't understand is that even if you discover the secrets of dark matter and dark energy, you and your colleagues must first ask allied teams to confirm your discoveries, then you publish papers in prestigious journals and send press releases. Rarely are there any monetary prizes.

Oh, sure, resident astronomers and telescope engineers make better salaries than island bartenders and therefore can buy overpriced houses in Waimea, Waikoloa Village, or Hilo. I understand the locals' envy of that and their resentment of well-paid *haole* of any profession, driving up housing costs simply because they can pay more.

Luckily, not all indigenous populations are so anti-astronomy. In fact, in other parts of the world, they're placated by the flush of money astronomy brings to remote areas. Observatory workers need housing, places to shop, places to dine, people to fix things, and more.

After all, my discovery several years ago of *Heimatstern* at Gran Telescopio Canarias atop Roque de los Muchachos on the island of La Palma generated lots of press. At that time, the Gran Telescopio was the largest optical scope in the world. The board of directors loved having their observatory associated with such brilliant work.

As for the Big Bend Observatory in Texas, they have built a fine eleven-meter instrument. But look where it is: set upon a piddly 4,000-foot hill near the "historic" town of Marathon in *Krähwinkel,* Texas. Several years ago, the observatory invited me to speak at a conference and housed me at a renowned historic inn. This meant not only did the floor creak, but the bed creaked too. Luckily, the hotel restaurant was a destination unto itself. Best braised wild boar shank ever, with pretzel *Spaetzle*.

Admittedly, Big Bend Observatory is doing decent spectroscopy in the areas of dark energy and black holes. But as for finding Earth's twin? It needs the power of the AWE-T.

Chapter Fifteen

MY BORED HUSBAND

Marie Ingles

After Nocona Parker's release, we knew we would have to say goodbye to Billy Bob and Natalie, but not before they begged for time off from Colleen and spent five days sightseeing with us.

We gave them the grand tour, from the northwestern tip of the island at Hāw'i, then around the Hamakua Coast to Hilo on the east side of the island, and then south to Volcano National Park. We hit the timing just right. Kīlauea was showing off with amazing twin lava fountains, reportedly almost a thousand feet high. We wore masks to protect our lungs and kept our distance to avoid what's called 'Pele's hair.' These are fine, hair-like strands of golden-brown volcanic glass that can get into your lungs if you don't protect yourself.

Despite the dangers and smell of the vog, each of us found the lava flows mesmerizing. The color of fresh lava is a searing golden red, perhaps nature's way of warning Earth's creatures not to touch it.

It was very late after we got back that night, so we saved a journey to South Point for two days later. Known as the southernmost point in the United States, South Point is a rocky prominence that juts out over the wildly rushing Pacific. Locals post fishing lines there, and tourists drive there to watch the adventurous cliff divers.

Natalie dared Billy Bob to dive into the cavernous hole that drops at least forty feet into the Pacific.

"Maybe in my younger days," he grinned as he patted his spare tire tummy.

For dinner, we drove back up the leeward side to Kona, where we dined seaside at Magic's Beach Grill and then drove back again to Hōkele Kilohana. We must have put five hundred miles on our rental car.

Billy Bob and Natalie *oohed* and *ahhed* appropriately at each venue, but Ryan and I found it slightly boring to be tour guides. The island's many sights that thrilled us on our first visit have become commonplace as we go about our daily lives. I fear we have developed the "been there, done that" problem.

One evening after sightseeing and partying, Ryan asked me privately, "When did you say they're heading back to Dallas?"

I chuckled. "Had enough, Mr. Tour Guide?"

"Let's just say my future is not in the tourism biz."

"They leave Friday. Just two more days."

He groaned in dismay.

After we hugged Billy Bob and Natalie goodbye at the airport, Ryan spent a few days happily doing nothing but watching cable TV *ad nauseum*. He even added a twenty-four-hour sports package to our already outlandish cable bill.

Times when I couldn't take another NFL battle, I'd go upstairs to play my cello. The condo's third bedroom turned out to be a good place for me to create a music studio. The room is positioned on an outside wall opposite our downstairs primary bedroom. My goal was to create a space where I could play at three a.m., but only the palm trees outside might hear me.

To help Ryan be more active, I signed him up for a men's golf group. He dutifully played once a week, but between rounds, he roamed the house aimlessly and contradicted almost anything he heard on television news. Likely, it's the lawyer in him, but the frequent, very vocal pushback became wearisome. I suspect married couples are not supposed to spend twenty-four hours a day together.

At breakfast, I read another news article about the case and nodded Ryan's way. "You should be proud. Nocona is free."

"But the murderer is still out there. Have you checked with Pua Akana? Has she questioned that local 'person of interest,' or does the FBI not interrogate sons of native heroes?"

"I'm sure Pua would arrest someone if she had solid evidence. FBI tests proved Nocona did not do it, but not that anyone else did."

"Are you another of those who don't think Native Hawaiians should be held to task, simply because their ancestors followed the birds and stars to arrive here a thousand years ago?"

"Ryan, that sounds like *haole* talk. That isn't your way."

He shrugged. "I might have picked it up from the guys you make me play golf with."

"Oh, now, I'm *making* you play golf?"

"Sorry. That didn't come out right. But yes, some guys in the golf group are quite racist."

"Well, racist is the last thing we need to be on this island. And, as for my calling the FBI, you always say we're not the police. What's the story?"

He sighed. "Oh, I don't know. I'm just unsettled. There's not a lot to do around here. I'm kind of 'beached.'"

"Let's plan a drive. Maybe to Hilo for lunch on the bay, then a bit of shopping. We could stop off in Volcano and rummage shops there."

"We just did that with Billy Bob and Natalie."

"Well, how about a swim at the beach club?"

"Oh gads," he sighed again. Then he grabbed his dishes and went inside.

Now, I was feeling unsettled. Ryan's attitude was so unlike him. I went inside to tidy the dishes, and from the kitchen, I heard him banging on plumbing in the half-bath.

I peeked in to see.

Plumbing parts were strewn everywhere. Flappers, flippers, and springs.

"Why not call for maintenance? We're renters, not owners."

"The last time we called, the guys didn't fix it right. You know. They were locals who didn't give a hoot about doing things right for *haole*."

"Ryan, again with the talk. How about I help? Do you need a spare pair of hands?"

"Do you fix toilets?" he barked.

"Not when I have your expertise, dear," I replied with a tinge of sarcasm, then went upstairs and madly played my cello for an hour.

It's my escape and release. I can forget all else and am never bored or angry when I play. But afterward, refreshed and replenished, I headed back downstairs. Ryan was still banging in the bathroom. So I decided to heck with Ryan. I'll go to the beach club myself. Leave him to the toilets or a replay of the K.C. Chiefs Super Bowl IV win.

Luckily, I did. As I searched the U-shaped sandy beach for a vacant cabana chair, a rather robust, dark-skinned woman wearing a deep-pink straw hat called out to me. "Would you like to share my cabana? I'm solo today."

Her smile was so charming, I took her up on her offer. "Thank you. My husband was too busy trying to be a plumber."

She tossed her head back and laughed.

I could see from the crinkles around her eyes, she was about my age, forty. And as we chatted, I was relieved to learn she lives in our HOA and is not a tourist.

She reached out to shake my hand. "Ailani Moreau. I'm so glad to meet another resident. That's one drawback to living in a resort community. Most humans we meet are here only for a week or two. They drive in, you chat with them at the pool, maybe have drinks and dinner at the beach club, and then they leave. The following week, another new couple drives in. I get so I don't even bother saying aloha, but something about your demeanor said, 'I live here.'"

As we talked more, I learned that Ailani was born on Oahu and was half Hawaiian and half Samoan. Her mother immigrated from Samoa to attend college here, then married a US Navy officer of mostly Hawaiian blood.

"The result is this large girl who grew up in Ewa Beach on Oahu. My parents moved to the Big Island after Daddy retired. It was less expensive to buy a house here, at least at that time. They live in Keauhou Estates, south of Kona. Takes me a good hour to drive there from here."

"Did you move here to keep an eye on them?"

"No, no, no...well, long story, I graduated from Punahou, a private school in Honolulu, then went to the University of British Columbia in Vancouver, Canada. I wanted to get off-island for a while. Find out what North America was like. Vancouver is where I met my husband, Gilles. He's French-Canadian. We've lived in Vancouver since our college days, but moved to the Big Island six months ago for his job. He works for the company that made the mirrors for HILT. You know, the new giant telescope."

"Oh, how exciting. I can't wait to see the first images."

Her straw hat flopped with a nod. "That will be a while.

The mirrors are only heading this way as we speak. That ought to stir up the protesters."

"I've read about that. I think it's sad that old-world cultures resent new-world science."

"Not only resent, but rebel," Ailani murmured. "Sorry, I get going on some topics. It's my poly-sci major. Although I have Hawaiian blood, I don't buy into the protest movement. Nor do I think Pele flies from volcano to volcano. Just call me sacrilegious."

As she and I chatted further, I got the feeling she may become a friend. Who knows? Maybe she needed a friend too.

Ailani patted my arm. "It's nice to meet you. Admittedly, I've felt a bit isolated here."

"Even when you're a local? You should feel what it's like as an Anglo *malihini*."

"But I'm a *malihini* on this island, anyway. Especially since I've lived in Canada for years."

"Maybe we need to start a support group. My dear husband, whom I love deeply, turns out to be a poor girlfriend. He was a defense attorney in Dallas. Almost daily, I remind myself that Ryan was trained to argue, and I cannot expect sympathy or advice. Each time I forget, we have communication dysfunction. He'll ask, 'What do you want me to do?' When I reply, 'I just need you to listen,' he'll say something macho, like, 'Well, if you need me to do anything, I'll be happy to do it, but I don't think complaining does much good.' That's when I pout and run upstairs to play my cello."

"You play classical music?"

"In Dallas, I was principal cellist with Metroplex Opera Orchestra, and I soloed with Dallas Symphony Orchestra now and then."

"Wow, I'm impressed."

"You may hear me practicing! I'm trying to stay fresh, so I

might take a solo gig. I quit the orchestra after Ryan got the wild idea of retiring and moving here. Not long after, he wound up with a murder case — the Texas astronomer arrested for killing that poor Japanese researcher."

"Your husband is the hunky 'Ryan Ingles' I saw on TV. You are one lucky *wahine*."

"Thank you for reminding me. I've known him since college, and he is far more handsome now that he doesn't wear thick glasses. His teammates used to call him 'Diver' because he wore prescription goggles during football games."

"Your husband was a football player?"

"Yes. Both husbands. Ryan is my second. He was an all-American linebacker on the same college team as my late husband, Cole Donovan. He was a pro quarterback. Portland Explorers. Super Bowls and all that."

"Cole Donovan? Being from the Pacific Northwest, my gosh, we were Explorers fans! Goodness, I've met a celebrity."

"Oh, I'm no celebrity, but Cole certainly thought he was."

I hesitated to say more. Admittedly, I'm still leery of opening up to *anybody*. Who wouldn't be, after being framed for murder by Lena, and *still* being blamed for who knows what by the D'Posse clique. I must be some sort of magnet for abuse: my father calling me his Ava Gardner but telling me how immoral I was, and Cole's philandering during our twenty-year marriage. Each remains difficult to forget.

Thankfully, both are dead and cannot abuse me anymore.

Ailani interrupted my memory lane. "So, after Cole died, you and Ryan got together?"

"That happened after my fifteen minutes of notoriety. You see, Cole went into finance in Dallas. Our marriage was in the toilet, but we had twin sons, and Cole was doing well financially, or so I thought. It seemed better to hang on. Then Cole died. At first, police thought it was suicide because Cole was running a Ponzi scheme that lost tons of money. But months later, partly because of Cole's schemes, Dallas Police arrested me for killing the opera's maestro. That's when Ryan came to my defense. In the end, it turned out my best friend had framed me. She was a serial murderer — she killed Cole and the maestro too."

"This sounds like a *Dateline* episode."

I laughed in exhaustion. "You would not believe how many people say that. You can tell my life has been anything but calm over the past several years."

"But Ryan was your 'knight'?"

"Exactly. But I'm afraid my knight is bored. Now that Nocona Parker's charges were dropped, we both wonder if he made the right choice to sell his law firm and move so far away. I guess they call this —"

"Island fever. After you've seen Hilo, well, you've seen Hilo. But at least you have your cello. Something meaningful. And, like you and Ryan, I need more to do than sunbathe. In B.C., I did a stint as Minister of Citizens' Services, a cabinet position."

"Wow, I'm impressed. Do you think you'll get into government here?"

She sighed in exasperation. "That might be like stepping on *kiawe* thorns. My parents say Hawai'i County is so dysfunctional, they should all be in the clink. It seems money greases a few too many *braddah* palms."

"I guess Hilo is too far to drive if you want a county post."

"The county has nine districts, and each has a dedicated council member. I considered running for our district's seat, but the number of years you've lived and worked here means a lot to voters, especially locals. The establishment does not want newbies telling them what to do."

I laughed. "The locals who work at the DMV in Kona certainly made that clear. We had to go back three times to get our Hawai'i driver's licenses because they wanted yet more proof of ID. It's chaotic."

"Oh, isn't that the truth? Try coming here with a Canadian license! Courteous customer service doesn't seem to be in the Hawai'i DMV training programs."

"To tell you the truth, I didn't expect all this animosity toward *malihini*. I mean, this is the *Aloha* State."

Ailani sighed. "Oh, I shouldn't dirty mouth my *braddah* and *sistah*. I imagine local workers have to put up with a lot of shit from arrogant tourists and mainlanders like me, demanding things run as efficiently as they do in Canada or wherever."

"Maybe you could campaign on the idea of better service for everyone."

"An idea. I'm sure my mother has bragged to everybody in Kona about my achievements, but that's why I've got to bide my time. Then again, maybe I'll run during the next cycle, simply to stay busy. Gilles says we'll be here quite some time since the mirrors will need adjusting and maintenance. His team handles all that."

"Besides Ryan's boredom, I'm also wondering what I might do on this island. I saw there's a philharmonic in Waimea."

She giggled at that. "If you wanna play for free."

A text dinged on Ailani's phone. "Oh, my gosh, Gilles is bringing a colleague home. The HILT project manager. He's a Swiss guy from Zürich. Jürgen something."

As she rose and gathered her gear, I rummaged in my beach bag. "Here's our social card. Let me know if you and your husband would like to have drinks sometime."

"Well, why not *pau hana* at Napua this Friday?"

"*Pau hana?*"

"Happy Hour. 'Done working.' It's like happy hour on the mainland. Time to relax and celebrate."

"Even if you don't work?"

She grinned. "We'll figure that part out."

"Just send me a text with your contact info, and I'll confirm with Ryan. He'll probably leap at the chance to do something other than have dinner with me on the lanai."

She waved goodbye as her husky legs loped toward the parking lot.

After she left, I spent half an hour staring at the lovely bay, with views of Kohala Mountain in the distance. Then I gathered my gear to head home. I was eager to tell Ryan about my new friend, Ailani. Perhaps "our" new friends, Ailani and Gilles. Then again, I reminded myself not to rush anything. As in music, pacing is key. If I force things, Ryan might think I wanted him to do something he didn't want to do, and that's always the kiss of death with men.

Chapter Sixteen

KANAKA ADVOCATE DAILY

Aussie Astronomer Dies in Freak Accident

HILO, Hawaii — An astronomer for the Infrared Telescope of the United Kingdom (ITUK) was found dead at sunset yesterday, near the summit of Maunakea.

At a press conference this morning, county police Deputy Chief Harold Koizumi released the astronomer's name as Dexter Zachary, 52. Originally from North Ryde, Australia, a suburb of Sydney, Mr. Zachary was married and was the father of three teenage children.

In response to reporters' questions, Koizumi remarked, "Mr. Zachary's wife Pamela, who lives in Hilo, said her husband called yesterday to say he was going snowboarding at the summit. But he did not return home as planned. A team of Maunakea Rangers searched the summit area that night and the following morning when they found his body."

According to Koizumi, "Mr. Zachary's body was flown to Honolulu for autopsy. It's too soon to know the cause of death. It may simply be a tragic accident. Even though the summit has snowpack in some areas after a big storm, it is very rocky up there. A tumble off-course might be fatal. We will announce autopsy results as soon as we know more."

When asked if this death is connected to the recent murder of astronomer Shin Watanabe, who was killed by an arrow while hunting last month at a Maunakea Puuhonua Holoholona (MPH), FBI Supervisory Special Agent (SSA) Pua Akana said, "At this time, Mr. Zachary's death does not appear connected, but our forensics team on Oahu has provided several key discoveries. And our task force on the Big Island is interviewing witnesses island-wide. Of course, we hope to have answers soon, but at this stage, we cannot say more."

Oliver Witherspoon, ITUK executive director, released a statement. "All of us at ITUK are devastated by the loss of our friend and stellar researcher, Dexter Zachary. He was devoted to the study of our universe, especially proving the existence of life forms beyond our solar system. In fact, above Dexter's monitor, he taped lines from the film *Contact*. Originally assigned to Carl Sagan, it says, 'The universe is a pretty big place. If it's just us, seems like an awful waste of space.' Dexter will be missed greatly, but his dedicated team will continue his work with renewed resolve."

For information, contact reporter Wallace Huppenthall at (808) 765-1212.

Chapter Seventeen

PONO-TV NEWS ONLINE

Breaking — Astronomer Poisoned

HONOLULU — Dr. Wendell Mahelona, Honolulu County chief medical examiner, announced today that the death atop Maunakea of Australian astronomer Dexter Zachary was likely caused by the effects of poison.

"A mass of toxicants was found in his blood, identified as alkaloids found in *brugmansia candida*, or what is commonly called 'Angel's Trumpet.' However, Mr. Zachary's death was caused by blunt force trauma to the head," Dr. Mahelona said.

This announcement prompted a barrage of questions from reporters because a Japanese astronomer was murdered recently on the Big Island, and the case remains unsolved.

"At this time, my office cannot label Mr. Zachary's death a homicide. Investigators will probably interview his family and associates about his lifestyle habits and search his home and grounds for evidence of this poison. I will say there were heavy doses of these alkaloids in Mr. Zachary's bloodstream — far more than if he had gardened it. Or smoked it, as some do."

When asked why someone would smoke this plant, Dr. Mahelona replied, "This particular species is invasive on Hawaii

Island. Some people dry it to smoke like a cigarette. Others brew a tea for hallucinatory effects, which I'm told are akin to taking LSD. But Angel's Trumpet is something you do not want to try. It can kill you. A scientist like Dexter Zachary would likely know that."

Colter Wynne, a CDC analyst in Atlanta, responded to our questions by email. "The danger in this plant is with the compounds known chemically as tropane alkaloids. Ingestion results in an alkaloid-induced central nervous system anticholinergic syndrome, characterized by symptoms such as fever, delirium, hallucinations, agitation, and persistent memory disturbances. Severe intoxication may cause flaccid paralysis, convulsions, and even death."

According to the plant identification website, floridata.com, "The Hawaiian name for this species is *nānāhonua*, which translates to 'looking at the ground.' It describes a plant whose flowers open toward the earth."

A cousin species is *datura candida*. Its flowers open up toward the sky.

Oliver Witherspoon, director of the Infrared Telescope of the United Kingdom, where Zachary was employed, expressed deep concern. "This is shocking news. I've known Dex for years. He's from down under, so of course he drank a *cuppa*, as we call hot tea. But after work, Dex was a gin and tonic man. In all this time, I never heard him talk about — nor have I ever seen him use — any illegal drug or even an herbal hallucinogenic."

FBI Supervisory Special Agent (SSA) Pua Akana said by phone that her team will investigate this development. "If any member of our island communities learns of suspicious activity, please call the FBI Hawaii Task Force tip line at (808) 999-1111," SSA Akana said.

Reported by Michelle Kimura. Stay tuned to PONO-TV.com for updates.

Chapter Eighteen

808 INSIDERS

Da Real Scoop

Today at 12:39 p.m.

H int, hint, local practitioners. All it takes to eliminate the polluting observatories that defile our sacred Maunakea is simply a hot cup of local tea. Perhaps if all the astronomers disappear, so will the telescopes?

❊

Most Relevant:
Da Kine Sailor — You got dat right, brah! Down with dose snobby astronomaters. Up with *da kanaka*!
Wahine Beekeeper — I'll be happy to drop by with a few cups of *da* hot stuff.
Got to Fish — Wahine Beekeeper, are you *da* hot stuff?
Ono Wrangler — I don't think she meant that.
Wahine Beekeeper — Mahalo, Ono Wrangler
Da Kine Sailor — Maybe we get rid of all *haole*. *Dey* order tea? Maybe fix them a cuppa *da kine*.

Chapter Nineteen

MY SIDE OF THE MIRRORS

Jürgen Bergen / Zeno Kühn

Such silly people, tumbling into my methodical puzzle. And for some unexpected reason, I've gained an ally with this 808 Insiders group. I wonder who the page administrator is. The "People" page lists the name Georgie J. Helm, clearly a false account. Just a quick search on Google yielded, "Hawaiian activist George Jarrett Helm Jr. helped found the Protecting Kahoʻolawe Ohana organization that eventually ended the US Navy bombing of the island. In 1976, he and nine activists occupied Kahoʻolawe but were arrested. On March 7, 1977, he returned to Kahoʻolawe but was injured after his boat was swamped. He disappeared."

Ja sicher, 808 Insiders is run by a fake account. But with thirty thousand members, MakeFriends is probably ecstatic to have such a vast audience for its ads. I wonder if the group admin is from the sovereignty group, Island Kingdom Now. It's the most organized, complete with a paid social media manager.

Regardless, killing Dexter Zachary was the easiest piece. He was eager to make his name. All I had to do was leave a voicemail from a burner phone I set up to display "Kekoa

Palakiko." In my best Hawaiian-flavored English, I said I wanted to learn more about astronomy and his work. I might be able to sway *nā kanaka*, or the local people. Would he give me a tour of ITUK? If so, I'd bring some picnic *grindz*. Oh, and I had a special *ki*, which means "tea," a brew made from a local *pua*, or "flower."

In an over-eager reply, Dexter gave me my choice of days and times.

Making the poisonous tea was easy enough. There are many resources online. My only problem was knowing how many vines to cut.

Truly, this stuff grows thickly, even in residential areas. Just driving around, I noticed a blooming crop of Angel's Trumpet hanging over a fence off Hina Lani Street in North Kona.

I returned the next day, dressed in my Kekoa Palakiko disguise and driving "his" black Jeep. I made a big deal out of parking just off the road. Then I got out and cut a bunch of vines with flowers, gathered them into two leaf and lawn black bags, and stuffed them into the tailgate. Then I drove toward the small home where Kekoa lives.

I'd already called his tour company to see if he worked that day, so I knew he wasn't home. I parked in front of his house for about an hour, giving the neighbors time to see the Jeep. I got out, messed around with the bags, pulled them out, opened them up, tightened them back, and put them inside. My goal was to have neighbors see Kekoa doing this stuff. I even waved and smiled at a few.

Then I drove back to my apartment in Waimea, where I stole in with the bags. I would have put the wines out to dry on my balcony, but it mists or rains almost every day in Waimea. Things never dry out. There's mold everywhere in the old buildings of this funky town. So I had to dry the leaves and flowers in my living room. *Mein Güte*, my furniture was covered with vines, and because of the humidity, it took several days for the leaves and flowers to dry fully.

Once the vines dried, I ground the leaves and flowers in a food processor. Luckily, my apartment had a big pot for me to simmer the grounds in. I bubbled the green mess for an hour, then added a dose of *rooibos* red tea for color and lots of sugar to mask any bitterness. I wasn't about to taste the concoction, for fear I might keel over before I could kill Dexter.

Tea and picnic lunch prepared, I again dressed as Kekoa, drove up Maunakea access road in my Jeep, and met Dexter at the VIS.

Regretfully, I found him to be a charming and talkative fellow, to the point I wished I didn't have to kill him. Tall, maybe six-feet-two, younger than me by ten years, his bright green eyes squinted at the sun arching above us in the thin air. Although I've practiced my Hawaiian-accented English to a decent state, I let him do most of the talking, while I threw in a "brah," "mahalo," and "rajah" now and then. Since Dexter was from Australia, what did he know?

He was wearing a turtleneck under a puffy jacket, with a ski cap and gloves, while I appeared very "braddah" in a puffy vest over a green Hawai'i Trail Explorers t-shirt, with the sleeves rolled to display my spray-bronzed, muscled arms. I was terribly cold but wanted to behave like an island-born tour guide, who's acclimated to all ranges of temperatures.

In Dexter's four-wheel-drive SUV, he drove us up the steep incline and twisting switchbacks to the almost fourteen-thousand-foot summit. At this elevation, you're in freezing air. You're also way above any clouds. All you see when you peer toward the ocean is blue, and you can't tell whether the blue is the ocean or the atmosphere.

Surrounding you are the hulking domes of the

observatories, my competitors, nestled in a curved row on the rust-colored terrain.

Inside ITUK, I truly enjoyed Dexter's chatty tour, but I said little. And despite my disguise, I had to avoid a couple of technicians I'd seen now and then at the bunkhouse.

During Dexter's tour, he strutted around, proud of his observatory's accomplishments. Proud, but perhaps quite jealous of HILT.

"After we finish here, I'll drive you down to the HILT site before we head back to the VIS. To appease activists, the site is five hundred feet below the summit. Every astronomer on this island wants to land time on HILT, once it's finished. A few of these older scopes will be obsolete as soon as HILT goes live."

"They should be taken down. Clear the sacred *mauna*," I spouted with my acting skills.

The two technicians across the way frowned.

Dexter reconsidered. "Perhaps I shouldn't have said 'obsolete.' Maunakea is the best site in the world for astronomical research and especially for education and training. Every scope up here provides something different. Our ITUK observatory is infrared, while HILT will be optical infrared. There are also sub-millimeter scopes and radio scopes. This technical jargon means there is tremendous variety in the research capacity atop Maunakea, so each telescope here is valuable and used to the max."

I silently nodded, as if impressed. I must give Dexter credit. He had much of value to say and was generous toward me, asking questions like, "Why do Native Hawaiians object to others doing astronomy atop Maunakea when your ancestors came up here to study the stars too?"

I struggled to answer his questions, trying to sound less informed than I was. After all, I was disguised as a rebel against the *haole* invasion of my land and culture. But my brain agreed with Dexter, so I had trouble sounding sincere. Mostly, I sounded defensive, spouting, "These are sacred sites. The only people allowed to come up here were *kahuna*! Not *haole*."

Again, the technicians across the way glared my way.

Dexter was not deterred by my belligerence. "You are old enough to know that over the past forty years, there has been a renaissance of what some consider to be native beliefs. But not all Hawaiians agree on what those are or should be. Do you want to return to the days when Maunakea was '*wahi kapu*,' and only *kahuna* were allowed at the summit? Or are the anti-HILT protests really a battle to gain money, concessions, and power?" Dexter gestured toward the open expanse around us. "There's plenty of room up here for all cultures to co-exist. We all originated from the same stardust."

That's when I surprised myself by summoning my acting talent. I didn't believe a word I said, but I knew I had to say it. "But why is co-existence always at our expense? Some time ago, a group sponsored a bill to create a committee of Native Hawaiians to manage all summits above 6,500 feet. I consulted with that group. The House bill passed through to the conference committee. But with no debate allowed at that stage, *nā haole* in the Leg turned the whole thing around. Astronomy was declared the 'policy of the state.'"

"That's because the activists demanded that *only* Native Hawaiians be on the governing body. That's unconstitutional on the mainland *and* in Hawai'i. It was clear their primary goal was to remove all observatories, creating huge losses to America's astronomy efforts and the islands' economy."

I didn't answer, for fear my acting talent wouldn't hold.

"Luckily, common sense prevailed. And despite a few weak protests that state police squashed, HILT is almost complete," Dexter reminded me.

I raised my eyebrows and nodded as if Kekoa didn't know

the status. But I was weary of my ruse. "Don't forget our picnic *grindz*," I said, hoping he would shorten this tour.

"Yes, I should get you back to the VIS. But first, we'll drive down to see HILT."

Dexter drove me downhill to view the completed HILT outer building that my alter-ego takes pride in guiding to completion, despite the protests Dexter mentioned.

Afterward, we bumped down the steep, twisting road to the VIS. Once there, Dexter helped me set up the picnic lunch at an outdoor table.

Again, this was a public stop where I hoped Kekoa would be seen. Because of the chilly weather, I'd taken precautions to keep everything warm in insulated containers.

With my back to several VIS security cameras I'd surveyed over the past weeks, I presented Dexter with a bowl of *saimin*. It's a local noodle soup full of *kamaboko* (fish cake), *char siu* (BBQ pork), and green onions. I didn't make it myself, but bought it at Ippy's in Waimea. I also bought some Spam *musubi*. It's an acquired taste. Sushi rice massaged into a rectangular patty, topped with fried Spam, some sauce, and then wrapped in dried seaweed. I top mine with Hoff & Pepper Haus Sauce, ordered from Berlin.

As Dexter slurped and chomped, I poured his fatal tea from one of my thermos containers.

"Thanks ever so, Kekoa. On work nights, I usually tote my own, how do you say it, '*grindz*?'"

I laughed heartily at his Aussie attempt to speak pidgin. I liked Dexter, so I told him the truth, but in a low voice, so the VIS workers seated nearby on lunch break would not hear me. "The tea is made from *nānāhonua*."

Poor Dexter innocently nodded, eager to show respect. "We Aussies love our tea, and it's wonderful to try a local version."

As he sipped, the surrounding chill caused steam to rise

from his cup, steam dense with tropane alkaloids. He downed his first cup and asked for another pour.

Mein Gott, my tea must be tasty. So tasty that two VIS workers asked for a sample.

I gruffly told the ladies I didn't have enough.

They gave me dubious looks, dismayed that the *braddah* wouldn't share.

They were lucky I didn't.

As Dexter yielded to the hallucinogenic effects, he looked at me with delirious pupils and slurred, "Mahalo for this lovely lunch. And especially your brilliant tea. You know, after the past week's blizzard, that patch of snow we saw today was tempting. Since I have the day off, I think I'll head back up...do a little snowboarding before the sunset tour crowds. I keep a board in my SUV, just in case we get enough snow."

Verflixt! Instead of this now woozy Dexter getting in his SUV and driving down the steep access road — with my black Jeep following closely — he wanted to drive back to the summit. That would ruin my plans to bump his car over the mountain's edge at a switchback. In my scheme, his car would roll down the steep slope, while "Kekoa's" Jeep continued down the mountain, and I disappeared. At first, authorities would think Dexter's crash was simply an accident until they found out who he had lunched with.

So I offered him another cup of tea, trying to keep him there. But he declined.

As Dexter rose, he wobbled. "Wow, that tea has a kick!"

We did the local fist bump, and I *mahalo'd* him again. Then Dexter gave me a shaka, swayed to his SUV, and aimed it up the mountain. Would he make it to the top? Would he veer off a hairpin turn and crash? I could only hope. I couldn't follow, bump him over, then head back down. Kekoa must be seen *doing* things, but never *caught* doing them, because my plans relied on having enough time for me to escape. It takes almost three hours for me to get back to my apartment and become Jürgen Bergen again. I certainly didn't want to be stopped on Mamalahoa Highway with Kekoa's fake plates.

What could I do? I decided to ensure more people saw Kekoa at the VIS. I went inside the gift shop and complained that it was making money by misappropriating my culture.

A young, mixed-race man smiled apologetically while taking my cash for a pack of Maui Style chips.

"Even more misappropriation! Those are made by a company based in Dallas," I said.

The young man nodded. "Sorry about that. But they're very good chips."

Convinced I'd made enough ruckus, I went back outside, climbed in the Jeep, and headed downhill, with Kekoa's fake plates shining in the sun for all security cameras to see.

Mein Glück, the next morning, Maunakea Rangers found Dexter's frozen body at the base of a snowy drift, his head fractured after his snowboard hit a pile of rocks.

You cannot imagine my relief. And, thanks to the toxicology reports, the medical examiner figured out the presence of Angel's Trumpet and as much said Dexter's crash was caused by delirium. So now all fingers point at the tea-maker, Kekoa Palakiko.

Plans awry. Plans fulfilled. *Wir hatten Glück.*

Chapter Twenty

BACK TO THE RAT RACE

Marie Ingles

W ho would have thought the investigative arm of Ryan's law firm would be hired to work on yet another Big Island murder case? But this morning, a video call blinged onto Ryan's laptop on the back lanai, although this time Colleen waited until 7:30 a.m. our time. Still, it was early for us lackadaisical retirees. Ryan and I had just sat down with our first mugs of coffee.

Ryan glowered at the screen. "May I at least have a sip of coffee before you begin?"

Colleen nervously chattered with a pasty smile. "Quickly, you lazy Hawaiians. Remember, I'm your boss now, and I must answer my clients by 1:00 p.m., my time."

"Good lord, I hope no 'real' Hawaiian overheard you. We are lazy *malihini* who will be delighted to sip our coffees as you give us the overview."

"I stand corrected. Sounds like you've got to watch your terminology over there on those rocks. But, well, here's what's going on. After the murder of the Australian astronomer on Maunakea, the state police came up with funding for — what did they call it — subject-matter experts to help with the FBI task force inquiries. This is because of the work you've already done with Special Agent Akana. She was so impressed, she asked for your team."

Ryan perked up. "When do we start?"

"Ryan, it's tricky. Most of these duties will fall on Billy Bob, Natalie, and Marie. I can only bill your attorney rate when a client needs a lawyer."

"Well, bill me at the investigator's rate. Shouldn't I be on the team? I'm the only one who's a registered officer of the Hawai'i court through Iona Law."

Colleen held up a finger to remind him. "That was *pro hac vice* for Nocona. I'll let the FBI, state investigators, and local police work out the legal hierarchies, but we've already booked Billy Bob and Natalie's plane tickets. You onboard, Marie?"

"Shit," was Ryan's reply. But he seemed to think better of his remark. "Apologies, Colleen. You're right. I'm not a detective, so I'll let you discuss the details with my lovely sleuth-spouse. And I will look forward to seeing Billy Bob and Natalie again."

Then off he went with his coffee to figure out what else he wanted to do.

I rolled my eyes to Colleen. "I suppose I'm game."

Colleen scowled at my tone. "You don't sound all that positive. What happened to my enthusiastic Nancy-D?"

"Colleen, you know I'm not much more than a legal secretary. Billy Bob and Natalie are both licensed PIs and have self-defense training. Now that we know more about this island, the state hiring me and two mainland investigators will cause another stir. Maybe even protests. Call me chicken, but I don't want to antagonize the local gentry. I came here to escape drama, not stir it up."

"Surely, the FBI and local police will see that you are safe."

"I don't know if they've got enough officers to do that. But I'll put on my brave face for the team, as long as Billy Bob is within arm's reach."

TWO DAYS LATER, RYAN AND I PICKED UP BILLY BOB AND Natalie at the airport, only the occasion was not as festive and fun as the first time. No flowery lei. No wild clothes-changing stunt in the crosswalk. We had two murders to solve now, and Billy Bob, Natalie, and I were supposedly the mainland brains who could solve cases like no one else. But I never felt more like an impostor. Billy Bob and Natalie were used to this pressure, but back when I worked for Ryan's firm, I was not out in the field. I Googled stuff, emailed, called, and schmoozed people into telling me things they didn't want to say. Basically, I did whatever Billy Bob or Natalie told me, and I kept records of what we'd found.

But on this island, the task force would look to me for ideas, contacts, or resources. I wondered what rat race I'd gotten myself into by saying, "I'm game."

Luckily for my nerves, our "boss" Pua Akana worked a standard five-day week, so the first weekend Billy Bob and Natalie were on-island, we played tour guide again. Ryan and I took them for a lovely and very expensive dinner at Mauna Kea Resort, where they met our new friends, Ailani and Gilles Moreau. Then, Saturday morning, we four drove to Waimea for brunch at Hawaiian Style Café. The food comes in gigantic proportions that make no sense to human capacity, but the owner knows his audience, predominantly tourists who line up outside, sometimes wait an hour, then order the famous *loco moco* so they can take photos and post them on social media.

Ryan and I ordered one *loco moco* to split, but Billy Bob

ordered the "Big Mok," a platter of rice topped with Spam, Portuguese sausage, link sausage, and one egg, all covered with beef and soy sauce brown gravy. And then there was Natalie, who went with the chicken-cutlet version, which is why she remains lanky as ever. She took half of hers home, but of course, Billy Bob ate every bite of his.

"Heart attack," she murmured, shaking her head as we walked out.

I whispered so the guys didn't hear, "What is it about some men that they pay no attention to their health?"

"Ryan the same?"

"Actually, he does okay. I buy a lot of seafood, fruit, and veggies. Luckily, we can afford it, because the prices are ridiculous. I was only being 'bad' today because of stress."

"These murders got you troubled?"

"Maybe it's because we live here, but I'm feeling added pressure due to the complex cultural issues here. And Ryan feels left out. He needs more to do than play golf and fix toilets."

"He won't do investigative?" Natalie asked.

"Colleen won't let him. He's billed at the attorney rate."

"She can't lower it for something this important?"

"You know Colleen. Straight-arrow accountant."

Natalie couldn't help but laugh. "Unless you get her drunk."

"Nat, who's getting drunk?" Billy Bob asked as we four walked the half block to our car.

Natalie scoffed. "Colleen."

"I kind of doubt that," Billy Bob said sarcastically. "But that does bring up memories of our dear Colleen, dancing her ass off at the Blind Rousette. Does the Big Island have anything as fun as that?"

"Not that I know, yet anyway."

Billy Bob's mention of the Blind Rousette ignited visions of our wild adventures two years ago to the Seychelles Islands in pursuit of Cole's Ponzi scheme funds. Our team got quite tipsy watching the island's annual Carnival parade. We later found a bar called the Blind Rousette, where our chalky pal Colleen danced her butt off far better than our friend Natalie did — a racial stereotype, surely, but it reminded me never to predict who will be great at anything by their ethnicity or skin color.

After we got home from breakfast, we separately napped at the condos before 5:00 p.m. cocktails on the lanai. A bit later, we drove north to Seafood Bar and Grill in Kawaihae, where we sat at the bar so Billy Bob and Natalie could get the gist of the Tiki-style restaurant. The bar extends the full length of it, and it's fun to chat with the bartenders, locals, and tourists.

All went well until we drove back to our condo, where we made the mistake of fixing one too many Mai Tais.

As we four gathered in the living room, I took a few sips and suddenly felt loose enough to blurt, "So, Billy Bob, is it safe to ask when you two will tie the knot?"

Billy Bob fumed. "Oh, God, that question!"

Natalie sighed too.

Ryan frowned. "Marie, when will you learn to keep your lovely lips in the closed position?"

Through the alcohol fog, Ryan's comment seemed patronizing, so I popped back, "Are only male lawyers allowed to ask probing questions?"

Looking back, I should have kept my "lovely lips in the closed position."

Ryan went to the kitchen, poured his Mai Tai down the drain, and then went down the hall, where he slammed our bedroom door.

Billy Bob looked stunned. "Wow. That is so unlike the boss. He's usually the one holding my temper back for me."

Natalie's eyes were sympathetic. "Trouble in paradise?"

"I'm sorry, you two. I shouldn't have popped off. I think

Ryan is concerned about whether he made the right choices. Selling the firm. Moving to Hawai'i. Heck, maybe he even wonders whether he should have married me."

Billy Bob made that game show buzzer sound when you've given a wrong answer. "Marie, no way Ryan regrets marrying you. Doreen drove him nuts for years. He told me stuff you would not believe. All she did was yammer. Never stopped talking. And I know for a fact, since I was best man at your wedding, that Ryan is deeply in love with Y.O.U."

Natalie took a moment, then patted my hand. "If you'll pardon my amateur psychoanalysis, maybe Ryan is dumping garbage from his first marriage?"

Now it was Billy Bob's turn to wish Natalie hadn't opened her mouth. "Is this some psychobabble women find on a secret male-bashing chat board? If so, call me gone." He groaned as he got up and took his Mai Tai to their condo.

Natalie sighed. "That went well."

"My fault. Just call me Loose Lips Marie."

"All you did was ask the same question I ask Billy Bob now and then. We're colleagues and best friends by day, then lovers at night. I'm ready to leap, but Billy Bob is not."

"Any chance that will change? I'd love to host your wedding at the beach club." I grabbed a white throw blanket from the sofa, wrapped it around my head, and mimicked how Natalie might look like a veiled bride sauntering down the aisle.

She laughed for a while, then grew quiet. "Woman to woman, both our guys are hauling a lot of baggage. During the throes of passion, Billy Bob sometimes calls me by his first wife's name. And Ryan's first wife was such a bitch, Billy Bob calls her 'DorScreach.' Whenever she came to the office, she acted like she was our boss. Maybe that's why the receptionist hated you. She figured you'd be just like DorScreach!"

We giggled after that, although I felt dismay brewing. "Maybe all marriages turn sour after the romance wears off."

"Let's hope not," she shrugged.

After we tidied up the Mai Tai mess, Natalie hugged me goodbye and went next door.

I climbed the stairs and slept in the non-studio guest room, not because I was angry with Ryan, but because I wanted to give him space. He must be working through something. I think any wife, even the most perfect wife on God's wonderful planet, would be the dumping ground for whatever garbage Ryan was sorting through. I just wish he didn't think Wife Number Two was the best place to aim his angst.

Admittedly, I got little sleep. Several times during the night, I woke with a start, wondering where I was, then remembered I was on a volcanic island in the middle of the Pacific Ocean. Talk about feeling anxious.

As for Ryan's behavior, I couldn't blame him. My prior history is one of feeling unloved and disrespected. Maybe old feelings never leave us. Yes, I'd overreacted to Ryan's comment. Maybe Ryan overreacted to mine too. Each of us because of past unhappiness.

***

THE NEXT MORNING OVER COFFEE ON THE LANAI, RYAN lightly touched my hand. "I apologize, Marie. I didn't mean to insult you, but I don't think you should pressure anyone to marry. Especially someone like Billy Bob. He's had it tough, romantically. Made some poor choices."

"Actually, I meant my comment to be a light-hearted tease, but the minute I said it, I realized it came out all wrong. Maybe thanks to the Mai Tai."

"We won't make that mistake again. Doreen and I had our worst arguments after we'd had a few too many."

I took his hand and looked into his morning-sea eyes. "Just try to remember. I'm not Doreen."

He nodded in attorney mode. "Right. And duly noted." Then he quickly changed the subject. "Since it's Sunday, I thought we four might go for a picnic up north. That little beach east of Hāwī. Remember? The park with the winding road, picnic tables, and peaceful views."

"That sounds lovely. I know you're weary of tour guiding, but thank you for planning something to do."

"This was self-serving. I want to celebrate a bit. Last night, as I questioned my reason for existing, I decided to take the Hawai'i bar exam. I don't think I'm ready to be retired."

Stunned, I stared at my coffee, unsure what to say next.

Ryan misinterpreted my silence. "Your silence tells me you're not pleased."

"No, it's not that. I just wonder why you want to go back to the rat race. Here we've got two murders to solve, and you may be involved when whatever legal aspects arise. Will you be able to study for the bar while Natalie, Billy Bob, and I run all over the island interrogating people and attending meetings in Kona with Special Agent Pua?"

"You've answered your own question. You're busy, but I have little to do."

"You can come along pro bono."

"As Colleen said, I'm a lawyer. Not a detective. While you and the team are busy, I'll study at my own pace. And after I get my license, I'll take only high-profile cases."

"High profile? From what I see on local news, it's mostly public defender work for meth-heads you wouldn't want to represent. We've only been here a few months, but I've seen TV reports of some meth-head abducting a teen off a beach. And another guy who was having an affair with his friend's wife, shooting the drugged-up husband. Or a drug dealer killing a guy and burning the corpse inside a car. It's scary to think you'd be dealing with that element. Besides that, I don't think most criminals on this island can afford a high-dollar lawyer."

"Maybe I'll take a few PD cases to break in. But high-profile cases do happen, mostly political or government stuff, bribery, embezzlement."

"Mostly on Oahu. And mostly a bunch of sleazy grifters."

"Marie, our justice system was designed so that all who've been charged with a crime deserve a good lawyer. Mike Iona told me I could rent space out of his office in Honolulu."

"So, now we're moving to Oahu so you can share an office with Mike and Sonya?" I hoped my voice didn't sound as uptight or paranoid as I was, but I feared it had touches.

He looked puzzled. "Not moving there. I'd just use an office now and then when I have to be on Oahu."

My 'Marie Needy' brain was whirling. *So now you're going to be an island-hopping attorney who's gone more often than he's here?* But I didn't say that out loud. Instead, I thought a moment and asked, "Are the classes on this island?"

"Most everything is online now, but the bar exam is taken in person."

A thousand images rushed through my brain. Ryan bent over a laptop day and night. Ryan waving goodbye before flights to Oahu. Ryan standing at the door of that tacky Sonya's office, "Miss Diamond Client Champion," before the two headed to lunch. And me alone on the Big Island, pretending to be an expert in criminal investigations.

Was this fair? Ryan's mid-life crisis somewhat forced me to give up my role at Metroplex Opera, where I enjoyed being good at something special. But now Ryan will go back to work, while I'll be left to what? Sunbathe with Ailani? Play my cello for free with a volunteer orchestra? Oh, I was spinning toward another of my meltdowns.

Suddenly, I wanted to run upstairs to calm my soul with an *au naturel* hour of Elgar, the way I did when Cole was out screwing sleazy barmaids or giddy groupies. Who knows? Some of them probably got pregnant, and my sons will discover their half-siblings on Ancestry one day.

This was how my mind was spiraling.

Luckily, Ryan's phone dinged with a text. "Natalie and Billy Bob are dressing for our picnic. We can stop at Foodland for goodies as we head out. But let's skip the booze."

I anxiously summoned my cheerleader smile and went to change, all to prevent Ryan from knowing just how much baggage was swirling inside his second wife's brain.

Chapter Twenty-One

808 INSIDERS
Da Real Scoop

Today at 7:15 a.m.

Heard the latest? The Dallas-based firm of Ballard / Ingles has been hired again to be "subject matter experts" — whatever that means — to the FBI Hawai'i Special Task Force. Seems the FBI, state, and county investigators need extra boots on the ground.

Aloha?

Licensed private investigators throughout the islands messaged 808 Insiders, asking us to find out why our state is hiring this firm and not a local group. However, the authorities have not returned our inquiries, so we couldn't glean more than what they'd heard through the coconut wireless.

The Ballard / Ingles bunch includes the VP of Investigative Services, William Robert Hughes, a.k.a. "Billy Bob," the classically corny name for a Texas football buddy of attorney Ryan Ingles, who now lives on the Big Island. Ingles is "of counsel" for Ballard / Ingles, whatever that means, but was lead counsel for Nocona Parker, the former defendant in the murder of Shin Watanabe.

Also along for this apparent working vacation is Billy Bob Hughes's squeeze Natalie Sherman, a so-called "computer analyst," again, whatever that means.

The team includes Ryan Ingles's drop-dead beauty and social butterfly wife Marie, who was once tried for murder in Dallas. She claims her best friend, funeral director Lena Verano, did the deed, although Verano fled to Dubai, so the case remains unresolved.

Not only that, but did you know Ryan Ingles and his island-hopping team were arrested a couple of years ago in the Seychelles Islands under suspicion of murder until the US Embassy and FBI International stepped in?

Doesn't all this smell like *Ono* left in the microwave too long? Just who are these people, and why aren't LICENSED Hawai'i-based PIs being hired, instead of some rather questionable...ahem, should we say the H-words?

✳

Most Relevant:
Laura's Honey B's — *Haole* is the word, Insider! And *dey* don't belong here.
Heather's Hilo Haven — My sister works for Aloha Investigations in Hilo, and her boss is big-eye pissed about this deal. *Nā haole* come and go, but my people were born here. We know where to go to get the right answers.
Grant's South Point Acres — I say a van full of C-4 can take care of *da* astronomater prob on Maunakea.
Kai Fisher — Whoa, **Grant's South Point Acres**, that's a whole lot extreme. Chill, Brah. Where's the aloha?

Grant's South Point Acres — I lost aloha for astronomaters when my auntie got arrested for protesting.

Nana Kai Braddah — Hey, **Grant's South Point Acres**, I get what you sayin'. I'm in construction near Waikoloa. DM me if you got some *kālā* and ideas.

Chapter Twenty-Two

FBI SPECIAL TASK FORCE

Marie Ingles

The next day, we three "subject matter experts" went to work, driving south to Kona for an eight o'clock FBI Hawai'i Special Task Force meeting with Pua, as she wants us to call her.

I have a hard time doing that with an FBI agent because this whole mess scares the devil out of me. Like the angry rants on 808 Insiders, I also wonder why I'm part of an FBI-led investigation in Hawai'i.

I especially wanted Ryan to come along pro bono. Not only would that reassure me, but it would also give him something to do other than dream up a Kona law firm with a spare office on Oahu. I agree we need more structure to our lives, but I worry what he's getting into. This is not the Mainland, and the crimes and perpetrators here are very different.

I didn't mention any of this to Natalie and Billy Bob. He drove this time, giving me a chance to take in the morning's clear skies and mountain views. Most afternoons, clouds obscure the summits. But this morning, we could see four of the island's five volcanic mountains to the top. And because it's "winter" by the calendar, Maunakea and Mauna Loa had summits of white from recent snows, while across the ocean channel, Haleakelā displayed a bit of dust on Maui.

When Billy Bob pulled into the police station, he announced, "I'm getting so used to this place, I feel like a local."

"Don't let anybody overhear you say that," Natalie scoffed.

"Guess I must delete 'local' from my vocabulary. But parts of this place remind me of funky beach towns on South Padre Island. Maybe I can at least pretend I live here."

I joked, "Well, I actually do, but I'm still not a 'local.'"

We tittered at that, aware that we were finding our way by stumbling over our mistakes.

Inside the station's conference room, Pua introduced us to Harold Koizumi, deputy chief of county police, and Sheriff Buckner Urima of the state police.

Harold grinned at us and boomed, "Call me Harold, but never Harry, and call him Bucky, or he'll get really mean."

We three smiled as we shook their hands and found a seat.

Both Harold and Bucky were probably of mixed-race Hawaiian descent, with piercing onyx eyes, dark brown hair, and widely angular facial features. Sheriff Bucky was the taller and younger of the two, while Harold was stocky and had your stereotypical spare tire that many older officers gain after they've turned fifty.

"Too many *grindz*," my mind joked internally, and I felt very "local" saying that.

Just then, the door opened. I was surprised to see Nocona Parker walk in and head to sit beside Pua.

She noticed my shock. "Nocona is also an SME — that's subject-matter expert. He'll be our scientific liaison."

I nodded and smiled to hide my amusement that Nocona

now sported a classic male cut instead of his long brown braids. He wore a lightweight sports jacket over a subdued Aloha shirt, looking very island-professional. Although when he pulled back his chair, I noticed he was still wearing *slippahs*.

After everyone settled, Pua began the meeting by asking Harold to say a few words.

He groaned a bit as he stood and somewhat frowned at us in frustration. "First off, I've been asked to say this: Hawai'i County did not hire you. Nor did we want to hire you. Nor did we want you involved. But SSA Akana did, the governor did, and the state police had the budget for it. So this is a somewhat forced, collaborative deal. The bottom line for Hawai'i County is, if you SMEs intend to serve as investigators on this island, you must be sworn in as 'Citizen Volunteers.' Is that clear?"

We nodded but gave each other confused, wide-eyed looks.

"Raise your right hand, please. Do you acknowledge and affirm that anything you see, hear, or discover related to the FBI Hawai'i Task Force investigation shall be conducted with aloha and remain confidential, on your oath?" Harold said.

Again, we all nodded.

"I need you to say yes out loud."

We quickly said yes in unison.

"And any violation of this oath may be punishable by jail terms of one to five years in a Hawai'i state prison. Do you acknowledge and affirm?"

Again, we all said yes, although his last phrase about prison terms raised a few eyebrows.

"Such as it is, I'm done, Pua. This is your task force. Take the point."

As the annoyed Harold sat, Pua rose but was interrupted when a young woman opened the door, strode in, and handed Pua a piece of paper.

She scanned it, then began with a surprising question.

"Gosh, I hate to bring this up again, but something appeared online moments ago, probably while you Ballard / Ingles people were driving our way. The county PR people in Hilo forwarded it by fax. That annoying 808 Insiders posted another statement condemning your firm's involvement with this task force. Says you were arrested in the Seychelles on suspicion of murder?"

Immediately, Billy Bob and I turned to Natalie, whose nervous scowl told us she was upset she had not tracked this during our drive.

"Sorry, I must have been distracted by this morning's views." She flipped open her laptop, found the group's page, and read the text to everyone aloud.

Billy Bob gave me a silent head shake as if saying he'd take the helm. "Pua, Bucky, Harold, I regret we didn't see this post earlier, or we'd have disputed it with an official statement. All I can say is, these insinuations are untrue."

"Care to enlighten us?" Harold said with a hint of disdain.

"In a nutshell, our firm traveled to the Seychelles Islands to help Marie claim the offshore account of her late husband, Cole Donovan."

Harold looked my way, a bit stunned. "Cole Donovan. The Explorers' quarterback?"

"Yes. But I was not involved in any of his business dealings."

Sheriff Bucky's eyes looked at me askance, probably wondering what *haole* the state police had to deal with now.

Billy Bob did his best to explain. "You see, the funds were from Cole Donovan's bogus Ponzi scheme, called Odyssey. Our investigations uncovered evidence of an offshore account in a foreign-owned bank in the Seychelles. As Cole's lawful heir, Marie flew there and requested the funds, knowing full well the FBI would impound them the minute the dollars hit her U.S.

bank. But the Seychelles bank manager was determined to keep the money. In fact, so determined, he sent a guy to kill Marie."

Harold, Bucky, and Pua looked at one another in shock.

"Luckily, the guy he sent was a bank teller by day, not a pro hitman. After his first shots missed, Ryan Ingles was able to overtake him."

Sheriff Bucky's eyebrows raised. "Who's Ryan Ingles?"

"Our law firm's managing partner."

"I'm confused. Was Ryan Ingles in Mrs. Donovan's room?"

Billy Bob took a breath to arrange his thoughts since that was Ryan's and my first night together. Billy Bob didn't tell any lies, but he sure quibbled a bit. "Ryan's room was next to Marie's. He heard the shots and her screams. I did too and came running from my room across the hall. We called the Seychelles police, but island politics were tricky and we four were detained. Luckily, Ryan's law partner, Colleen Ballard, was still on-island and got the American Consulate and FBI International involved."

"*Oi Oi*, you guys get around, don't you?" Harold sneered.

Billy Bob said firmly, "International offshore banking can be tricky. A lot of third-world nations have banks there."

Natalie jumped in, perhaps a bit too defensively. "As for the other comment about Marie's murder trial, we've already explained it to Pua. Marie was framed but quickly exonerated. A married couple on the FBI Most Wanted Fugitives list will be charged as soon as they're extradited."

I gave her a silent thank you with my eyes.

Harold blew out a huge puff between his full lips. "All of this is one big *mōkākī*, so I'll let state police look into it now. After all, Bucky's paying the tab."

Sheriff Bucky groaned sarcastically. "Mahalo, Harold. I know nothing about this Seychelles stuff, but PIs statewide are downright *huhū* about this mainland firm being paid from state police coffers. I'm going to need statements about each of these accusations. That way, our PR people will have answers for anyone else who points fingers."

"Yes, sir, Bucky. We'll take care of it this afternoon…again," Billy Bob said.

Pua seized on that point. "Thank you, Bucky. Sheila Huber from the county has already done a lot to curtail 808 Insiders, and we appreciate state police help with this as well. Please make it clear to the public that our SMEs are citizen volunteers, not officers of the law. The work they'll be doing is conducting inquiries. They're not carrying weapons or arresting anyone. This is a vast island to cover, and we need people to ask questions. So, let's move on from jurisdictional hierarchies and social media fake news to the facts."

Wow, that silenced Harold and Bucky. At least for a while.

As Pua pointed to a large LED display, she summarized what had been discovered to this point. On the screen were bloody and horrifying images of both victims. Then came close-ups of the bloody arrow plunged into Shin Watanabe's neck. Next was Dexter Zachary's blood-splattered snowboard atop Maunakea, and a close-up of poor Dexter's head bashed in. I shuddered and looked away until the next photo flashed green leafy vines with orange flowers that Pua called Angel's Trumpet.

"Bottom line: We have two deceased astrophysicists from different nations who died from two different MOs."

Bucky interrupted. "That means *modus operandi*, in case you SMEs do not know."

Our team nodded, although the mystified look on Nocona's face told us he did not.

Pua continued, "But when you know more about Hawai'i, the arrow and the poison are actually similar in that both are used by indigenous practitioners — the arrows to hunt and the

Angel's Trumpet to get high, not that anyone should drink Angel's Trumpet tea, because you can wind up dead."

Next, Pua pointed to a photo of the mystery guy she had referenced at our first meeting. In his fifties, he was coarsely handsome, with short-clipped black hair, caramel skin, high cheekbones, a broad-bridged nose, full lips, and wide dark eyes.

"At this time, the only person of interest in the death of Shin Watanabe is Kekoa Palakiko. Related to the Dexter Zachary case, we are waiting for the results of new forensic tests. Kekoa is a local celebrity, son of a long-ago hero-activist. Kekoa himself actively took part in anti-HILT protests several years ago. And only last year, he consulted with a legislative group that attempted to give Native Hawaiians sole control of all Hawai'i summits. For you who are *malihini*, many Hawaiians resent that their lands were taken over illegally. And some want to secede from the United States and return governance of these islands to the Kingdom that Hawai'i once was."

Nocona murmured, "Kinda like Native Americans."

Harold blurted, "They are way ahead of us. They have partial sovereignty — their own lands and governance."

"Please, guys, I realize these are sensitive and concerning issues, but let's stay clear," Pua said.

Natalie raised her hand, then made a point out of using Pua's title, perhaps to be supportive. "SSA Akana, have you interviewed Mr. Palakiko yet?"

"Once by phone. Once in person at his home. He said he was line fishing west of South Point the day Shin Watanabe was killed. And he insists he was hiking on Mauna Loa the afternoon Dexter Zachary died. However, no one can vouch for him at either location."

"How about his day job?" Billy Bob asked.

Harold answered in a somewhat softer tone. "He's a guide for Hawai'i Trail Explorers, a local tour company. His specialty is Mauna Loa. He's a naturalist, so he goes off by himself on his days off. Who wouldn't after spending your workdays trying to please entitled tourists? So, when Kekoa goes fishing, he goes where no one else is. As for hiking, he quickly named the trails he took, and I believed him."

"He could spout those from his tour guide job," Pua said.

Harold frowned. Obviously, he did not like having Kekoa as a person of interest.

Natalie again raised her hand. "Can Kekoa's wife or family vouch for his whereabouts?"

"Kekoa and his wife divorced some time ago, reportedly over his anti-HILT activism. Mrs. Palakiko is the executive director of the 'Imiloa Astronomy Center, a part of the University of Hawai'i at Hilo. So, she wants HILT to be completed, of course," Pua said.

"Any kids?" I asked, although I immediately regretted it. Good gosh, Marie, what do children have to do with anything? You're being simplistic, a mom where moms do not belong.

Pua gave me a frown, confused as I was with the value of my question. "Two adult kids live on the mainland."

Billy Bob asked, "What about digital tracing or CCTV?"

"According to our analysts, Kekoa did not use a credit card on either day of these murders, so we can't track him that way. As for video, Mauna Loa is a massive space with few security cameras, and there aren't any near his remote fishing spot. Turns out Kekoa's mobile phone is pay-as-you-call, and he told us his vintage Jeep's mapping software is on the blink."

Harold chuckled. "His Jeep thinks he's in Idaho."

I was glad to see him smile. His joke provided a pleasant break to the tension since Harold and Bucky have made it clear they don't want us mainlanders on this team.

Unlike my stupid "mom question," Natalie had an idea. "What astronomy projects was Dexter Zachary working on?"

Everybody looked to Nocona. "Like most spectrographic researchers, he was trying to confirm the existence of water and earth-like surfaces on exoplanets, or at least that's what his website bio said. I didn't know the guy, but I know his boss, Oliver Witherspoon. He's the ITUK director. I'm no detective, but I'll interview him if you'll give me a list of questions."

"Will do, Nocona," Pua said.

With Ryan not there, I struggled to think of a probing question his keen mind might ask. I nervously raised my hand. "Who was Dexter's competition? I mean, who would be upset if Dexter were the first to confirm water on the — Nocona, what did you call them?"

"Exoplanets. These are planets beyond our solar system. Astronomers have confirmed many thousands within our range of sight. We can't see them with optical telescopes because exoplanets don't shine like stars. So, we observe how they orbit their suns, which are the stars we can see."

Billy Bob looked amazed. "Nocona, I'm just a dumb PI from Dallas. How can you observe exoplanets if you can't actually see them?"

"That's not a stupid question. In fact, it was only answered within the last few decades. There are two methods. One is by seeing the light of the parent star dim as the exoplanet passes by. The other is by detecting a wobble in the parent star, like our sun. That wobble is caused by the gravitational pull of an orbiting planet."

Our team fell silent as our non-scientist brains attempted to visualize these events. My mind could imagine the light of a parent sun-star dimming, but the wobble thing escaped me.

"Over my head, Nocona," I laughed.

He leaned toward me to explain. "Think of a sun-star as a gigantic magnet, and its planets as much smaller magnets. Both have a gravitational pull, but the sun-star is far more powerful.

So, if the sun-star moves, you'd probably expect its planets to follow. But what's been discovered is that, when the sun-star's orbiting planets move, the sun-star wobbles a bit too."

"Wow. Great stuff, Nocona. And I see why we need you on this team," Billy Bob said.

"Yes, Nocona, excellent input. And returning to Marie's question, did Dexter Zachary or Shin Watanabe have competitors who might want to prevent them from succeeding?" Pua asked.

Nocona shook his head. "Not anybody I know. The universe may be infinite, but Earth's astronomy community is a world of its own. Of course, we guard our discoveries, but globally, we correspond by group lists or video calls. Trusted colleagues help confirm each other's findings, and if the same discovery is made at almost the same time, or if one astronomer adds to a discovery by another astronomer, we team up to publish papers and send press releases. Then again, our various governments and universities compete, as if it's the World Cup."

Harold scowled. "But why, Nocona?

"Sir, humans have always asked, 'How did our world, our universe come about?' To see into our past, we build bigger and better telescopes. HILT would have seen first light by now, but there've been so many delays caused by legal wranglings and activist protests."

"We've suffered from them too," Harold said.

"Yeah, but HILT is now years behind. The Europeans are almost at first light with AWE-T — that's the Astrophysical Wide European Telescope — in the Southern Hemisphere. We Americans jokingly call it 'Haughty.' You see, only astronomers from European member nations can use it. It's almost as large as HILT. Just one meter less in width."

"But what about NASA's...what's it called, that space telescope?" Harold asked.

"The James Webb Space Telescope is an amazing resource, but it doesn't have the light-gathering power of a HILT or AWE-T. The Webb's primary mirror is six and a half meters wide, while HILT's mirrors will be forty meters wide. Besides that, the Webb cost $10 billion to build and launch, while the HILT project will cost about $2 billion. But most importantly, the Webb doesn't have hands-on access. To reach it, you'd have to travel a million miles, so it can't be repaired or updated. The instruments on it were determined well over a decade ago. And if an asteroid ever pings it, well, computers can't repair —"

Pua interrupted. "So that's why there's a big push to complete HILT here."

"That, and the fact it's in the Northern Hemisphere, while AWE-T is on a mountaintop in Chile. But after the Hawai'i protests several years ago — you know, with VIS workers threatened, old ladies arrested, and movie stars and rock stars getting themselves in viral video clips — HILT's directors had to beg for federal funding. This meant delays from environmental studies, time spent for public input, and more protests — well, you know the history. The outer building is now complete. And it's a stunner. But the telescope mirrors, electronics, and hardware aren't installed yet. All of this takes years to 'tweak' before HILT sees first light. So, America lags well behind Europe, thanks to the, well, I don't want to be disrespectful, but these protestors simply don't understand the importance and urgency —" Nocona trailed off.

Pua took over. "Nocona, no need to fear. We all understand the issues."

Nocona looked chagrined. "Sorry, it's just that I want my nation to be able to compete."

Harold countered sharply. "I thought you said astronomers didn't compete."

Nocona grimaced, clearly frustrated by the chief's retort.

"These giant scopes will open up worlds, and I don't want American astronomers left out."

Sheriff Bucky finally spoke up. "Astronomy, astronomy, astronomy. I thought all this was behind us after the Leg declared astronomy a state policy, whatever that meant. Arresting this Palakiko *brah* will give activists more Koa for their fire. The Kia'i 'promise keepers' will pull on their skirts, drag out their *kūpuna* and Hollywood stars, and start the big-eye, tongue-out dance to block the access road. Meanwhile, our wishy-washy governor will make state police the bad guys who have to drag off someone's auntie. That's why I caution you, SSA Akana. Tread lightly. I do not want another civil war, with island police left to clean up the FBI's chaos."

With that, both Harold and Bucky slid back their chairs and disgruntledly headed out, leaving us fiddling with our coffee cups.

I glanced over at Pua. "I see where your pressures come from."

She nodded and sighed quietly. "Ever since HILT construction began, activist fervor has not diminished. The governor even brought in the Army National Guard to keep Maunakea access roads clear. That debacle and the need to protect state-managed lands stimulated the creation of a state police force. But as you can see, both state and county officials are my reluctant partners. As of now, I am relying on the team in this room."

"Pua, we'll do what I can, but wow. We're *malihini* and didn't know there were all these political issues," Billy Bob said.

We five sat silently, considering the complexities. When I glanced over at Billy Bob, he shrugged, probably as uncomfortable as I was at what seemed foreign and insoluble.

My goodness, this meeting took such a turn, none of us said much after we shook Pua's hand goodbye. Even driving through the gated entry of our gorgeous condo development made me feel foreign here.

To Kekoa Palakiko, I'm a cello-playing *haole* transplant with the nerve to investigate a Native-born Hawaiian for defending his cultural beliefs.

Even so, if he is the murderer, he was wrong to kill.

Chapter Twenty-Three

A BREAK IN THE CASE

Marie Ingles

E arly the next morning, as we relished *malasadas* and coffee on the lanai, Pua called Billy Bob's phone. He put her on speaker, joking, "Pua, you've got the Ballard / Ingles SMEs at your disposal, or disposable, whichever."

She laughed. "I lucked out, didn't I? First off, thank you for your written statements to Sheriff Bucky about Marie's trial and the Seychelles incident. He stopped in to tell me that his PR team verified your details, then sent a message to the 808 Insiders administrator — whoever that might be — to say that state police would not tolerate libelous assertions that may interfere with island murder investigations."

Billy Bob nodded at me. "Wow, this is good news. Now we have both county and state support. Thank you for your help with this."

"I'm merely the messenger. But, moving on, I want you to hear several tips that came over the FBI task force hotline yesterday afternoon. It's just your team there, right?"

Billy Bob's eyes grew wider as he realized we were within

earshot of neighbors. "Yes, but come to think of it, we'd better move this meeting inside."

We four shuffled up from our lanai chairs and made our way back through the slider.

Billy Bob motioned a halt sign to us and went into his private investigator mode. He locked the slider door, peered out the glass as if an intruder might be there, then closed the shades. Sealed in, he silently pointed us to the living room for even more privacy, then placed his phone in the center of the coffee table. "I've got us corralled, Pua, but Ryan is with us too. Is that okay?"

"I imagine so, since he is a registered officer of the court."

She left off *pro hac vice* for Nocona's case, like Colleen would've reminded us, but I wasn't about to bring that up.

We waited silently until we heard two different male voices on a recording.

The first voice was a low baritone with a British accent. "My colleague and I want you to know that a local man, a muscular fellow, was up at the ITUK observatory with Dex Zachary the morning before his body was found. We wondered if this bloke might have something to do with Dex's murder."

The second voice chimed in, much younger, but sounded American. "Yeah, this dude had a real attitude. Dex was showing him around, but he acted like he was King Kamehameha. Spouted a lot of anti-astronomy stuff."

Then the British voice said, "If you want to speak with us in person ..."

As he left their names and numbers, I wrote them down.

Billy Bob asked, "Pua, are you contacting these guys or do you want us to?"

"We'll talk to them. But I wanted you to know about their description of the local man. It sounds like Kekoa Palakiko."

"Was there an official record, like a sign-in sheet or appointment calendar? Natalie asked."

"We called the ITUK office in Hilo to see if they had a record of this visit, but they didn't. They said Mr. Zachary had taken a personal day off, so he wasn't officially at work. Sometimes astronomers go up to the summit without jumping through official hoops. Our FBI analysts just got access to Dexter's email, so they will scour it for us."

Natalie leaned into the phone speaker. "You said there were more tips?"

"Yes, two VIS workers. These ladies saw what they called a 'suspicious looking *braddah*' — their word — having lunch with Mr. Zachary in the picnic area."

Billy Bob laughed. "What made *da braddah* look suspicious to them?"

"Here's what they said on the recording."

We three listened as Pua fiddled with the recording. And then it began.

"We were outside on lunch break when this *braddah* made a big deal out of the *grindz* he brought for Mr. Zachary. We know Mr. Zachary because he stops in once or twice a week. It's cold up here, so my friend kept hinting about trying some of *da braddah's* hot tea he kept bragging about. But he said he didn't have enough. Usually, locals love to share stuff, but the way he avoided us seemed kind of weird."

Billy Bob glanced around to see if we all had the same thought. "Did they say this guy was Kekoa Palakiko?"

Pua replied, "The cashiers didn't know who he was, but described him as a 'big dude' wearing a camo ball cap and camo vest, with bare arms. He kept his back to the security cameras. Maybe he knew where they were. But from the back, he looked enough like Kekoa."

"Ryan here, Pua. Although I'm not officially on the task

force, I wondered if you need help from Billy Bob or me. We are a pair of big guys and would be happy to escort you to in-person interviews with Kekoa."

That delighted me. Ryan might rejoin the team?

Pua laughed. "Thanks for your offer, Ryan, but Sheriff Bucky is a big guy too. He and I will intercept Mr. Palakiko after he returns home. An officer is watching his house. We'll let you know as we learn more."

"Pua, how about I call Nocona to interview those two ITUK technical guys? Sometimes people will be more open with a guy they know — not me, but Nocona," Billy Bob said.

"Great idea, and thanks. This is the sort of support I need from you SMEs," Pua said with a hint of relief in her voice.

Ryan spoke up again. "Right, Billy Bob. And maybe Nancy-D and Natalie should go to ITUK's base operations in Hilo. Ask around about Dexter Zachary. Why anybody would want to kill him."

"Nancy-D?" Pua asked.

"Oh, that's Marie's nickname. Long story —" Ryan trailed off, perhaps remembering days gone by at his Dallas firm. Then he looked wistful. "Well, while all of you try to track down this killer, I suppose I'll twiddle my thumbs."

Chapter Twenty-Four

HAWAII PU HERALD

Kia'i Hero Held for Questioning

KAILUA-KONA, Hawaii — Anti-HILT activist Kekoa Palakiko of Keauhou, age 54, is being held for questioning related to the murder of Dexter Zachary, an Australian citizen and senior resident astronomer for the Infrared Telescope of the United Kingdom (ITUK) atop Maunakea, with base offices in Hilo.

Zachary died recently at the summit of Maunakea. FBI special task force investigators, led by FBI Supervisory Special Agent (SSA) Pua Akana, at first presumed Zachary died after a snowboarding accident. However, county autopsy and FBI toxicology reports revealed he had ingested concentrated toxins.

At a press conference outside the police station in Kona, with about a hundred Island Kingdom Now activists in attendance, Harold Koizumi, deputy chief for Hawaii County's Kona station, remarked, "Mr. Palakiko has not been charged with a crime. We brought him in for questioning after receiving tips that he was at ITUK and the VIS with Dexter Zachary. Mr. Palakiko has been read his rights and has an attorney. If he presents no danger to the community, he will be released."

According to Palakiko's attorney, Victor Thielens, "This is racial profiling. Kekoa is a hero who is trying to prevent the desecration of Hawaii's sacred lands."

Thielens often handles cases for the activist secession group Island Kingdom Now, of which Palakiko is on the board of directors.

SSA Akana replied to Thielens's remark, "The deadly poison Mr. Zachary ingested was the same chemical composition as toxins from trumpet flowers, the family of plants that some cultural practitioners use to brew hallucinogenic teas."

Her remarks were followed by loud jeers from the crowd.

Palakiko is revered by locals as the only son of Tangaroa Palakiko, an activist with Stop the Steal Ohana. In the years preceding 2012, this loosely formed group protested the sale of Parker Ranch to billionaire vegetarian Eller Lawrence Pryor. The sale eventually did not go through, but the elder Palakiko died from a heart attack suffered when police attempted to arrest him for the destruction of property.

A Kealakehe High School graduate, Kekoa Palakiko is an avid naturalist, employed as a guide for Hawaii Trail Explorers.

In response to this reporter's question about whether the arrest could be seen as racial profiling, Koizumi remarked, "Hey, you guys know I'm local, right? Born here. Went to Hilo High School. UH-Hilo grad. The FBI wouldn't arrest a local guy if they didn't have a good reason. Trouble is, too many locals give us too many reasons."

In response, the activist crowd booed loudly.

SSA Akana tried to overcome the jeers. "As we said, Mr. Palakiko has not been charged. He's being questioned."

The crowd erupted in a chant demanding Palakiko's release.

Contact our crime reporter Ikaika Kelekolio at Ikaika.Kelekolio@hawaiipuherald.com.

Chapter Twenty-Five

MY SIDE OF THE MIRRORS

Jürgen Bergen / Zeno Kühn

This island may be a banana republic, but the special task force was smart enough to fall for every one of my clues. And now that Kekoa Palakiko has been jailed for questioning, there will be *ein clusterfehler* of protests.

TV's "Island News Now" says activists are threatening to block the Maunakea access road again unless Kekoa is released.

This is typical of these born-again types, opposing the very science that brings Nobel awards, dollars, jobs, and prestige to their backwater island state, not to mention tax dollars to fund their monthly subsidy checks, healthcare programs, and children's schools.

Tomorrow, a local-run children's charity will tow away my version of Kekoa's black Jeep. I donated it online and gave the pickup location as a city park in Waimea. I dressed up as Kekoa, and when the tow driver arrived, I simply signed the paperwork and showed him Kekoa's ID. What did the driver know? And I doubt some underpaid county clerk in Hilo will notice a duplicate Jeep registration in Kekoa's name.

Hopefully, I'll be long gone from this island before they do.

But, in case Kekoa's neighbors have security cameras, I also sold the SUV I used a few months ago to survey his house. In its place, I went online and bought a new Hummer SUV from a dealer in Honolulu. It will be shipped over and delivered right to our door.

I say "our" since the title is in Jürgen's name.

Even on an island in the middle of nowhere, it's amazing what you can do online.

Chapter Twenty-Six

HAWAII PU HERALD

Palakiko Charged in Death of Astronomer

HONOLULU — An Oahu grand jury handed down an indictment yesterday afternoon, charging Big Island activist Kekoa Palakiko with felony murder in the death of Japanese astronomer Shin Watanabe. Palakiko is expected to be arraigned in federal court within the next few weeks.

Watanabe was killed last month during a hunt at Maunakea Puuhonua Holoholona, commonly called MPH.

On the Big Island, Hawaii State Police Deputy Sheriff Buckner Urima spoke at a video press conference from the county police station in Kona. Also on the video call were two members of the recently formed FBI Hawai'i Special Task Force, including FBI Supervisory Special Agent (SSA) Pua Akana and Hawai'i County Police Deputy Chief Harold Koizumi.

Sources say the announcement was made via video because of the number of protestors who've gathered at the Kona station to protest the indictment.

Urima began the conference by saying, "SSA Pua Akana, who leads the task force, directed me to make this announcement. In this way, local islanders can be reassured that federal, state, and county authorities have fully examined all evidence presented to the grand jury. The charging document is available on county, state, and FBI websites and includes the following evidence:

1. Mr. Palakiko attempted to enter the gate at MPH early on the same morning Mr. Watanabe was killed.

2. The license plate and make-model of his vehicle matched Mr. Palakiko's.

3. Security cameras recorded Mr. Palakiko arriving at and departing from a state recreation area near MPH that same day.

4. Five witnesses saw Mr. Palakiko fleeing the same hunting section where Mr. Watanabe was killed.

5. Mr. Palakiko's Jeep was seen speeding from the area

6. A search of his Jeep produced physical evidence of a package containing archery equipment that was delivered to Nocona Parker, who was initially arrested in this case."

After the video announcement, task force members refused to answer reporters' questions, but SSA Akana concluded by saying, "Please review the charging document. This case is now under the authority of the federal prosecutor's office in Honolulu. Further comments will be at their discretion."

Kekoa Palakiko is being held without bond at the Federal Detention Center in Honolulu. He does not yet have a public defender assigned, although Island Kingdom Now attorney Victor Thielens is advising.

Contact our crime reporter Ikaika Kelekolio at Ikaika.Kelekolio@hawaiipuherald.com.

Chapter Twenty-Seven

REDISCOVERY

Marie Ingles

After reading that Kekoa Palakiko has been formally charged with murder and is in the federal detention center on Oahu, I texted the news to Ryan. He was in Honolulu for a special class for the Hawai'i bar test.

"Right. All over local media. Billy Bob and Natalie know?" he texted back.

I texted them too, copying Ryan.

Billy Bob replied, "Already had a call. And there's more."

Just then, Pua rang me, and I conferenced her in with Billy Bob, Ryan, and Natalie.

"Good morning. As I just told Billy Bob, this formal murder charge means you SMEs are off duty. I didn't invite you and Nocona to this morning's video conference, because I didn't want you four exposed to potential harassment."

"This must be a blow to Kekoa's supporters," I said.

"Several hundred are in front of the station right now, wearing 'Free Hawai'i' t-shirts and pounding drums to intimidate us for doing our jobs. Some of these people are real bullies. They get in your face and glare with their big, scary eyes. Even when you pack a Glock 19M, like I do, it can be frightening for a female to face down one of these big-bellied guys, or some of the angrier *wahine*," she said.

"Pua, earlier, you said something about there being more?" Billy Bob asked.

"Yes, and this is confidential because you remain sworn in, but a second indictment is in the works for the murder of Dexter Zachary."

"Oh, my gosh. So Kekoa killed both of them?" I asked.

"Evidence led our prosecutors to that conclusion."

"Wow. When will the second charge be announced?"

"Tomorrow, the trial attorney thinks. The grand jury met this morning."

"I wish you all good luck. But let us know if you need any further help," Billy Bob said. Then, after Pua got off the call, he mumbled to the rest of us, "Guess I'd better call Colleen and get our marching orders. If we're not billing hours, we're probably done here."

After they hung up, I felt sad to think our friends were leaving. But I also felt relief because the killer had been found. Also, I had no more Nancy-D duties.

Admittedly, these recent cases reminded me that "work" meant spending long hours doing something very stressful, often the opposite of what you'd rather pursue. What I'd rather pursue remained the question.

A half-hour later, Billy Bob group-texted Ryan, Colleen, and me that Colleen wanted him and Natalie to stay on-island for two weeks in case they are needed for anything here. In the meantime, the pair would focus on other Dallas-based cases but manage them remotely.

"This means we have to be on duty by 4:00 a.m. I am an early bird, but not a rooster," Natalie texted.

None of this drew a response from Ryan on Oahu, which

made me wonder what he was doing and who he was with. Hopefully not that seedy Sonya.

Okay, so there I went again, being insecure. I must not keep doing that to myself.

But now, what was I to do? My beach pal Ailani was in Canada with Gilles for two weeks, something about mirrors for another telescope project. And so, as I always do when I need an escape, I went upstairs and played my cello.

Over the past month, I hired an interior designer to add sound-dampening drapes over each window and tack acoustic fabrics high on the walls, all to prevent the sound from bothering Ryan. We don't own this condo, so I can't completely renovate the room, but Ryan complains now and then when he's studying online.

Alone in my "studio," I gathered up my hair and tucked it in place with two of my cherry blossom hairpins. Then I slipped out of my clothes, put a fresh towel over my cello bench, and held my instrument between my bare legs, inhaling the stillness of the room before I stroked the first dramatic notes of Dvořák's *Cello Concerto in B Minor.*

Something about playing in the nude brings out the beast in me. I become one with my instrument, unafraid of how someone might see or hear me. And when I play with such emotion, I recall how good I am. That may sound like bragging, but there are times I know I am good, not just my mother saying, "Oh, you are wonderful, Marie!" But my educated and practiced self *hearing* that I am good. And that reminded me I'm still young enough to have dreams.

But what is my dream? Certainly not returning to Dallas. But being a musician again, being part of an orchestra.

That revelation inspired me to mail my resume to Devon Chua, the new music director of the Oahu Philharmonic. Online, I looked up his photo, a rather striking thirty-year-old from Singapore, whose web videos revealed a British accent. Seems he studied at the Royal College of Music in London.

I didn't tell Ryan about this until a week later, when I received a return phone call from Maestro Chua himself, who cheerily invited me to Honolulu for an interview. I could barely contain my glee until Ryan asked who the call was from, and I told him my news.

Over afternoon cocktails on our lanai, his eyes took on a worrisome frown. "So, now I'll ask you the same question. Are you sure you want to go back to all that? The rehearsals. Performances. Formal wear. Glad handing."

"I only pitched myself as a guest soloist, so this would not be 'all that.' A week at the most. Then again, I might contact a West Coast orchestra too. Who knows, maybe they'd be intrigued by a female cellist with two Dallas orchestras on her CV."

Ryan nodded reluctantly. "As gorgeous as you are, and as beautifully as you play, they probably would, but you'd be traveling all the time."

"Nothing different from what you're doing now. It's only five hours to LA or San Francisco, and you could come along."

"With the new office, I'll be pretty busy."

"I know. But your plans for a new firm helped me understand that I'm directionless. Sunning at the pool or beach with Ailani is fun, but I can't do that every day. As you found out, fixing toilets, playing golf with a bunch of racist white guys, and being cranky was a bored and frustrated version of you, trying to find something to do. I'm glad you are pursuing a Hawai'i law license. You'll be happier being the wonderful lawyer you are. And I'll be happier pursuing what I enjoy. So, while you were gone last week, I practiced my cello a lot. Really *played* it. I didn't worry about disturbing you, and I realized how much I've missed performing."

Ryan stared at his coffee and chose his words carefully. "I certainly don't want to interfere with your dreams, but I thought *this* was your dream. Living here. Being an islander. Helping raise funds for that wonderful bio-reserve in Hilo, joining a do-gooder group in Kona, or playing with that philharmonic in Waimea. These murder cases have interfered with our opportunities to get connected."

"But the driving. It's forty-five minutes to Kona, an hour and a half to Hilo, and thirty-five to Waimea. I don't want to spend my life in a car. And I suspect we'd be shut out of any board roles until people get to know us better."

He paused for a moment. "I understand. Truly. Despite our visits here, we didn't expect the amount of driving needed to take part in events."

"We were spoiled living in Highland Park, zipping down the Tollway for ten minutes to get downtown," I said.

"Wow, with these thoughts on the table, I'm wondering if we should stay on the Big Island or move to Oahu when our lease is up. I'd certainly have access to a lot more cases. And if you're going to solo with mainland orchestras, you'd need easier flights than the red-eye out of Kona. Maybe I shouldn't focus so much energy on a Kona office."

"First, let's get you licensed. Then let's see what my interview brings. After that, we can decide. I always loved the Big Island's expanse, but for concerts, shows, or more varied restaurants, we either have to fly, fly, fly to Oahu, or drive, drive, drive."

"And when we arrive, we see 'closed because of staffing shortages,'" Ryan joked.

"Or something else funky or quirky or disappointing, like the toilets broke, or the floor fell in." I sighed, then thought for a moment. "Gosh, that sounds terribly *haole*."

Ryan winked at me with those sapphire eyes. "You and I are

probably the exact definition of *haole,* the mainlanders locals love to hate. Still, I *am* studying for the Hawai'i bar and want to contribute my skills to help people. Heck, I might even get some of them out of a jam. So, to make Hawai'i work for us, Oahu might be the better choice. It has more white-collar clients — or I should say, 'Aloha-wear' clients. Bribery. Embezzlement. Tax dodging."

"And you should help those guys?"

He chuckled. "At least they can pay. I've gotta keep my lovely wife in gowns for her San Francisco cello solos."

"Just remember, my lovely gowns are tax write-offs."

"Wow, aren't we an elite pair?"

We both shrugged at our snobby Dallas-ness, and I felt somewhat guilty for moving to the Big Island without understanding how different our wants were from the daily lifestyle. Our goal was to enjoy the island's beauty, weather, culture, and history. And yet, over the past few months, we've wished so many things were less funky or quirky or dysfunctional. And expensive. Although Ryan and I don't worry about money like so many do, paying $10.99 for a loaf of bread disturbs me, not for my finances but for working-class people.

And then there's the issue of things to do. The beach, well, you get used to that. Ever since the Big Island was discovered by tourists, the main areas have been very crowded. But there are the mountains, yes, always love those summit views. Ryan and I have done some hiking, but mountains don't talk to you, at least not to me. And the sunsets. Glorious. We walk down to the beach for "the gathering" every day. But then what? Do I try golf? Take hula lessons? Join a do-gooder group or pinch hit with the local philharmonic, as Ryan suggested?

I went to the kitchen to start dinner, saddened by the thought that he and I had made a mistake moving here. A concert cellist and a white-collar defense attorney aren't right for this island. We're too snobby-Dallas. A pair of the dreaded *haoles*.

But as I unwrapped the gorgeous mahi-mahi we bought from the fish mamas at the corner of Waikoloa Road and Queen K, I also felt a sense of anticipation. Ryan and I had something to explore together. Maybe we might fit in better on Oahu. Not just Ryan practicing law, but me pursuing solo gigs.

Chapter Twenty-Eight

PONO-TV NEWS ONLINE

Exclusive Report

H ONOLULU — This morning, during an hour-long exclusive interview with PONO reporters, Kekoa Palakiko reiterated his innocence in the recent murders of foreign astronomers. But more importantly, he announced his support for the completion of the Hawaii Island Large Telescope (HILT) atop the state's tallest mountain, Maunakea.

According to sources, this is a complete turnaround for Palakiko, who has been involved in many anti-astronomy protests over the years.

Asked why the sudden change, Palakiko expressed concern about demonstrations that continue to rock the Big Island and Maui since his arrest. To date, the exteriors of six observatory offices have been vandalized. State sheriffs have arrested several hundred protestors who once again attempted to block the access roads to Maunakea's summit. Workers at the visitor center, dormitories, and observatories have been told to stay home, rather than face the angry protestors.

Palakiko remarked, "They even vandalized my wife's office at 'Imiloa Astronomy Center. My wife could have been hurt.

This is mob disorder, and I want to clarify that astronomy is not our enemy. My supporters must not terrorize the observatories or astronomy offices. This issue is not about one telescope. Someone has set me up for murder. We need to find out who and why."

Palakiko has a long history of activism in Hawaii, reaching back to the early 2000s as the son of Tangaroa Palakiko, who died after protesting the sale of Parker Ranch to a billionaire vegetarian from San Francisco.

Also interviewed for this report, Jürgen Bergen, the Swiss project manager for the installation of HILT's telescope, remarked, "This is a surprising and welcome turn, especially since Kekoa took part in protests that delayed construction of HILT. I was not here then, but those delays cost the observatory, not only in time but in dollars," Bergen said.

Kailei Sayama, president of Island Kingdom Now, remarked, "Kekoa must've drunk some magic tea. Or else he wants out of jail so bad, he'll say anything. His lifelong quest has been one with ours: sovereignty for the Hawaiian people. To have him say he now supports HILT is a spear through my gut. I can only think his surrender was because of personal issues, like his wife's office being ransacked."

In closing, Palakiko read from a prepared news release. "I was never against the science of astronomy, but the way HILT leaders ignored the significance of the mauna. With HILT's funds pledged to support Native Hawaiian affairs, I think my people will benefit from this new telescope project. After all, studying the stars was how our ancestors got here. And Queen Liliuokalani long ago said, 'I believe astronomy can help us understand our place in the universe and appreciate the interconnectedness of all things.' Like our Queen, HILT will look backward in time to seek our origins, our spirit. I just want to be sure that anyone who ascends Maunakea does so with respect and care."

Queen Liliuokalani was Hawaii's last reigning monarch and a keen amateur astronomer. She was particularly interested in studying planets and often wrote about astronomy in her journals and letters.

One earlier monarch who was fond of astronomy was Kamehameha III, who reigned from 1825 to 1854. He was a vigorous supporter of education and culture and was particularly interested in astronomy. He had a telescope installed at his palace and often spent time observing the stars and planets. Kamehameha III also commissioned the construction of an observatory atop Maunakea.

Of him, Palakiko remarked, "Our early leaders were passionate that the Hawaiian people have the very best education and technology. Astronomy provides opportunities for small businesses and jobs. It's not something we should force out. But malihini must respect our heritage and culture."

Reported by Michelle Kimura. Stay tuned to PONO-TV.com for updates.

Chapter Twenty-Nine

NEW AND OLD INSECURITIES

Marie Ingles

R yan and I were stunned to see a news report about Kekoa Palakiko's flip-flop on HILT. The story came on our bedroom TV as we frantically dressed for our early flight to Honolulu.

I asked Ryan, "This is surprising. Do you think he's concerned about the threats to his wife, or simply trying to turn potential jury opinion in his favor?"

"I don't think this would, that is, if the jury is made up of Native Hawaiians. But I'm glad to hear of this change. It's been horrifying to see scientists attacked, all in the name of what? Ancient religious beliefs? Or is there more going on than we newbies realize? I'm guessing there are political and monetary issues that you and I are not privy to," Ryan said.

"Maybe Kekoa's announcement will help stop the violence."

"We can hope," Ryan said as he headed upstairs. "I'll get your cello loaded. You don't need any music, do you?"

"I already packed it inside the case."

"See you in the garage."

OFF WE THREE HEADED TO OAHU, RYAN, MY CELLO, AND me. Ryan was enrolled in a course for licensed mainland lawyers, something about how state laws differ here. And I was going along because I had an 11:00 a.m. interview with Devon Chua at the Oahu Philharmonic offices.

As we awaited our flight inside a little cafe, I asked Ryan, "Why doesn't Hawai'i have a ferry system like Washington State or the United Kingdom? It would be great to drive our car onto a ferry and glide north to whatever island we were headed to."

"Big Mike told me they had a so-called 'Super Ferry' in the early 2000s, but there were environmental, political, and logistical issues. Environmentalists didn't want it. Can you imagine a ship going thirty knots and running into whale birthing channels? Also, one major shipper lobbied against it. And evidently, there wasn't enough money to build the necessary piers. So, the state shut it down — used some excuse about the timing of impact statements."

"Gads. I realize these are big waters, with reefs and wildlife to protect. Again, this is my outsider perspective, but gosh, you'd think there would be a way."

Our pony-tailed server leaned close and whispered, "Sorry for interrupting, but I agree. Driving to Kona, then going through Ag security, TSA security, check-in, and waiting for your flight takes far more hours than actually flying to any island, even all the way to Kauai."

Ryan nodded. "Right. Our flight to Honolulu takes less time than driving to the airport from Waikoloa."

"And I see you've got a third passenger," the server joked.

I explained we were lugging my cello for an audition. "The case rolls, so it's easy enough to cart around. The biggest issue is getting it on the plane. First, we buy it an extra seat in my name, then overcome all sorts of pushbacks at security."

Ryan chuckled. "Oh, and you should see the panic on flight attendants' faces when we bring it on board. Once again, we explain that it goes in an extra paid seat, and we'll need a belt extension to strap it in."

As the server grinned, we heard our flight called. Luckily, it was on time and without too much hassle over my cello.

On Oahu, Ryan had requested an early check-in at Prince Waikiki so he could get to his class by 10:00 a.m., and I could be in our room until time to leave for my interview.

Our suite was lovely, with a view of Ala Wai Boat Harbor.

As I unpacked our bags, Ryan kissed me good luck and headed for the door. But he stopped short. "I forgot to tell you. I made a dinner reservation at Orchids at Halekulani. I thought we'd meet Mike Iona and Sonya there."

My gut cringed, but I countered it with a forced smile. "What about Mike's wife? Shouldn't we invite her?"

"She died several years ago. Breast cancer. Sonya's single. I wasn't sure if the two were dating or not, so I thought this might be a fun get-together." He grinned like a Cheshire cat. "You always ask me to be more social."

"Sounds like a lovely evening," I cheerleader-smiled back. Hopefully, Ryan couldn't tell I was faking.

After I unpacked our bags, I dressed in black orchestra basics, wore my hair in an updo with invisible hairpins, and then rolled my cello case out the door and into the elevator. In the lobby, I requested a ride for my interview with Maestro Chua.

At the Oahu Philharmonic offices, I greeted Maestro Chua with my best smile, although my heart sank a bit. He seemed so much younger than I and so more androgynously handsome than I expected, late twenties or early thirties. And here I was, a fading middle-aged beauty.

Still, I could tell from the glint in his almond-shaped eyes, he thought I was still attractive. Heterosexual men simply cannot hide that look.

I gave him a shy smile. I didn't want to be phony or brazen.

Over bottled water in his somewhat cramped office, he asked, "Why Oahu Philharmonic?"

"I miss the joy of playing with an orchestra."

"But aren't you rusty?"

"I practice almost every day."

"Who made your instrument?"

"It's a Guarneri del Gesù."

"Wow, it must be worth millions."

"Expensive, yes. Ryan and I bought it as an investment. I chose it because it has a rich tone and is more complex than Stradivarius cellos."

"Must be nice to have that kind of funding," he murmured.

"We sold two houses at just the right time, and we're only leasing now," I said, not wanting to reveal that Ryan and I are so well-heeled.

"Well, a multi-million-dollar cello would be a standout here, especially since our programming is sometimes what I call 'island-ized.' Don't quote me on that. But as an example, the holiday performances of *The Nutcracker* that we play for the Oahu Ballet weave local legends into the traditional story."

"I saw a clip on the news. Something about an owl or, what do they call it, '*pueo*'?"

"Yes. The *pueo*. It's sacred to many Hawaiians. I'm told the owl is a physical manifestation of ancestral guardians who protect native people from harm."

"I have a lot to learn about the depth of Hawaiian symbols."

"Don't feel alone. The culture is rich with fables, symbols, and unwritten rules. My PR person helps keep me from stepping on toes. Still, I hope our audiences will enjoy the classical works as much as island favorites. I didn't come here to conduct slack guitar. Or, as I'm also finding out, begging for dollars to pay our musicians."

"I was involved with fundraising for the Metroplex Opera before I became its principal cellist. I was president of the Metroplex Opera Guild."

"Socialite turned musician? That's highly unusual."

"It was more, musician turned socialite turned musician. I majored in music at the University of Texas and also studied with a wonderful instructor in Oregon."

"Yes, I noted these things on your resume," he murmured.

"Surely there's a lot of money on Oahu, as far as donors."

"Yes, but this island's demographics are such that music written by dead white Europeans doesn't appeal to certain populations — or to tourists who are only here for fun in the sun. That's why our programming features so many multicultural and pop works."

"In Dallas, we started a group just for the guys, called the 'Cavaliers.' They host an annual golf tournament that brings in about $250,000 each year. Maybe your staff could start a Cavaliers group here. What would be the equivalent of Cavaliers? *Aliʻi?*"

"That means 'chief.' Maybe Kahunas would be better. But I'll ask, even though I hate golf."

"Me too," I chuckled.

"Now, back to your music education. You mentioned a cello teacher in Oregon?"

"Eric LeBeau," I said, but my eyes suddenly teared up with memories of my long-ago cello instructor. And lover. As clichéd as it sounds, he and I had an affair. It ended when Cole retired from pro football, and we moved back to Dallas.

"And?" Maestro Chua interrupted.

I blinked to clear my eyes and emotions. "Yes, sorry, I lost my train of thought. Even back in college, I felt I could play with an orchestra, but life took other turns. Eric helped me find my way."

"Did you bring your cello?"

"It's with your front office."

"We only have a small studio here. You'll be auditioning for soloist duties, not a position with the orchestra. Because of union rules, I'd have to hold a blind audition for that."

"Yes, of course. Although I currently live on the Big Island, my husband is studying for the Hawai'i bar. That means we might move to Oahu in the future."

His smile told me he liked the idea.

He stood then, as did I, and off we scurried to the studio. While I nervously unpacked my cello and music, Maestro Chua sat about ten feet away. Even more nervously, I put my music on a rack, then sat and tuned my cello to a recorded "A" Maestro Chua's assistant played on her iPhone. At least the sound was an oboe.

"What will you play for us today?"

"Chopin Cello Sonata in G Minor, without the piano. I hope that will work okay."

"Should be fine." Then he lowered his eyes as if to listen, not watch.

I positioned my bow and fingers, took a breath, remembered Eric's long-ago encouragements, and then began.

The Chopin is a soulful piece that can bring out my emotions, so after the first few tentative strokes, I felt myself dissolve into the work. Suddenly, I lost connection with anything beyond the music and my cello, until I heard the maestro's voice shouting, "That's enough. That's enough."

Startled, I looked up and asked, "Was that all right?" I sounded like a young girl, afraid she'd failed her math test.

Maestro Chua got up and walked toward the door, but then he turned back with a slight bow. "I'll be in touch." Then he left.

His assistant came to help me get the cello back in the case, then she walked me out to the elevator.

"Thanks for your help," I nodded, trying to smile.

"He'll be in touch," was all she said.

With that, I fumbled for my phone, scheduled a ride, and wondered what to tell Ryan. Did I get a gig? Or should I stick to being Nancy-D on cases Ryan might defend?

⁂

AT THE HOTEL, I CHECKED MY CELLO WITH SECURITY, freshened up in the room, and got a ride to the Halekulani Hotel, where I met Ryan at Cattleya Wine Bar. Luckily, Mike and Sonya had not arrived, so I had a moment to tell Ryan about my audition and interview.

"He said nothing? Not even, 'Very nice'?"

"No. But I think I played well."

"Was anybody else there?"

"Just his shy admin."

"I thought auditions were blind."

"Not for soloists."

"Hmmm. I should have accompanied you."

"Why?"

"He's a guy. And you are one beautiful woman." He winked, then took a sip of Scotch.

"Well, thank you, but he's at least ten years younger and looks like an Asian Johnny Depp. Before Johnny Depp started wearing all that eye makeup, anyway. Besides, I imagine the maestro is interested in younger women. Or, who knows, maybe guys?"

We both chuckled, and I enjoyed Ryan being protective and flirtatious as if we were reviving our dating relationship.

But just then, Big Mike Iona marched in, wearing an off-white linen jacket over a blue and white floral silk shirt. And beside him was the raunchy Sonya in a too-low, orange top.

Suddenly, my evening went from a romantic interlude with my husband to an insufferable dinner, where I had to resist stabbing Sonya with a hairpin.

Dressed in an off-white linen sport jacket over an Aloha shirt, Big Mike did not wait two minutes before telling Ryan, "I got two cases for ya, Brah."

"Big ones," Sonya nodded eagerly, making a sign with her hands as if the big one was a penis.

My instincts about her had been right. Her glistening pupils made me wonder if she was high on something, but perhaps she was simply in heat.

Ryan grinned back. "Tell me more."

"Kekoa Palakiko," Big Mike said.

"You're kidding me. I thought that was a done deal."

From there, Big Mike's discussion involved Ryan representing Kekoa on what are now two federal charges of murder, which stunned me because Ryan rarely represents anyone who is not stinking rich, and this guy wasn't.

"I thought these charges were slam-dunks for the feds," Ryan said.

Mike held up a hand. "Kekoa says he's been set up. For one thing, his wallet was stolen a while back. Lost all his IDs. He didn't report the theft. Just drifted along, island style. But after getting arrested, he's put two and two together."

"But he was spotted at the MPH gate and driving from the murder scene. And weeks later, he was seen on a tour with

Dexter Zachary up at ITUK and the VIS. Not to mention the feather they found and something about shipping tape. Connect the dots."

"That's why he needs you. Kekoa swears he was nowhere near any of the places he was supposedly seen. And I believe him. The guy's a fisherman, hunter, and hiker. Not a murderer. He's matured over the past several years. Lost his marriage over his astronomy protests. His wife, well, his ex-wife works in astronomy education. Thanks to her office being ransacked — you know how it is when it's your house that's burning and not your enemy's — he's turned one-eighty on his views. So now, Island Kingdom Now leaders are pissed and won't pay for a lawyer," Mike said.

Leering at Ryan again, Sonya crooned, "He needs your expertise. Your talents."

I wanted to stab her with my hairpins. I glanced at Ryan, hoping for his reassurance, but the sparkle in his eyes told me he was flattered. Darn it. Good ol' lunky "Diver" Ingles was now experiencing the delights that a handsome guy like Cole Donovan relished from puberty. Unadulterated worship from the female population for being handsome, a football player, and rich. Ryan did not have this until after laser vision surgery rid him of thick-lensed glasses, but now that he's my husband, I don't want him manipulated by girlie adulation.

Ryan leaned my way. "Okay if we postpone our return flight and interview Kekoa?"

At least he asked.

"Oh, goodie," Sonya squeaked.

I gave her a deadly smile. "Ryan is an expert at spotting a phony," I said pointedly. Then I added my sweet cheerleader smile to soften the bite.

"Marie's a superb judge of character too. It would be a great help to have her with me."

"Of course, darling," I replied, patting his knee and again smiling Sonya's way.

She averted her eyes, clearly displeased at seeing Ryan and me as a team.

Mike grinned widely. "I'll set up the interviews. Check your text first thing tomorrow for the appointment time, probably late morning. And if you decide to take the case, come by the office after to discuss fees."

"Who's paying the tab?"

Mike angled his head. "We are. Pro bono. We'll pay you, however."

"Gosh, Mike, I don't want to get into a protracted pro bono case that costs your firm a lot in time and expenses."

"No worry. We can talk story tomorrow. Now, let's get some *grindz*. I'm hungry."

From there, we perused Orchids' elaborate and elegant menu, enjoyed several delectable courses, and made conversation as best we could.

I complimented Mike on his Aloha wear, and he told me, "Sig Zane in Hilo. You should buy Ryan something when you're over on that side."

However, even during such ordinary, pleasant exchanges, Sonya's glassy eyes kept leering at Ryan as if to say, "I want to suck your cock."

To counter this, I kept putting my arm around Ryan's shoulder to remind him — and her — that his loving wife was right there.

I doubt Ryan would ever stray, but he is male. So, I will do what I must to keep my husband close. Or, should I say, I will stay close to my husband, since it's increasingly apparent my insecurities refuse to leave me, even when you've outlived your abusers and know in your gut your husband would never stray.

That night, I made a special effort to be sexually loving to

Ryan, the way a man hopes his woman will. I didn't want to put on an act, but women sometimes must be part actress. So, I put on my black vacation nightie, put on a bit more makeup and a dab of perfume, and then slid into bed beside him. I purposely left my hairpins in because Ryan usually likes to take them down himself. Then I curled up on his chest, nuzzled his fuzz and nipples, and then, well, both of us were a bit surprised by my ardent gestures.

Afterward, as we lay cuddling, he asked, "What brought that on?"

"I just wanted to remind you I love you. It seems we've settled into *marriage*, but it's important to remind ourselves how we felt when we first fell in love. We couldn't get enough of each other."

He thought about that. "I haven't been that good of a husband to you lately."

"We've both been distracted."

"Maybe it's island fever, but I've felt lost."

"You're not alone. I guess we'll know more with time, especially if you take this case, and if I get solos. I'm not sure whether Maestro Chua liked my playing. It was such an odd audition. He didn't watch me play but closed his eyes, so I somewhat lost myself in Chopin. Maybe that was his point."

My ramble was interrupted by Ryan's snore. I doubt he'd heard any of my remarks.

Trying not to wake him, I slid out of bed and went to take a quick shower. As I toweled off, I leaned in and whispered to the mirror image of myself. "Still needy, aren't you? Why can't you feel confident Ryan will love you? Do you think you have to perform to make a guy happy?"

THE NEXT MORNING, AFTER COFFEE AND BREAKFAST IN THE room, Ryan checked his texts, got our appointment time, and off we went to the Federal Detention Center, a beige multistory building with a curved frontage.

Once inside and past security, we waited for Kekoa in a private interview room, where Ryan pulled out a small recording device. "This will be confidential, not to worry about that, but if you ask questions or mention anything, just remember, it will be on this recording."

I nodded. "But the guards?"

He smiled and patted my hand. "It's against Hawai'i law to record or listen to defendant/attorney interviews. Hey, I learned that in my class, and it's already paying off."

About that time, Kekoa shuffled in. He was tough-looking, muscular, with an angry scowl. Although his ankles were chained and his hands cuffed, I felt anxious, especially when the officers unshackled him.

One officer said, "In Hawai'i, defendants do not have to be shackled when they meet their attorneys. That is, unless there's a reason they should be. You two fine with that?"

"No problem, officer," Ryan said firmly. But to me, he whispered, "Don't worry. You've got a six-foot-three linebacker here. I can take him."

I nervously whispered back. "You'd better."

When Kekoa sat across from us at the table, his visage softened, and he looked like a wounded ram. He was a bulky guy, maybe played football in his youth. Or surely did a lot of surfing or canoeing.

"Kekoa, aloha. I'm defense attorney Ryan Ingles, and this is my legal assistant, Marie."

I noted Ryan did not call me his wife. Probably better for the recording.

Kekoa's deeply set dark eyes searched the room. "Where's Big Mike?"

"He asked me to talk with you. I'm from Dallas, but I live on the Big Island now."

"Ah, the *hale* rock."

"Right. That's why Big Mike asked me to help. Since I'm based on the Big Island, my team can handle investigations more easily than Big Mike's team can, you know, having to fly back and forth. My team includes three professional investigators."

Kekoa looked up optimistically. "Okay, so when do I get outa here?"

"Not soon. Big Mike's firm will represent you at arraignment and bail hearings, but since you're under two homicide indictments, you're not likely to be released on bail. The primary reason I'm here is to ask a few questions so Big Mike and I can get to work on your behalf."

From there, Ryan peppered Kekoa with every question one might imagine, even down to, "Did you kill Shin Watanabe?" and "Did you kill Dexter Zachary?"

Kekoa answered each question sincerely. He did not fidget, avoid eye contact, or touch his face, each a telltale sign that someone is lying.

When I was a full-time Nancy-D, Billy Bob instructed me, "Liars will talk faster or more quietly, or their voices might sound higher pitched. Sometimes they'll stutter or use filler words like 'um' and 'like.' They'll clam up about details, but if they talk a lot, they'll forget and contradict themselves. Another tip-off is when they seem anxious or defensive."

As far as I could tell, Kekoa did none of these things.

After our interview, Ryan buzzed for the guards. They cuffed and shackled Kekoa, then led him to the door, where he turned anxiously to say, "Please get me out of this place. I didn't kill nobody, man. You gotta believe me."

"I've got your back, Kekoa," Ryan called out as Kekoa disappeared and the door slammed.

"Hmmm. So, you've got his back?"

"Marie, I don't think this guy killed anybody. Either this is a case of mistaken identity, or somebody is working hard to set him up. The circumstantial evidence reminds me of your case. Remember how Lena planted your cherry blossom pins that killed Luca?"

"All this seems too layered. Feathers. Arrows. A black Jeep. Poison tea."

I showed Ryan my notes. In big block letters, I'd written, "Kekoa is not lying. So, who's killing astronomers? And why?"

Ryan kissed me on my cheek with a big smack. "Great minds think alike, Marie. I'd better call Colleen to get Iona Law Firm on the account list, and I'm only going to bill at half my hourly rate. Hopefully, she'll loan us Billy Bob and Natalie. I'm glad they stuck around."

So much for a break from being Nancy-D.

Chapter Thirty

KANAKA ADVOCATE DAILY

Texas Attorney Hired to Represent Palakiko

HILO, Hawaii — Honolulu's Iona Law Firm has hired Big Island attorney Ryan Ingles to defend activist Kekoa Palakiko, according to Makoa "Big Mike" Iona, who will serve as local counsel in the case.

"Ryan was the best choice, since we already sponsored him *pro hac vice* on another case, and he lives on the Big Island. Although Ryan's not yet licensed in Hawaii, our firm will provide oversight. My associate Sonya Pruitt will work closely with Ryan and his Dallas-based legal team that includes top-notch investigators," Iona said in a press release.

Palakiko has not been released on bail, which has motivated ongoing demonstrations on the Big Island, Lanai, and Oahu by members of Island Kingdom Now. Based on Oahu, but with associate groups on each island, Island Kingdom Now is the state's largest secessionist group.

Russell Chong, a longtime Big Island politico, told the *Kanaka Advocate Daily*, "From what I've heard, Island Kingdom Now still supports Kekoa's rights, although they're miffed with him over his change of heart over HILT."

According to Island Kingdom Now's website, the group aims to protect the cultural heritage and rights of Native Hawaiians, advocate for Hawaii's independence from the United States of America, and campaign for the removal of all observatories from atop Maunakea.

Interviewed by phone, Ingles remarked, "I understand the activists' frustrations. We are working diligently to represent Kekoa's right to be free on bail until he is tried. We also hope to uncover evidence that proves his innocence."

Ingles' team includes his wife, Marie Ingles, widow of two-time Super Bowl champion quarterback Cole Donovan; Billy Bob Hughes, a licensed private investigator in Texas; and computer analyst Natalie Sherman.

Iona remarked, "Before Kekoa's arrest, Ryan's team represented Texas astronomer Nocona Parker, who was arrested for killing Shin Watanabe. But the feds quickly released him after evidence pointed to Kekoa. But we think he's been set up."

Ingles declined to name potential suspects. "The only similarity between the two murders was that both astronomers were working to find Earth's twin planet beyond our Milky Way. Both Mr. Watanabe and Mr. Zachary were leading researchers in this field."

Ingles admitted that other Big Island astronomers also work on similar projects. This reporter asked if that would make them suspects.

"I'm told competition between observatories is keen, as each wants to make major discoveries. Which begs the question, what was Kekoa's motive? He has reversed his stance against astronomy in Hawaii and announced his support for HILT. To me, that says the FBI does not have the right guy."

According to Knight Observatory Director Monty Lundquist, "Astronomy on the Big Island and Maui is a close-knit community of scientists, technicians, and administrative personnel who work on a variety of projects. Finding Earth's twin is just one of them. Astronomers from all over the world request time on our amazing instruments. From the late Shin Watanabe and Dexter Zachary to international stars like Germany's Zeno Kühn of AWE-T, Sweden's Claudia Walser, Spain's Santiago Velazco, and France's Raphaël Gachet, the research is competitive. But it's also collaborative. Otherwise, anyone could say they discovered evidence of a taco shop on another planet, and we'd have to believe them," Lundquist joked.

Kimberley Ensley, executive director of HILT's board, remarked by phone from Boston, "We are pleased to see activists like Kekoa Palakiko appreciate the value HILT will bring to Hawaii. HILT's amazing mirrors are on their way here from Canada. We hope to see the shipment arrive at the summit soon."

As for the arrest of Palakiko, FBI Supervisory Special Agent Pua Akana remarked, "Although the Ballard / Ingles legal team now insists he's innocent, three of their investigators served on the FBI Hawaii Special Task Force. At that time, they had a different opinion of Mr. Palakiko's role in these tragic murders. We still think we've got the right guy. The islands' astronomy community can return to making Nobel Prize-winning discoveries, rather than worrying whether someone will try to murder them."

For information, contact reporter Wallace Huppenthall at (808) 765-1212.

Chapter Thirty-One

MY SIDE OF THE MIRRORS

Jürgen Bergen / Zeno Kühn

M*ein Gott*, the *Kanaka Advocate Daily* reporter mentioned my real name. *Ach je*, now the FBI will want to interview the real me, Zeno Kühn. Have investigators discovered he's six months into a one-year sabbatical from AWE-T? If so, they've probably scoured my MakeFriends page that says I'm on Madagascar Island.

Throughout my planning, I've kept the MakeFriends page fresh, posting phony photos and highlights of my visits. Hopefully, the FBI will not attempt to trace me there. I never mention hotels, but maybe I should book rentals with Zeno's credit card and check in and out online.

Not sure what to do. Ever since Kekoa's pro-astronomy speech, he's suddenly of no value. My plans rely on the anti-astronomy masses to prevent a future rebuild of HILT.

These twists are pressuring our timelines. As Jürgen nervously awaits HILT's equipment to arrive, I, Zeno, am eager to destroy it, flee this island prison, and return to real life.

We need a new scapegoat. A new activist for the FBI to chase. *Ach je*, this means another performance. I truly hate spraying on cosmetic bronzers and masquerading in native costumes. They itch! But I must keep the activists stirred.

As soon as the mirrors arrive, I will escalate Jürgen's actions. Zeno needs to resume work at AWE-T sooner than expected.

From my office in Vitacura, Chile, I will take joy in reading an article in *Astronomy Today* that says something like, "The new Maunakea Authority recently voted not to approve the rebuild of the Hawai'i Island Large Telescope (HILT) because of opposition to the project from the indigenous population. And in other news, the FBI continues its search for HILT's former project manager, Jürgen Bergen, as a person of interest in the explosive destruction of the giant HILT observatory and the deaths of three astronomers."

Haha, I look forward to being interviewed about Jürgen. How mortified I'll appear to have recommended him for the HILT job. "You just never know a person, not really, even when you work with them for years," I'll say, deeply chagrined.

Chapter Thirty-Two

HAWAII PU HERALD

Third Astronomer Killed! Island Frantic.

HILO, Hawaii — A third prominent astronomer has been killed on the Big Island. FBI authorities would not release the victim's name until family members were notified. However, anonymous sources say he was a French National working with the Franco-Canadian Observatory (FCO) on Maunakea, with base operations in Kamuela.

FCO Director, Emile Tremblay said, "At this time, we ask the public's patience while we notify family members and provide the FBI task force with details to help capture whoever is murdering our world's finest astronomers. We are stunned that a beneficial scientific field like astronomy is under attack."

According to FCO employees who asked to remain anonymous, the most recent murder victim was working on deep-field imaging projects.

"This is a different arena from the previous victims' research," Tremblay said.

After learning of this event, hundreds of sovereignty activists gathered outside the Federal Detention Center in Honolulu to demand the release of Kekoa Palakiko, the Big

Island activist who awaits trial for the murder of two other prominent astronomers.

Palakiko has professed his innocence from the time of his arrest. Asked whether this recent killing proves Palakiko was falsely charged, FBI Supervisory Special Agent (SSA) Pua Akana remarked, "Each case may be a separate circumstance. Or, this latest could be a copycat to force authorities off target."

Well-known Native Hawaiian sovereignty activist Alohi Akamu remarked, "We need to fire this money-grubbing Ballard / Ingles firm, from Dallas, Texas, of all places. What do they know about islanders' issues? Kekoa wouldn't still be in jail if he had kamaaina counsel, and I don't mean Big Mike Iona's law firm paying the tab."

SSA Akana added, "Should the public have information about these murders, please contact the FBI Hawaii Task Force tip line at (808) 999-1111."

Contact   reporter   Ikaika   Kelekolio   at Ikaika.Kelekolio@hawaiipuherald.com

Chapter Thirty-Three

808 INSIDERS

Da Real Scoop

Today at 4:32 a.m.

808 Insiders are oh-so *hauʻoli* to see Native Hawaiians demanding the removal of Ballard / Ingles as Kekoa Palakiko's defense team! If you want to help, call Big Mike at Iona Law Firm and tell him to fire Ballard / Ingles. *Deyʻre* from Dallas. Hire LOCAL.

❀

Most Relevant:

AstroExplorer — Right on, 808 Insiders. Kekoa Palakiko deserves the best!

Ono Wrangler — I get you *mauka* and *makai*, AstroExplorer.

Wahine Beekeeper — AstroExplorer, you one of *dem* astronomaters?

AstroExplorer — I'm LOCAL, but I got a nice telescope. Cost me $12k.

South Point Angler — $12k for a telescope? You must be *fookin' haole*!

Hāwī Haole — I got here soon as I could, Brah!

Wahine Beekeeper — **Hāwī Haole** How long you been on the rock?

Hāwī Haole — 15 *makahiki*

Wahine Beekeeper — Takes 20 to be local. LOL

Crazy Macheco — Too many *haole* coming here.

Waikoloa Night Skies — Too many meth-head locals already. Can't even get into restaurants without having to jump a hobo.

South Point Angler — **Waikoloa Night Skies** your *haole*, for sure, asshole!

808 Insiders — Comments have been discontinued.

Chapter Thirty-Four

WHO'S COPYING WHOM?

Marie Ingles

Wow! We are in a mess! As we four sat with our laptops around the breakfast table, Natalie was madly trying to trace the IP addresses of users on 808 Insiders who wanted to get us fired. Her complaints to the 808 Insiders admins have gone unanswered.

"There's no way to talk to a human. How do these social media giants get away with only AI customer service? Not only does this page's admin not respond, but there's a new user called AstroExplorer who is cheering on the activists. Because of his username, I wondered if he's connected to astronomy. What local guy would spend $12k on a telescope?"

Billy Bob chuckled sarcastically. "We are playing whack-a-mole, only on Hawai'i, would that be, 'Whack-a-mongoose'?"

"Whack a rooster!" Especially the one that wakes me up at 5:30 a.m.," Ryan laughed.

THE NEXT DAY, WE FOUR FLEW TO OAHU TO RE-INTERVIEW Kekoa. Federal prosecutors refused to drop the charges based on this third murder.

As the FBI trial attorney told Ryan by phone, "Although the most recent murder was committed while Mr. Palakiko was incarcerated, this does not erase the evidence we have for the other two killings. Until we know more, the charges stand."

After we four took a taxi to the detention center and made our way to the interview room, we squeezed around one side of a too-small table for a pair of former linebackers and their ladies, then waited until the guards brought in Kekoa.

At first glance, he looked thinner but a bit more hopeful. His first question was, "You t'ink I might get outa here after this new murder?"

"Not according to the FBI," Ryan replied. "That's why we're here. We wondered if this latest killing might be a team effort. The French astronomer was researching different projects from the other astronomers. Did any of this factor into any actions you might have taken?"

Ryan's question puzzled me. I looked to him for an answer, but he didn't budge. Then I looked across at Billy Bob. He gave me a piercing stare and the slightest shake of his head.

Kekoa was also confused and blurted, "What actions? Now you think I'm the killer?"

Ryan took his time before replying. "Kekoa, what we are trying to uncover is the best way to defend you. If there's anything you can share, that is, if you want to help us understand why anyone would kill these astronomers, please do that now. We are trying to defend you, but we also want to stop further killings. For example, if you were working with someone, perhaps from Island Kingdom Now…"

Kekoa sat back, looking puzzled and wounded.

I didn't blame him. Did Ryan think Kekoa had partners

who were continuing these attacks? When did Ryan start thinking Kekoa was guilty?

Kekoa fumed in dismay. "If you try to hang this on me, Big Mike will lawyer me instead. I ain't a killer. I'm a fisherman. A hunter. A tour guide. And I've changed my mind about this damn HILT. Announced I'm okay with it being built, but only if they do what they say they're gonna do to help Hawaiians. My wife, well, ex-wife, she and I argued about HILT. She's gung-ho about astronomy. But some jerks vandalized her offices! My own wife. Everybody knows she's my wife, and to do that, well, that got me thinking. I agreed to okay HILT if she gives our marriage another try. Island Kingdom Now thinks I'm selling out my beliefs, but I don't want her hurt."

With that, he pounded the table with his fists, scaring the life out of me, but I told myself, "Do not flinch."

Ryan reached out to calm Kekoa. "Kekoa, before I commit to representing anyone, I try to make sure I know if they're guilty. Your answers today seem as sincere as your earlier replies."

Kekoa realized Ryan had tested him. "I'm no liar." His eyes flooded with tears, and he sniffed, trying to stifle them.

Natalie handed him a tissue. "Don't feel alone. Ryan pushes me all the time too."

Kekoa sniffed, blew his nose, and then managed a limp, downturned smile.

Natalie looked to Ryan to see if she could begin.

He nodded back.

"Kekoa, I handle the technical aspects of your case. Yesterday, we received a copy of the security video at MPH taken on the day Shin Watanabe was killed. Your black Jeep was spotted there, license plates and all. I know you swear that wasn't you, but the MPH gate attendant picked you out in a photo lineup. Please look at this footage and see if you notice anything unusual."

When Natalie handed Kekoa her iPad, he peered closely. After a while, he sat back in shock. "That's not my Jeep. I swear. Play that again."

Natalie replayed the video.

Kekoa frowned. "I don't know the *brah* driving, but I know that ain't my steering wheel. Mine is custom. Has Koa wood inlay. Did it myself."

We four squinted at the video again. This steering wheel was plain black.

Ryan reached across and patted Kekoa on the shoulder. "We'll point this out to Pua Akana at the FBI. She's impounded your Jeep, right?"

"Hell if I know."

"She'll check it out."

"Play that again, please." Kekoa leaned closer, then sat back aghast. "And look at that *braddah's* nose!" He pointed to the driver on the screen and then pointed to his nose. It was quite broad at the nostrils and somewhat flat at the bridge, while the man in the Jeep had a narrow, aquiline nose.

We four stared at the video, then looked at Kekoa.

"Why didn't we notice that?" Billy Bob said.

"You ain't local," Kekoa scowled.

Billy Bob scoffed. "Well, Big Mike Iona, local police, the MPH guard, and even FBI facial rec software didn't notice that difference either."

"It looks like someone is playing an elaborate game to convict Kekoa for these murders. But he didn't know about the Koa wood inlay or how to use a fake nose," Ryan said.

All of us were elated at this fresh evidence. We even hugged Kekoa before we left. His prison uniform smelled like moldy bread, but I tried to ignore that. He wasn't the murderer. Hopefully, we can get him out of jail soon.

That afternoon, Ryan alerted the FBI trial attorney and Pua about the steering wheel and nose differences. Then he had a thought. "Pua, can you get county officials to run all sales transactions for black Jeeps over, say, the past twelve months?"

Several days passed before we heard back, but Pua called via conference. "First off, we watched the video several times. Even had a cosmetic surgeon give us advice since facial rec was confused by the blurry images. We agree. The nose is not Kekoa Palakiko's. On top of that, we've located a second black Jeep, the same model year, but also titled in Mr. Palakiko's name. It was recently parted-out by a junk dealer who buys cars from charity organizations. There's a signature on the title. Our analyst compared it to Kekoa Palakiko's. It doesn't match."

"Well, well. Somebody is disguising themselves as a local to kill astronomers," Ryan said.

"You've brought in key evidence, Ryan and team, for which my task force thanks you. Based on these discoveries, I'm told Mr. Palakiko will be released. But this sends us back to square one, and begs the question, who?"

The four on our end collectively blew out frustrated sighs, because we knew we were probably going back to work on the task force.

Chapter Thirty-Five

MAKING MORE NEWS

Marie Ingles

B illy Bob, Natalie, and my friend Ailani gathered on our sectional to watch the "Breaking News Special" on PONO-TV's 5:00 p.m. news.

Oh, my, in front of the Federal Detention Center, there was a Hawaiian-style extravaganza, with local activists dressed in traditional costumes thumping large gourds. Ailani told us they were called *ipu*. A group of *hula kahiko* dancers swayed and chanted in traditional costumes, while local dignitaries exchanged colorful *lei* and *ohana* kisses.

Standing before the crowd, a young male Hawaiian reporter with an amazingly deep baritone interviewed an array of celebrities but kept glancing back to the front doors, waiting for Kekoa to come outside.

First, he interviewed two movie stars, George "Lava" Jenkins and "Big Max" Hekekia, followed by rock star Kamo Hasegawa.

Ailani heaved a sarcastic sigh. "Those three guys show up whenever they can get their gorgeous faces on the news, but Lava Jenkins isn't Hawaiian at all, just part Tongan. Kamo was at least born on Oahu, but his parents were from somewhere in

Central America. Big Max is the only one with Hawaiian blood through his mother, but the rest of the gorgeous beast is Italian and Swedish."

"Well, he can be one hundred percent of anything around me any day," Natalie laughed.

"Sorry if I seem resentful, but everybody claims to be Hawaiian these days."

"Are you?" Natalie asked.

"I have Hawaiian heritage through my father. He and I were born on Oahu, but my mother is fully Samoan. Then again, that means her ancestors came to Samoa from Southeast Asia, so I've got a lot of Asians in there too. How Samoans got so large, I haven't a clue, and I fight my weight every effing day."

"You ain't alone," Billy Bob groaned. "Maybe I'm Samoan."

"I kind of doubt that, Billy Bob. But if you can tolerate another of my factoids, I saw a TV report about that. It's called 'the thrifty gene.' The theory is that early Samoans faced tremendous food insecurity when settling in the South Pacific islands. Those with the thrifty gene could store more energy, survive, then pass the thrifty gene along."

"To me. Well, great. Now I know —" Ailani began.

Interrupting Ailani on TV just then, the front doors of the detention center opened. Out marched Ryan, Big Mike Iona, and the ever-trashy Sonya in a shiny chartreuse two-piece suit. She was standing between Ryan and the previously charged Kekoa Palakiko, dressed in what I imagine was a brand-new sports jacket over an aloha shirt and slacks.

Standing at a makeshift podium with about ten microphones attached to the front of it, Ryan, Big Mike, Sonya, and Kekoa each had five or six lushly colored *lei* stacked so high around their necks, they kept pressing them down to keep their chins above the flowers.

"I can barely see our man for the stack of *leis*," Billy Bob shouted.

"Actually, the plural is simply *lei*. In ʻŌlelo Hawaiʻi, there isn't a distinction between singular and plural," Natalie said.

Billy Bob shook his head. "It's gotten so I can't utter a freakin' word without being a failed Hawaiian." Then he suddenly peered intently at the TV. "More importantly, why is that woman hanging all over the boss?"

Ailani asked me with a wink. "Is that your pal Sonya?"

"Yes, Sonya is the sleaze with her arm around Ryan's waist," I gritted through my teeth.

Billy Bob glanced my way. "Whoa! Something you're not telling me?"

"Well, sad to say, but Sonya Pruitt has the hots for my husband. Please don't say a word to Ryan. It's not his fault, and he gets prickly when accused."

"Okay…" Billy Bob gave me a doubtful glance.

Natalie interrupted. "Uh-oh, turn it up. Ryan might be next to speak."

Ryan's classic-cut brown hair was windblown as he stood in front of the Detention Center, wearing a blue floral Aloha shirt under the lightweight navy sport jacket I'd picked out.

Kekoa stood on Ryan's right, with Sonya and Big Mike on Ryan's left. Again, I could see that Sonya kept her right arm around Ryan's waist.

Did he also have his arm around her? *Argggghhhhhh*. I couldn't tell. My mind was reeling.

As reporters and camera operators circled him, he began. "Thank you for coming today and for helping us celebrate Kekoa Palakiko's release. Justice has been well served. Someone on the Big Island framed Kekoa for two brutal and tragic murders. But this someone's lust to kill is so strong, he committed a third murder while Kekoa was in jail. This led us to suspect that Kekoa's identity had been stolen, and a security video revealed concrete evidence that someone was impersonating him. As a result, prosecutors dropped the charges. But now, the FBI Hawaiʻi task force authorities are back to square one. Someone in these islands is trying to kill the world's top astronomers. Who and why? Authorities wasted a lot of time targeting our client when they should have been asking who really committed these horrific murders?"

"Gosh, Ryan, don't piss off Pua and the task force," Billy Bob shouted at the TV.

On-screen, just then, Ryan turned to shake Kekoa's hand. But before he did, I could see Ryan had to move his arm from around Sonya's waist, while she kept her hand on his back, the way a woman might if he was her man.

I was furious and looked to see if Ailani had noticed. Her grimace told me she did. Natalie averted her eyes and exhaled a sigh, while Billy Bob gave me a sympathetic wince.

"I don't like this. Don't like it at all," Billy Bob said.

Then we four went silent, listening to Big Mike say things like, "This was a team effort, with inter-island collaboration between federal, state, and county authorities."

"More inter-island discombobulation," Billy Bob snarled.

After Ryan's speech, I rose to gather our snack and drink dishes, again wondering if my amazing new husband was having a fling with Ms. Diamond Client Champion.

Ailani stuck around after Billy Bob and Natalie left for their condo. "You okay? I couldn't believe how that woman was fawning over your husband."

"He looked like he was doing a bit of fawning as well."

"Marie, don't put too much into this. Maybe it was just colleagues celebrating, you know, proud of getting Kekoa released. I mean, when Gilles and his mirrors team finish a project, they celebrate with a champagne party. And there are usually lots of hugs. But that's what happens when colleagues are thrilled about achieving something together. I don't let it bother me."

"Ailani, I told myself the same thing, but I've got a history — emotional abuse from the past. Anytime the possibility of rejection rears its ugly head, I relapse into what I call my 'Marie Needy' response."

"At least you know what's going on. What famous lady once said, 'Sometimes it's best to turn a blind eye.'?"

I laughed. "I think that was Queen Elizabeth in *The Crown* series on Netflix. The real queen probably didn't say that. But I never thought I'd have to worry about Ryan."

"That attorney, what's her name, Sonya? She looks like some aging rock star."

"Britney Spears."

"Oh, my gosh, that's it. Britney Spears, well past her prime."

"Are you being ageist?"

"Just between us, since we are both over the forty-yard line. Don't you worry. You are the most talented and beautiful *wahine* on this island, and I wouldn't say that if I didn't think it was true. I'll take second place to you any day."

"Ailani, I appreciate your flattery, but my having lucked out, appearance-wise, shouldn't be the reason Ryan remains loyal. I want him to love me just for me. The way I look with sand all over me at the beach. The way I look when I'm in my world playing my cello. The way I look when I'm exhausted and sweaty after exercising, have my hair in a George Washington, and just want to veg."

"I guarantee you he does. Do yourself a favor and don't mention the Sonya thing. Just greet him when he returns and give him a big kiss."

"More showmanship, huh?"

"It's a sad fact, but sometimes we *wahine* gotta put on a smile and do the *hula*."

I laughed but shook my head in frustration. "I found myself 'performing' the other night for my very own husband and wondered why I felt I must."

At the door, she gave me another hug. "If you need to talk, just let me know. I understand how you feel. Gilles is a good-looking guy, too, and women are always making a pass. Normal-sized women. Skinny women. Not a large-bodied Samoan woman like me. That pisses me off, but again, it's not his fault. Simply remind Ryan who he loves and why."

After Ailani left, I felt relieved to have a friend I could talk to. Not to ignore Natalie, who's a brilliant colleague, but she's tougher than I am. She'd probably blister Billy Bob's tush if he behaved like Ryan did today with Sonya. Part of me wishes I could be more like Natalie. Assertive. Fearless.

I was loading the dishwasher when I got a brief text from Ryan. "Home by ten. Last flight out of Oahu. Sorry. Only flight I could get."

Of course, this made me wonder if he'd delayed a flight to have dinner with Sonya. Perhaps they'd had an interlude after, since his flight was leaving so late. Oh, my imagination ran foul. I sighed and repeated what Ailani had told me, "Simply remind him who he loves and why."

I turned the TV to another local channel and saw the same video of Ryan speaking, Sonya squeezing, but more horrifying that Ryan squeezing back. Oh, gosh. I turned off the TV, wishing I hadn't watched it again, wishing I could call Ailani again. But I didn't want to be a bother.

Who else could I call? For a moment, I even wished I could call Lena Verano, the Lena who used to be my good friend. Of course, this thought spiraled into anxious questions about Lena, why she killed Cole, why she killed Luca, and if she regretted what she did.

"I'm sorry," her email had said. Should I believe the words of a pathological liar, murderer, and sociopath?

Oh, dear, this was going to be a long night, what with Ryan coming home late. I'd better go upstairs and practice my cello before he arrives. Release my tensions, then get dolled up. I had more performing to do.

Chapter Thirty-Six

CELLIST, NANCY-D, OR MOMMY?

Marie Ingles

The next day, Colleen Ballard video-called Ryan and me to say in her tax attorney's voice that we were out of a job. "Now that Kekoa's case is complete, we'll wrap up Ryan's legal billings to Iona Law Firm and the investigative billings for Hawai'i State Police to pay. But if the FBI wants any of you back on the task force, someone else has to pay."

"I guess that means Billy Bob and Natalie should head back to Dallas," Ryan said.

"Right. I will let you know if the FBI figures anything out, or if another case comes up."

"Thanks, Colleen, but I'm pretty overwhelmed right now with bar test prep."

"How are your studies going? 'Made any decisions about opening a firm?"

"The studies are going okay, but my Kona office plans are on hold. I'm trying to decide whether to open my office on Oahu or partner with Mike Iona's firm."

"As you know, it would be much cheaper and perhaps wiser

to partner with an established firm with a well-known local attorney at the helm."

"I hear you, Colleen. Every time I try to do something on my own here, I'm reminded we are in foreign territory. A yearlong partnership could be a better choice. Marie is pursuing opportunities with the symphony orchestra on Oahu. And our lease comes up soon, so we have decisions to make on that as well."

Ryan nodded my way, but I shrugged since I hadn't heard from Devon Chua about scheduling a concert appearance. So, having the task force on hold and losing the workday companionship of Billy Bob and Natalie meant I was footloose.

Of course, I could still meet Ailani at the pool or beach on Thursdays. If I didn't have her friendship, I'd go nuts. With Ryan studying night and day, or flying off for another class, our romantic life is at a standstill. When I foolishly brought it up over brunch at a Waikoloa Beach bistro the next Sunday, Ryan became defensive.

After a few sips of my Mai Tai, I felt bold enough to ask, "Shall we repair to our boudoir this afternoon and not come up for air until tomorrow?"

Glancing to see who might have overheard, Ryan whispered, "Marie, what is it lately? You've never been a horny vamp. Can't we just enjoy this ridiculously expensive brunch and the surrounding mountain views without delving into the status of my sexual urges?"

Uh-oh, now I was a "horny vamp." His insult disturbed me, but I didn't want to make a scene, so I murmured a demure, "I shouldn't have brought it up here. But the last time we had an encounter was on Oahu, after our dinner with Mike and Sonya. And after Kekoa's release, I got dolled up for you, but you said you were too tired."

Again, Ryan glanced around and fumed under his breath.

"Marie, we can discuss this after we get back to the condo. Today, I wanted to take a break from studying or stress of any kind. I thought maybe we could take a nice drive to the north shore. Does that interest you, or is my sex organ the only thing you have on your mind lately?"

I felt under attack. "Okay. I give. I shouldn't have brought it up here."

"Right. Now, do you want to take that drive? Go to the special little beach park?"

I gave him a forced smile. "Of course, I'd love to."

There I went, smiling again. Natalie wouldn't put up with this shit.

Nor would Lena Verano. Heck, she'd simply kill any guy who pissed her off.

And stupid me. I had thought Lena was my best friend. Am I a poor judge of character? Do the people I love attack me because I'm the problem, not them?

Maybe it was what they call "island fever," but as a humid breeze blew over our outdoor table, a wave of anxiety passed through me. As I reached to take another sip of my Mai Tai, I suddenly felt that nothing was going to work for me because I didn't belong in this universe.

Ryan noticed my distress. He reached to take my shaking hand. "I'm sorry, Marie. I overreacted. Some of what's going on with me is a combination of stress and all these bar classes — lectures and practicum on countering witnesses, refuting arguments, and getting witnesses to recant. I'm always looking for a way to argue my point or dispute what opposition counsel has just said, even when they're right. Even when you're right."

I raised my eyes, and he could see they were teary. I hated that. I didn't want to be the weepy society beauty he first represented. But darn it, Marie Needy kept bubbling to the surface. Even after the adventures Ryan and I had in the

Seychelles, when I'd been so brave and confident, helping to find Cole's millions. So reassured after winning first-chair with Metroplex Opera Orchestra. So convinced I was on my way to being a concert cellist, that I forgot my weakness is the unrelenting fear that a man I love might stop loving me.

I couldn't speak right then.

Ryan blew out in dismay. Then he raised his hand to signal our server. "Check, please."

After we returned to the condo, he went straight to his laptop study courses and did not mention the afternoon drive.

Frustrated, I stepped upstairs to my studio and played in the nude for an hour, escaping to my passionate world. Something about Elgar's romantic chords returns me to the woman I so want to be, a woman with a lot of love to give and the courage and power to pursue my dreams.

When I went back downstairs, Ryan had left a note. "I couldn't think with all the noise. I'm in the business center."

Great. Even my soundproofing had failed. My cello playing was now "noise."

That evening after Ryan returned, he silently fixed a Scotch and turned on the local channel news.

I listened to the announcers' depressing reports about the lack of clues in the astronomy murders and silently fixed two lovely chefs' salads with grilled chicken, sliced avocado, chopped bacon, provolone cheese slices, pineapple chunks, macadamia nuts, and Maui onion dressing. We took our salads out to the lanai, where the sunlight turned deeply orange, and the last foursome finished putting on the lake green. Ryan was pleasant enough. Chatted about some $11 million county embezzlement case he'd heard on the news.

"Two local attorneys and a private investor. Mike Iona is their lawyer."

"Maybe we watch local news too often, but there seem to be quite a few embezzlement cases in these islands."

"Big-time corruption, sad to say."

"Yes, it is sad. We love the Big Island for the beauty and peace it brings us. Still brings us. But amid the corruption cases, locals killing locals, and these astronomy killings, island authorities must be overwhelmed. I'm disappointed Colleen put a hold on our investigations. We might find out who did this. You're a whiz at questioning people, and I've learned a lot from Billy Bob and Natalie. Maybe we should simply volunteer."

"Marie, until I pass the bar, I'm too busy to play investigator. You are welcome to offer your services to Pua, but I think you need to decide whether you are a cellist or a 'Nancy-D.' You can't be successful at both."

Now it was my turn to overreact. I looked Ryan dead in the eyes and said, "Again, more rebuttal to make the witness recant?"

That seemed to shut him up. And later on, he apologized for his caustic remark. But still. Ryan and I were crumbling in a rocky period. I forgot that the bloom of a new marriage wears off over time, but I did not imagine that a love as natural, comfortable, and secure as ours could suddenly go so hot with anger and cold with disdain.

Maybe all married couples fall in and out of love. Maybe I expect too much.

That night, we slept together, but not touching. And the next morning at 6:00 a.m., my phone rang.

At first, I thought it was Colleen, but I checked the caller ID and saw it was my son Shawn in New York.

"Hey, Mom, how about Avery and I come to see you?"

I was stunned. Even though these were my twin sons, my flesh and blood, this was not a good time. But how could I tell them no?

"Just a moment," I whispered.

To avoid waking Ryan, I scrambled out of bed and went on the lanai. I tried to sound positive about Avery's plans, tried to feel excited about their upcoming trip, but with all that was going on, adding two young adult males to the mix seemed too much.

I knew Ryan would think so too. But how could I say no? They're my sons, although staying in touch with them lately has not been easy. During daylight saving time, there's a six-hour time lag between Hawai'i and New York. We've made appointments now and then to chat on Zoom, but, well, age-twenty-something males are often out for cocktails after work, hustling age-twenty-something females. So, I have not spoken to them often.

I hope they have matured a bit and especially remembered the promise I made them recite a couple of years ago, a behavior pledge. I gave them each a signed copy. They'd better follow through, or I'll feel as if I've failed.

But more urgently, I had to figure out a way to placate Ryan about my twin sons coming to visit.

Chapter Thirty-Seven

TWINS IN NAME ONLY

Marie Ingles

To say my twin sons' visit did not go well is an understatement. Or perhaps I should say, the end to my sons' visit was a disaster.

When I told Ryan the boys were coming that next weekend, he rolled his eyes, clearly annoyed. But I must give him credit. He tried to be step-fatherly. After they arrived, he cooked steaks on the grill, and the next day we took the boys — guys — on a sunset boat tour out of Kona.

At least they looked healthy. Both are in their early twenties and New York stockbrokers, thanks to Ryan getting them their first jobs in Dallas. Those starter posts helped them gain enough experience to post profiles on various job boards. Before long, they got offers from Oppenheimer and moved to New York.

Ever since they moved, I've been too busy or relieved that I didn't have to parent them anymore. Both had been total pains after their father died and during my murder trial. Angry, acting out, getting arrested, and resentful of me.

At the same time, I was grieving my loss of Cole in a confused way, not to mention enduring a murder trial a few months later. Even after that ordeal, Ryan and I became so consumed with our new relationship and eventual marriage, along with our work for his Dallas firm and the opera, I guess I simply took the chance to escape from parenting problematic young men. After all, they were twenty-one when Cole died, and twenty-two by the time they went to New York.

Was it wrong of me to feel a sense of relief when they left?

Avery has always been difficult because he was much like his father. Brash, handsome, entitled, gonna do things his way, and darn any woman who had different ideas. Shawn was difficult because he felt less than his father, endlessly needing me to soothe his wounded spirit.

Little in them was different during this recent visit.

I posted photos of the four of us on MakeFriends with a deep orange sunset in the background. I hoped my brother saw us grinning as if we were happy to be together. But like most photos people post, the pictures don't tell the full story.

After being a devoted stepfather for a weekend, Ryan pleaded "busy" and left me to entertain the guys.

I took them to our development's private beach — well, I shouldn't say "private," since all Hawai'i beaches are public, but ours has a private parking lot, bathrooms for residents only, and a full-service restaurant. The guys were duly impressed and snorkeled for hours. That next night, they went by themselves to a manta ray dive out in front of the Hōkele Kilohana Resort Hotel.

The following day, I sent them on a tour to see Kīlauea Volcano. The stinky thing has been erupting for weeks and reportedly had lava fountains almost a thousand feet high. Since Ryan and I have already been there, done that, I took advantage of having the guys on a tour bus for twelve hours and lazily played my cello, then booked a massage to destress from the tension.

Later in the week, the twins and I drove to Hilo to see the Merrie Monarch Festival, an amazing display of hula dance, Hawaiian music, and arts. The festival began in the early 1960s to honor Hawaiian King David Kalākaua, "the Merrie Monarch," who wanted to conserve Hawaiian traditions, language, and arts. From most of the eight islands — and even foreign countries — hula clubs called *hālau* traveled to Hilo to perform. The women danced in traditional grass skirts, as well as brilliantly colored long dresses. The men performed in traditional wear and danced to the beat of huge *ipu* gourds.

My sons were amazed by the male group performances, which are powerful and rhythmic. As for the women's hula, I regretted that Avery found a few of the females too "old and fat" for his taste.

His words, not mine.

"Avery, it's not about the size of their bodies. It's about the dance. The history, music, and culture," I reminded him. "A lot of women take hula lessons, but I never felt I should. To me, that would seem disrespectful."

"Well, I'd respect them more if some of those *wahines* would lose a few," Avery sneered.

I gave him a mother's glare. Right then, he reminded me of his father, who used to make fun of any Portland Explorers wives who'd gained a few pounds after having babies.

Perhaps that was an unfair comparison. I will always love my sons, but I've moved on from being a mommy. I would like to enjoy their company as adults, but time will tell on that. They are still brash young men with much to learn about life.

By the time we drove back to our condo, a cross-island trip that took a good ninety minutes, I was exhausted from entertaining them. Oh, they were on good behavior the first couple of days, but by the end of their five-day stay, Avery pushed one of Ryan's buttons by making a snide remark about lawyers.

"In New York state, these insider traders get high-dollar lawyers to keep them out of jail. Makes me think I shouldn't bother playing by SEC rules when some asshole defense attorney makes gazillions getting these crooks off."

Ryan peered up from his laptop and almost roared. "Asshole defense attorney, eh? Well, if you ever need me to defend you for insider trading, think again. Your mother raised you to be honorable men. And you'd better follow her tutelage because I won't save your arrogant asses."

With that, he slammed his laptop shut and then left for the business center.

I sighed. "Avery, do you ever apply a filter before you let a remark out of your mouth?"

"Gosh, Mom, I didn't..." he trailed off. "...Ryan's different than he used to be. Now he seems like an ass."

I sighed. "Don't deflect. Ryan is unusually tense right now. He didn't mean to lose it. But truly, you promised, both of you did, to be honorable, trustworthy, and reliable men. So please be that and don't tempt yourselves to go over that line."

Shawn gave me a shrug. "There you go, Mom, blaming me for what Avery said. We only look alike. I'm different from him. You never seem to get that. Nobody does. It's like I disappear when Avery's around."

"Shawn, don't push my buttons either." With that, I finished loading the dishwasher, wordlessly hugged each twin, and went to take a shower before bed.

Ryan returned much later and silently slid in beside me.

I glanced over to see if he wanted to talk.

He gave me a weary look, weary of having my sons here.

"I'm sorry Shawn pissed you off, but I'm happy you gave

him some of your own back. And, of course, I greatly appreciate your helping them get their starter jobs back in Dallas."

"I got your sons those first jobs, so they'd get out of your house." With that, Ryan made a big deal out of turning over and aiming his back at me.

Great. Now my husband was acting like a brat. I scoffed in disgust, then went upstairs to my studio, where I curled up on the daybed.

In the kitchen the next morning, I was still miffed and gave Ryan a look that could melt ice. He'd been unfair. Natalie would have been proud of me for my glare.

After breakfast, I drove the twins to the airport. But before we left, Ryan at least shook their hands and said something unoffensive, like "Thanks for visiting your mom. I know she appreciates it."

At the airport, I hugged each twin goodbye and kissed them. As they walked past security, each turned back to wave a final, "Bye, Mom." For just a moment's flash, I could see them as my young sons, smiling and waving as they got on the first-grade bus. My heart rose with maternal emotions as I relived that, and it helped me feel love for my sons again. I hoped that life would teach them whatever Cole and I did not.

Chapter Thirty-Eight

HOLES IN OUR SWISS?

Marie Ingles

When I got home from dropping off the twins, Ryan wasn't there. A note on the dining table said he'd taken a flight to Oahu for yet another study class. What? This was unplanned, and I became obsessed with jealousy. Even playing my cello would not ease my angst, so, in a rebellious move, I called Pua Akana.

"You've got three tragic deaths on your hands. I have investigative skills. Do you need some help? I can do it pro bono. I'm already sworn in, and I want to find this killer."

"We've interviewed every known astronomer on-island, but beyond what we knew before we charged Kekoa Palakiko, there is some new evidence."

"Are you willing to discuss this with me?"

"Well, I suppose I can since you've been sworn in, but this can go no further than your team. On your honor, agreed?"

"Of course, Pua."

"FBI tests on the tape used to reseal Nocona's package revealed that the tape was made by a Swiss manufacturer. I may not pronounce the name correctly, but it's a paper tape called

'Klebeband eco Kraft,' made by OZG Industrial, located in a suburb north of Zürich."

"That's odd. Are we looking for someone from Switzerland?"

"Maybe, but this particular tape is sold throughout Europe. Heck, it's even available online. So the person could be from France or Italy, Germany, Belgium, and so forth."

"There are a lot of European nationals on this island."

"Yes, but our DNA and fingerprint tests didn't reveal a thing. Beyond that, our analysts scoured the tape manufacturer's list of customers. They found one that ordered the same type of tape, but the name turned out to be a bogus company. That means someone probably ordered this logo tape to frame Kekoa."

"That's more good news for Kekoa. Wow. The guy was set up."

"Takes one to know one, right?"

I laughed. "I imagine he's as relieved as I was. Maybe more."

"I'll keep you posted and ask our trial attorneys about you doing pro bono work."

"Great. I'm having a hard time being un-busy. If I can make calls or send emails, just let me know. In Dallas, I had my paralegal certificate. Ryan's firm required it, so I did online coursework and completed testing. That while also playing first-chair cello. I'm a multi-tasker!"

She laughed. "Wow, I'm impressed. If I use you pro bono, I suspect that anything you do would be an unofficial assistant to me. Maybe research, phone calls, setting appointments, that sort of thing. I'll let you know. Thanks very much for your call."

Chapter Thirty-Nine

PONO-TV NEWS ONLINE

Breaking – Astronomer Shot

K AILUA-KONA, Hawaii — Brazilian astronomer Flavia
Valente was critically wounded by a gunshot at close
range last night, about 11 p.m. Valente was working with Virgo
North Observatory, with base operations in Hilo.

According to island police, the assailant remains at large.

Before being shot, Valente called 911 to report the break-in.
County police arrived within minutes, found her wounded, and
then called for an ambulance. She was stabilized at Ali'i
Community Hospital and later flown by Island Medevac to
Kings Community Hospital in Honolulu for surgery.

FBI Supervisory Special Agent (SSA) Pua Akana said at a
press conference, "Ms. Valente told police she had videoed the
intruder, but her smartphone was missing. However, a security
camera caught an image of what appears to be a male fleeing the
office after 11 p.m. He was about six feet tall, with dark hair
and dark skin, and was dressed in a traditional Hawaiian *malo*
(loincloth) and feathered headdress."

In an exclusive interview, Virgo North Observatory
Director Michel Steinbring told PONO-TV, "We are

devastated. A serial killer is targeting astronomers. Why? To get us to leave? If we did that, the islands would suffer huge economic losses, not to mention global prestige."

Steinbring added, "The observatories atop Maunakea are nonprofit research centers. Our funding comes from grants, donations, and sponsoring nations. We don't make money but generate millions in revenues for Hawaii, not from discoveries — nobody pays you millions for finding an exoplanet — but from the dollars observatories pay for equipment, maintenance, and staffing. And there are the dollars our employees pay for housing, food, services, automobiles, and goods our employees require. Many locally-owned businesses provide these things to the one thousand people employed in the state's astronomy community. Astronomy is not the enemy of the Hawaiian people. For years, it's helped provide economic value and educational programs for all."

Valente, age 35, is married and the mother of two children, ages 8 and 10. The family resides in São Paulo, Brazil.

Hawaii Governor Garrison Loden remarked, "This series of attacks not only has devastated the families and colleagues of those who've lost their lives but also damaged the reputation of the island state we love. Scientists worldwide, along with the businesses and services that supply them, are asking whether they should continue to do business here. That's why I am asking the state legislature to convene an emergency session to authorize funds for additional investigative experts. We cannot plead 'short of staff.' We must find who is responsible and stop this serial killer now."

Asked whether the governor thinks the perpetrator is a sole operator, he replied, "I pray it is a lone wolf. But if it's a concerted effort by a specific anti-astronomy group, the state will shut them down. I have no idea why anyone would want to harm people who are as passionate about studying the stars as the early Native Hawaiians once were."

According to Steinbring, Valente was analyzing data late into the night because she planned to return to Brazil this weekend.

Steinbring continued, "Virgo Observatories is a global organization. These days, astronomers don't need to ascend the summits to peer at the heavens. Instead, our telescopes are managed by engineer operators who collaborate with astronomers. There are two Virgo telescopes, Virgo North in Hawaii and Virgo South in Argentina. Each observatory is integrated with the latest networking technologies to allow remote operations. Flavia Valente expected to finish her work after she returned to Brazil. Now, she'll have to stay here much longer," Steinbring said.

Akana urged island residents to call the FBI Hawaii Task Force tip line at (808) 999-1111 if they know anything about this attack.

Reported by Michelle Kimura. Stay tuned to PONO-TV.com for updates.

Chapter Forty

MY SIDE OF THE MIRRORS

Jürgen Bergen / Zeno Kühn

Mein Gott, I shot a mother of two *kinder*. I hadn't planned another killing. All I meant to do was vandalize the offices. I knew there would be security cameras, so I dressed in full native regalia, a new bully activist with a black ponytail wig. My mission was to keep authorities focused on local activists so they would not question Jürgen or try to locate Zeno Kühn.

But within moments after I broke in, I was facing a lovely brunette with bushy, long hair, a Brazilian, they said.

When she saw me, bronzed and half-naked in my outfit, she began screaming and would not stop. Then she ran into an office, where she slammed the door and locked it.

I leaned near and could hear her telling the police, "*Preciso de ajuda agora!*" And then she paused and stuttered out, "Help to Virgo now!"

I backed away, intent on leaving, since my appearance and break-in were enough to achieve my objectives, but suddenly she unlocked the door and walked out with a smartphone camera aimed directly at me.

She said in a heavy accent, "Police coming. I filming you."

Just in case, I'd tucked a pistol into the waistband of my wrapped skirt, but because I'd worn gloves to prevent fingerprints, I fumbled to get the gun out. *Ach du liebe Zeit*, I did not want to shoot this woman, but I aimed clumsily and frantically shot twice. One bullet hit, and she buckled into a pile, still clutching her smartphone.

Through the phone's speaker, I heard the dispatcher's frantic voice ask if she was all right. I leaned over the comatose woman, grabbed her phone, ended the call, and then ran outside to my car, where I remembered the phone's GPS capability. So I stomped it with a rock until the phone's screen went blank, then picked up the smashed remains, drove back to Waimea, and dumped the phone in Merriman's waste bin. Who would look for it there?

Ach je! As I sat on my apartment sofa, I felt terrible dismay. I'd made more of a mess than intended. I only wanted to keep investigators distracted from interviewing Zeno, so Jürgen could proceed with his plans to stop HILT.

Over the past eight months, we've amassed a supply of explosives and detonation materials, ordered in small, varying amounts for HILT construction purposes. We store them in locked cabinets. No one questions Jürgen, the project manager. Requisitions signed by Jürgen, filed in his office at Knight Observatory, are just some of the many scattered clues in our plans. The Swiss-manufactured tape will point to Jürgen for the deed. And to finish transporting our varied explosive devices to the top, Jürgen bought that Hummer. Huge thing. He and I feel very powerful driving it. Nothing will stop us. Rather, me.

While authorities chase Jürgen to oblivion, I will return to Berlin, reconnect with friends, then head to Chile to reclaim my position with AWE-T. And after it sees first light, I will take the role of chief astronomer.

I look forward to the Nobel prizes I will win with AWE-T.

Perhaps I should start calling it, "The Zeno Kühn Triple XLT." Or Kühn Triple X.

I liked the sound of that, and my mood lifted. I felt so giddy, my handle "AstroExplorer" on 808 Insiders posted that the FBI task force must now suspect a local activist. A bunch of users called me a racist *haole*.

Mein Gott, these social media nuts get stirred up quickly. You dare not say one word against a local, even when they deserve it.

Chapter Forty-One

NOT AGAIN. A GROUPIE

Marie Ingles

Right in the middle of something so scary as a killer loose on the Big Island, Ryan and I had to fly to Oahu so he could take his bar exam. I didn't have to go, but I wanted to be supportive. And I admit, getting away from the Big Island's serial killings was a relief.

The local media constantly issue alerts. The cable company interrupts broadcasts with blurry images of the activist and loudly beeping alerts asking if we know this man, whom to call, and what to do if you see him.

These were all good things to do, but everywhere you go, islanders are jumpy. My favorite local checker at our small Foodland grocery always asks me if there's been any progress. He saw my name in the news and thinks we are still on the job.

My hairstylist is fearful that the killer might be one of her clients. "I see a lot of local guys, so who knows? I might be cutting the hair of a killer!"

And the 808 Insiders page is full of posts that say things like, "I saw a man in a hoodie running down the street near my house. What should I do?" And then the idiot posts a Ring camera shot of a local guy simply jogging in the wee hours, wearing a hoodie. But to the hysterical, he must be the killer.

That's why I didn't mind escaping the Big Island for a while.

Also, after the fourth attempted murder, Pua Akana emailed me to say my idea of pro bono "Nancy-D" work was on hold. "The FBI trial attorney told me I can't work with you. I explained you'd been sworn in, but he said that was for the first case only. If the governor gets new funds, I hope the state can bring your team back to our task force soon."

With all that was going on in Ryan's and my world, I wasn't disappointed. But, although we weren't currently involved in the investigations, the posts about us on 808 Insiders remained toxic. I read several to Ryan while we waited for the plane.

"'That Ryan Ingles and his wife effed everything for us. Now the cops pull us over just for being local,' Ono Wrangler says. And a post from a guy called AstroExplorer says, '*Yessah*, but that Ingles lady ain't no attorney. Why she on *da* case? She play cello. Get *dat*?'"

Ryan hemmed. "What does your being a cellist have to do with anything?"

"More importantly, how does he know I'm a cellist?"

"If this keeps up, we'll ask Natalie to make a complaint," Ryan murmured.

"Would Colleen approve that time billing?" I asked back, but Ryan was intensely focused.

Which was more important? At that moment, his studies. The Hawai'i Bar Exam is a two-day test over about twelve hours that covers several areas.

Ryan studied during the hour-long flight, and even in the cab as we headed to our four-night stay at the Royal Hawaiian.

We stayed in a suite in the hotel's Mailani Tower, which offers all-ocean-view rooms and a contemporary take on old Hawaiian elegance. In addition to the beautiful interior design,

I love this property because you're steps from Waikiki Beach. So many of the larger resorts have such expansive grounds, you must walk forever to be near the ocean, or so it seems.

That first evening, I ordered room service and did my best to let Ryan be. I'd brought a novel along to read, and I think Ryan noticed I was trying not to be my chit-chatting self.

After my bath, I slipped beside him into bed.

He turned to me, saying, "Thank you. Hopefully, this will be over in two days."

After a room service breakfast the next morning, he was anxious before he went downstairs to catch his ride.

I wished him good luck, gave him a peck, then put on my bathing suit and went to the beach. It was so early, there were lots of lounge chairs, so I grabbed one and stretched out.

I was surprised how wonderful it felt to be on my own, relieved to be rid of the intense guy Ryan has become after moving to the Big Island. Did he simply need more to do? Was the stress from the bar test too much? Or was there more going on?

After day one of his bar exam, our evening was a repeat of the one before. Dinner in the room. No drinks. Ryan studying. Early bath and bed.

At least I finished my novel!

The next morning, I gave Ryan a good luck kiss and handed him his briefcase.

Right before he left, he said, "I'm too old for this. The last time I took a bar test, I was twenty-three!"

Aha, there was more going on. Not simply a mid-career crisis, but a mid-life crisis.

Understanding how he felt, I spent another morning at the beach, wondering how Ryan was doing, hoping he was doing well, and also wondering about my future as a solo cellist. Was I too old to begin that part of my career? And what about Ryan?

What if he doesn't pass the bar? What will he do then? Want us to return to Dallas?

I went back to the room, booked a massage, and hoped that would help my angst.

About 4:00 p.m., Ryan texted. "All done. Meet me in the Mai Tai bar."

Delighted, I showered and donned a slinky ruby sundress, pinned up my hair with my new, white plumeria hairpins, and went down to the bar.

On a stool, Ryan looked exhausted but was in a celebratory mood, which was fun until he said, "Mike and Sonya will meet us at the restaurant."

My face fell, and he noticed.

"Sorry, guess I should have mentioned it earlier. Big Mike suggested it yesterday. He got reservations at one of his favorite places. He knows the owner."

"Well, let's get that cab," was all I could manage. The evening I'd looked forward to, spending time with my husband to celebrate his efforts and patch up our marital rift, had turned into dread at seeing Sonya make more moves.

The reservation was at an upscale Sicilian bistro in Waikiki's Beach Walk area.

As we greeted Mike and Sonya in the lobby, I noticed she had worn her ratty blond hair in a messy updo, which was not unusual, but the stinker had copied me by wearing decorative hair pins. I didn't know whether to be offended or complimented. Her dress was a gauzy tan thing that matched her skin color, so the effect was that she was wearing nothing. Only one shoulder strap held it up, while the strapless side revealed far too much of her left boob, likely an implant.

Maybe I shouldn't have spent so much time analyzing Sonya's boobs, because after we headed to our table, she quickly took a seat across from Ryan, not from me.

Cagey move. That meant I sat on Ryan's right, but across from Big Mike. For his sake, I was determined to be congenial. "Mike, I was delighted you chose Italian food. There are such limited options on the Big Island, and they're not what Ryan and I call 'Snobby Dallas Good.'"

Ryan agreed. "Admittedly, we were spoiled in Dallas, but most of the Big Island's restaurants, except for the few five-star types, still have a bit to learn."

"I hear ya. It's a staffing and education issue. There are just not enough trained chefs on the Big Island. Too many tourists come here each year. And the *malihini* 'splosion over there...I tell ya, that island is gonna wind up like Oahu. High housing costs. Oh, there I go...island issues."

"That's okay, Big Mike. Being on the Big Island has taught us a lot about living in a tourist destination."

"All sorts of troubles in these islands, for sure. I guess you heard about those embezzlement cases that landed in our laps. These *braddah* stole $12 million that was meant for local housing and our *keiki* schools."

Sonya tittered and leaned as far across the table as her boobs would allow. "He gave one of those cases to me, but I doubt I can do as good a job as you would, Ryan. How do you sincerely represent clients you know are guilty and should spend years behind bars?"

"I stick to the evidence, or the lack of it. And the law. But I must say my closing statements may not be as passionate as when I know my client is not guilty."

I wanted to change the subject away from Sonya's crooning. "Big Mike, would you represent the astronomy serial killer when he's caught?"

"That depends on who he is. Ya know, the astronomy thing is a mess. You've got some true believers of the old ways, the Kia'i, they call them. The Protectors. You know, the ones who dance in traditional gear, make the gigantic eyes, stick out their tongues." He chuckled. "Scare the devil outa me."

"I've seen them on TV," I said.

He nodded. "Well, those are the ones who want to kick everybody off their sacred *mauna*. But I tell ya, when I was a *keiki* on the Big Island, that mountain wasn't 'sacred.' Seems it got more sacred when some of these born-again types went back to the old ways."

"Huh. Sounds like some of the stuff fundamentalists do on the Mainland," Ryan said.

"*Rajah*, but along with the religious types, there truly are sensible factions that want fair value for leases. That makes sense; help fund schools and provide for those who can't."

"You're right, Mike. That seems more sensible than trying to make multimillion-dollar observatories leave."

"You'd think, but along with these groups, there are a bunch of swindlers who set up bogus Hawaiian kingdoms or advocacy groups. They want *lots'a kālā* for granting summit access, but won't let anybody know where that money goes. And the hard-nosed political types do whatever they can to move up the state's power structure. So, which group does this killer come from? That would tell me whether I'd represent him."

"Wow. This really *is* a mess," Ryan said. "It's challenging for newcomers like us to understand. On the news, I see a lot of politicians say things to appease Native Hawaiians, but then they do something else."

Mike's huge black eyes looked sad. "The real power is behind closed doors. On and on, the political wrangling goes."

We four were silent for a moment. Then Big Mike raised his wine glass in a toast. "There I go again…island issues. Let's forget those tonight. I hope you'll find your meal to be 'Snobby Dallas Good.'" He took a sip but swallowed quickly, remembering what I dreaded to hear. "Oh, damn, I hate to bring this up, but I'm worried about this 808 Insiders stuff."

"I hear ya, Big Mike. They keep hammering at us, but there doesn't seem to be a way to shut them down," Ryan said.

"Well, we gotta try. I'll have our PR firm post a few rebuttal comments tomorrow."

I remembered what Natalie had said. "Mike, our computer guru suggested that your PR firm should post a comment on the *original* post, not simply reply to someone else. She said that replying to someone else makes that post disappear."

Mike nodded, slightly confused. "I'm not into this MakeFriends stuff, but maybe that'll help. I hope so, anyway. Anytime someone badmouths you guys, it smacks us, especially if you're coming to work with us soon."

Ryan exhaled heavily. "Hopefully."

Gosh, did that mean they've sealed a deal? I wanted to change the subject. "Ryan and I didn't expect that our dreams to live on the Big Island would turn into a barrage of antagonism against us."

Big Mike gave me a sympathetic nod. "That social media junk makes me sad."

Sonya glanced up to leer at Ryan, her eyes glistening with lust. "Ryan, as soon as you get your test results, let us know. We've got office space right next to mine, right, Big Mike?"

"We'd like to have you on the team, Ryan."

Ryan nodded toward me. "We are discussing our options. Marie is a wonderful cellist and might want to play for the Oahu Orchestra. As it is now, she's only able to do solos."

Sonya said nothing to me or about my cello and leaned so far toward Ryan, her implant almost escaped the gauzy top. Her hazel eyes were electric, and her lips were in a pooch. "This should be your decision, Ryan. You're the attorney. Some freelance musician doesn't have the same commitments."

I was stunned. Did she think I couldn't hear? What was I to do? I couldn't reach far enough under the table to kick her "accidentally." Should I cause a ruckus? Get up to leave in a huff? I'd been so determined to get through this dinner congenially for Ryan's sake.

I looked across to Mike, hoping he might step in.

He pursed his lips and feigned interest in the antipasti.

I glanced over to Ryan.

Darn if he wasn't giving Sonya a glistening goo-eye back.

I felt a rush of mortification, shocked that this was happening in front of me. It reminded me of Metroplex Opera cast parties, when the overdressed, wine-infused ladies of D'Posse would swoop over to Ryan's side and flutter about, as if he were not married to me. And it reminded me of country club dances when Cole was alive, and I'd find him on the dance floor rocking out with a bunch of vampish women.

Was I supposed to turn a blind eye then — and now?

My new husband was almost salivating.

Luckily, a server interrupted my angst with our entrées.

After he served Sonya her porcini risotto with foie gras, he began making his way around to my side of the table. As he did, I quietly leaned forward, pretending to admire Sonya's dish, but instead whispered through my so-sweet smile, "Sonya, dear, you might want to keep your left breast inside your top, lest the steam from your risotto melt your breast implants."

Her eyes narrowed as if in a dare.

"And for you, Miss," the server said to me.

"Perfect timing, *mahalo*," I said with another smile.

Thanks to the Scotches, my tipsy husband seemed oblivious to my exchange with Sonya.

But across the table, Big Mike gave me a wink and a knowing glance. "I love those plumeria hairpins you wear, Mrs. Ingles. They're classy, just like you."

Innocently as possible, I said, "*Mahalo*, Mike. I appreciate the compliment. Oh, I forgot to mention, I was curious what your first name means. It's Makoa, right?"

He nodded.

"I looked that up on wehewehe.com. It means 'fearless, courageous, and brave.' Is that a good translation?"

"Don't know if I'm all that," Big Mike smiled.

"Well, I think you are named appropriately. Right, Ryan?"

He nodded a yes and was about to say something when the server came around to freshen Ryan's water glass.

I took the opportunity to glance at Sonya again. Her glower told me she was pissed, so I smiled sweetly and asked, "How's that steamy risotto?"

She scowled back, so I smiled sweetly again.

Mike and Ryan were oblivious, talking across the table, supposing this or that about their future alliance. That is, if there will be an alliance, and I hoped not.

After we finished our entrees and the server brought us espressos and biscotti, I excused myself for the ladies' room.

When I walked out minutes later, I was surprised to see Big Mike waiting for me.

He took my hand inside his huge, rough palms and gave me the most earnest look with his large, *pueo* eyes. "Don't worry about Sonya. She's a trashy flirt. And Ryan, well, the man is under a lot of stress. Passing the bar is hell, ya know?"

"But she's throwing herself at my husband."

"Ah, no worry. Sonya is grocery-store *pokē*, but you, Mrs. Ingles, *you* are *Maguro Toro*."

I shook my head and smiled at the sashimi metaphor. "I hope that's a compliment. Ryan has never been the type to stray, but with all that's going on, he's not himself right now."

"If Ryan joins my firm, I'll make sure Sonya keeps her distance. *Ho'ohiki!*"

"I don't know what you've just said, but I imagine it's a good thing."

"Promise." With both thumbs and pinky fingers up, he gave me the double *shaka*.

I returned a clumsy single *shaka*. Then we both laughed at my *malihini* attempt.

After dinner, we four waited outside for our rides. I made a point of putting my arm around Ryan's shoulder to keep Sonya from getting anywhere near.

She did attempt to give Ryan a sideways hug/kiss, but Big Mike reached between her and Ryan to give him a *Braddah* handshake. When our car arrived, Mike opened the door for us, winked at me, and went back to stand beside Sonya.

I gave her my best fake smile and a wave, then rolled down my window to say to Mike, "I'm counting on you, Makoa."

He grinned.

Back in our suite, I wondered what I could do to make everything right again between Ryan and me, but I stupidly did not learn from my earlier life lessons.

I slipped in beside him and curled closely as my fingers fiddled with his hairy chest. And then they slid down to his tummy button and lower.

Ryan tried to oblige, but he was so weary from test taking, not to mention a whole lot of Scotches and dessert wine, well, for the first time in our experiences together, his you-know remained a limp sausage.

"I think I'm just too tired."

"But you seemed so amorous at dinner." I paused, then regretfully heard myself stupidly add, "Toward Sonya, anyway."

"Oh, Marie, let's not do this. "

"Ryan, I did my best not to cause a scene, but that woman was coming on to you. And you flirted back. I did not appreciate that. And I didn't expect it, either, not from you."

"Marie, it was just the booze. She was drunk and so was I. Just two colleagues who've worked on a case together but forgot how to behave."

I rolled off him. "I'm telling you, Ryan, that woman has a thing for you. And you'd better not have a thing for her."

He sat up with his back to me, hands wiping his hair. "Marie, where is this coming from? I've never fooled around on you. I'm not the type."

"But when you're drinking, well, at cast parties back in Dallas, you didn't seem to understand it's not okay to let women flutter all over you, especially while I'm standing there. And it's not okay for you to flirt over a dinner table the way you and Sonya did tonight. Bottom line for me: we need to talk when you're not so weary and full of booze."

With that, I went to the bathroom and took a long soak. I was proud of myself for speaking up, but still furious that I had to deal with this kind of shit, not at my age, and not with Ryan. I'd had enough of that with Cole.

The next morning, Ryan was conciliatory. He got up early, ordered breakfast, and set it up on our lanai.

As I silently sipped coffee and watched the distant surfers, he touched my arm.

"Marie, maybe too much booze made me oblivious. As you well know, I dated only Doreen in college. Two decades later, we got divorced, and you and I fell in love out of the blue. I mean, you were Cole Donovan's wife. I never once thought you might be interested. For most of my life, women like you saw me as downright ugly."

"You were just unapproachable. Doreen always hanging off you. Those horn-rims."

"All long gone."

"I understand what you're saying, but you were ogling Sonya as if I weren't there. I was mortified. Almost got up and left, but I didn't want to make a scene in front of Big Mike or leave you alone with Sonya."

"Marie, don't you think you're being a wee bit paranoid?"

"Paranoid? Even Big Mike took me aside over by the restrooms. He told me she was grocery-store *pokē*, while I'm some sort of fish I can't remember the name of."

Ryan chuckled. "Probably Toro. Big Mike's always talking about Toro."

"I took it as a compliment, and his support was affirming."

"Okay, so paranoid might be too strong, but I do think you're being insecure. Cole fooling around left a mark on you."

"Yes, it did, but it's not wrong to be angry when some 'Diamond Client Champion' twit threatens my marriage."

Weary of Ryan's argumentative brick wall, I got up and went inside, giving the slider a bit of a thump. As I walked by the room's desk, his open laptop dinged with a new email. I glanced out the slider to see if he was still on the lanai.

He was pouring another cup of coffee from the room service pitcher.

Yes, I had time. And yes, I was paranoid. But I quickly scanned his email to see if there was anything from Sonya. And there it was, an email from late the night before, sent by Sonya Pruitt and slugged CONFIDENTIAL and PERSONAL.

With my fingers shaking, I opened it.

The text read: "Ryan, I so enjoyed last night. Being with you. And I could tell you enjoyed being close to me, that is, as near as your wife would let you. Wow. She's really a prima donna. That's why I hope to see you privately, away from Big Mike too. You see, ever since we met, my aura has been consumed by visions of you. Sincerely, I cannot stop seeing your blue, blue eyes, your soft, full lips, your luscious head of hair. So, I'm taking a chance. If you feel the same, please let me know. But if you don't, please don't tell Big Mike or anyone, especially not your dominatrix. Since you're still under our firm's ethical authority, by law, you must keep the content of this email CONFIDENTIAL. As supervising local counsel, I'm saying you may never tell anyone about this email. I know I can count on you and can't wait to be with you soon. Please text or call me at 808-777-2121."

Signed "Sonya."

I was so angry, I was hyperventilating. I glanced out the slider to see if Ryan was still occupied. He was flipping through the newspaper, probably avoiding his dominatrix.

I whispered to myself, "What would Natalie do? She'd give me a stern look and say, 'Marie, do *not* delete the email. Let Ryan read it, but make sure he can't know you read it. First, forward it to your own email account. That way you have it. Next, go to Ryan's sent folder and delete the forwarded email so he won't see the forward. Then go to his trash folder and permanently delete the sent message again. And finally, mark Sonya's email as 'unread' in Ryan's inbox. That way, he won't know you've been snooping.'"

I followed Natalie's imaginary instructions and left his laptop open as I'd found it. Then I went back outside, kissed Ryan on the cheek, and smiled. "I'm sorry I lost my temper. You're right. I probably overreacted."

For the rest of our stay, I did my best to be cheery. Except for Ryan's naïveté, the Sonya problem wasn't his fault. But he must learn how to manage it. And sometimes within a marriage, you have to forgive and forget. But my mind whirled with ideas on how to get revenge on Ms. Diamond Client Champion.

Chapter Forty-Two

808 INSIDERS

Da Real Scoop

Today at 9:19 a.m.

Did you smell corruption in your morning cuppa Kona? Today's media announced that Governor Garrison Loden has dedicated a fat $5 million of the state's Rainy-Day Fund to aid authorities with investigations. Guess who's first up with a hand in the state's coffers?

Dallas-based Ballard / Ingles. After all, they've been ever so successful, haven't they?

Does this smell like our pasty-white governor might be greasing even more *haole* palms? As we all know, our dear Gov has not one ounce of Hawaiian blood and only rose through the ranks because his wife descends from King Kalākaua. Agreed, the governor's background as a mainland hospital chief made him popular with voters who want better medical care in these islands. Despite that, the state chooses a mainland firm to bill up to $5 million.

As 808 Insiders sees it, this is those dreaded H-words taking *kālā* from locals.

Most Relevant:

AstroExplorer — You are so right on this, *Braddah*! Give the bucks to local firms.

Hilo Rain Man — Secession is the answer. As Haunani-Kay Trask once said, "We are not American. We will die as Hawaiians. We will never be Americans!"

Kona Wave Rider — The $5 mil should go to islanders on the list for rightful lands. My Tūtū has been waiting for years!

AstroExplorer — Here's how to stop HILT. Decommission all *haole* telescopes from the sacred *mauna*. The *'āina* does not belong to the invaders.

Chapter Forty-Three

BACK IN BUSINESS

Marie Ingles

A fter Ryan and I returned to our condo the next afternoon, Sheriff Buckner Urima called.

Ryan answered. "Aloha, Sheriff Bucky, let me put you on speaker so my paralegal can hear you too."

Guess I've been promoted to paralegal. I gave him a wink to show I'd noticed. Maybe he was trying to soothe my angst.

Sheriff Bucky boomed on the speaker. "Ryan, Mrs. Ingles, as you may know from media reports, Governor Loden allocated $5 million in funds to help find this serial killer because of the extraordinary nature of the situation. The state assigned me and two state police investigators to help with SSA Akana's FBI Special Task Force. This is in addition to Hawai'i County police officers and the FBI analysts on Oahu. But we need more bodies to conduct inquiries. Because this is on the state's tab, I've been asked to re-hire your team as SMEs, especially since you're familiar with the cases. We will meet twice weekly by Zoom. I know video calls are not ideal, but given the miles on this Big Island, any centralized meeting point seems a waste of time and high-dollar gasoline."

"Before I say yes, I need to check with our managing partner in Dallas."

"*Mahalo*. You see, these murders are terrifying for local residents, but also, there's been an enormous impact on tourism. Like it or not, the state's ten million annual visitors drive our economy. But after these killings made the mainland news, over a million bookings were canceled this past week."

"I didn't realize the impact —"

"Huge losses. Almost as terrible as the Maui fires and the COVID lockdown. So, for more reasons than the obvious, we've got to stop these attacks."

Ryan looked at me, and I looked at Ryan. We shrugged a silent, but reluctant yes. "Sheriff Bucky, I will call Colleen Ballard immediately."

"*Mahalo*. Our next meeting is tomorrow, 9:00 a.m. Pua Akana will send you the link."

THE NEXT MORNING, RYAN AND I WENT ON ZOOM FROM separate laptops in separate rooms to avoid the echo problem.

One by one, up popped the rectangular images of Pua Akana, Harold Koizumi, Nocona, several FBI analysts, two state police investigators, and a governor's office liaison.

Natalie and Billy Bob were on the video call too, but from Phoenix, where they were on a layover. I sent them happy-face emojis via private chat.

Billy Bob chatted back. "Our flight from Phoenix arrives at KOA at 2:27 p.m. Can you pick us up?"

I texted back, "Happy to do it. I'll tell Ryan. It will relieve his boredom." I added a sarcastic-face emoji to that.

When I turned back to the video images, I was surprised to see an image of Kekoa Palakiko pop up on the screen.

Sheriff Bucky smiled. "Welcome, Kekoa. Just to let everyone know, Kekoa is on the team to help us question members of various activist groups. FBI and state police have formally apologized to Kekoa and Nocona for our false assumptions and mistaken indictments. Each will be compensated for their time in detention, as well as their services to help us find these killers. And now, Harold, how about you swear in our SMEs."

Deputy Chief Harold Koizumi again led us through his citizen volunteer speech, but this time he did it more pleasantly. That was probably because the state was paying the tab.

After we said our "I do's," Pua summarized everything known to date.

Mid-presentation, Natalie raised her virtual hand to speak. "Pua, Sheriff Bucky, since three out of the four victims were working on projects to find Earth's twin planet, I wondered if the third murder — the astronomer who was doing deep-field imaging — might have been a one-off to put investigators off course. Also, he was, well, simply shot with a gun. There wasn't some elaborate hunting scheme or poison tea."

Pua nodded. "Good thinking."

"Dale Luckland, here, FBI Behavioral Analysis Unit. We also noticed the difference. Our unit provides insights into the psychology of the killer, so if you uncover quirks in this case that might help us profile this guy, please keep us in the loop."

Natalie replied, "Besides my earlier thoughts, I'm suspicious about the 808 Insiders page on MakeFriends.com. The page admin is openly prejudiced against Ballard / Ingles, as well as the observatories. But lately, there have been several comments by a user called AstroExplorer. At first, he seemed like an Anglo with an expensive telescope, and his username suggests a connection to astronomy, but now he's posting as if he's a local and making negative comments about foreign invaders and clearing the mountain. It seems like an anomaly."

"We will check it out, Natalie. Unfortunately, with no credible threats to life, we cannot get a warrant to uncloak user profiles on MakeFriends.com. It has to do with privacy issues. But if you see posts from this AstroExplorer or another user that could be considered a threat to someone's life, please flag them for us," Dale Luckland said.

After that, Pua's presentation continued until we each knew everything the authorities knew, which wasn't much beyond what we already knew: the killer was definitely male.

I raised my virtual hand. "Kekoa, the Virgo Observatory killer was dressed in traditional Hawaiian wear. Do you think he's a local activist? Someone you might have met?"

Kekoa's mute button was on, so we couldn't hear him for a while, but Pua helped him get live. "Here we go, *haole* blaming locals for everything. Dat's why there's a lot of resentment, ya' know?"

I was mortified. Another *malihini* foot-in-mouth, but Pua Akana jumped to my defense.

"Kekoa, if you look for prejudice, you'll find it, but no one investigating this case is unfairly targeting locals. But we must look at all potential suspects," she said.

He shrugged disgruntledly. "All I know is, he's not from Island Kingdom Now. But he might be a *brah* from one of those phony 'kingdom' governments that want the observatories, tour companies, and tourists to pay millions to use the summit land. I'm not sure where the *kālā* would go, other than into the group's bank accounts."

"Good input, Kekoa. As Pua said, we're not targeting locals. But we're trying to stop a murderer, whoever he is," Sheriff Bucky replied. "Now, for the rest of the team's assignments, Pua has a list of people for you to interview, depending on your expertise. And the FBI team prepared a list of interview questions. If you learn anything new, report it to Pua, and she will disseminate it to all team members."

OVER THE NEXT TWO DAYS, OUR TEAM INTERVIEWED OUR assigned witnesses in the Waikoloa, Waimea, Kohala, and Puako communities, where many observatory employees live. Their job descriptions ran from telescope engineers to PR gurus and administrative assistants. Meanwhile, Nocona handled the scientific side of things, like resident astronomers and visiting astrophysicists. And Kekoa, Harold, Bucky, and Pua handled the locals.

When our Zoom session reconvened three days later, the four of us from Ballard / Ingles hoped the others had found something extraordinary. That's because we felt guilty about not finding anything new. But as we went round the table, we realized even the FBI top dogs remained as puzzled as we were.

Pua and Kekoa had interviewed activist suspects and found all had verifiable alibis. Nocona had interviewed astronomers and astrophysicists. All had seemed as horrified and innocent as Nocona when he was arrested. And our team had found similar results from the observatory employees we had interviewed.

Since our team was earning the big bucks, Billy Bob tried to make us look good in some way. "Everyone has been so eager to help. We even met a fellow who invited us up to HILT for a tour. What was his name, Nat?"

"Jürgen Bergen," she replied.

I could see Billy Bob checking his notes. "Right. Jürgen Bergen. Swiss fellow from Zürich. Project manager for HILT. He gave us a lot of detail about how these gigantic scopes work. We wish we had more to report."

Dale Luckland perked up. "Swiss guy? That tape used on Nocona's package was from a Swiss company, right?"

Billy Bob looked at his notes. "I hear ya, Dale, but this guy is, well, you're a profiler. Jürgen's skin color is more olive than brown, and he volunteered that he's Jewish. Besides that, he's super-pro-astronomy, currently building the world's largest telescope. And when we asked to see proof of his work schedules, he printed out his whereabouts during those times."

Nocona sighed in dismay. "I feel inept, but I'm learning a lot from my fellow Texans. Ask for proof. Don't just take their word for it. I'll do better on my next interviews. Promise."

Sheriff Bucky shrugged. "Don't kick yourself, Nocona. We're asking you to do things outside your line of work."

"Well said, Sheriff. And I understand everyone's frustration. All we know about this killer is he's male with a narrow, aquiline nose, or so our analysts call it. That means it's arched. A Roman nose or hook nose are other terms I've heard. Is he truly a local? Nothing reveals much beyond the costumed creature we've seen on security videos. Certainly, the first killing was by someone disguised as Kekoa. Did any of you interview suspects who are the same build? What are you, Kekoa, six feet?" Pua asked.

"'Bout that," Kekoa said.

One of the FBI analysts piped in. "Our software estimates the killer's height at just over 5'11", and he weighs a muscular 190 pounds. His hair and skin tone are similar to Native Hawaiians, at least in the videos, but he could be using hair dye and skin bronzers."

Ryan perked up. "Well, that adds a few nuances to the composite. We're looking for a male, 5'11" and 190 pounds, with black hair and bronze skin, hair possibly dyed, skin possibly sprayed with toners. But, unlike many Native Hawaiians, our killer has a narrow-bridged, arched nose."

Pua added, "Everyone, please scan your lists and ID those who fit this profile. If you can't recall what they looked like, go back and visit them again. Or Zoom call them. You are all sworn in and have the authority."

"We need to get 'dis guy in the pokey — and I don't mean 'da fish kind," Sheriff Bucky said with a sardonic grin.

Chapter Forty-Four

MY SIDE OF THE MIRRORS

Jürgen Bergen / Zeno Kühn

I only offered a sunset tour of HILT to keep these investigators from suspecting me, but HILT's mirrors arrived in Honolulu a week earlier than expected.

Gilles Moreau excitedly delivered the news by phone. "The ship had lighter headwinds than usual in winter, so you'll get almost a full week's head start."

What to do? Delay installation for a day so I can take these four investigators on a delightful sunset tour? Or proceed with my plans and escape this *Riesenstein*.

After the interisland barges delivered the containers to Kawaihae Harbor, multiple trucks arduously ground their way up and down the summit access road. These trips were timed to happen during the wee hours and were escorted by state police and Army National Guard at the request of Governor Loden. My alter-ego Jürgen coordinated with the authorities to keep transport times secret from the media, but *natürlich*, word eventually leaked out. A few pitifully costumed protestors showed up. But this time, the state was ready with an executive order signed by the Governor and a full set of armed sheriffs to enforce it. So the protestors did not have their way.

There may be more demonstrations, but HILT has twenty-four-hour security. Jürgen made sure of that, especially because we wanted the guards to know who he was. When it's time to destroy HILT, everything Jürgen does will appear as natural as him coming to work.

The grass-skirted protestors will get the blame.

I must say, Jürgen and I have had trouble dividing our personas. He cared deeply that the mirrors reached the top. I hope his persona won't suddenly capitulate.

I can control us, can't I?

Chapter Forty-Five

TOUR THE SUMMIT

Marie Ingles

Ryan and Billy Bob returned empty-handed again from their in-person interviews at the dorms on Maunakea, save for finding a few men who fit the physical profile.

As Ryan fixed himself a Scotch and a beer for Billy Bob, he dejectedly told me, "We met about twenty people up there. But they were all somewhere else when the murders happened. It was exhausting to re-interview so many."

Billy Bob chuckled. "The ones we could find, anyway. Workers come and go, on for a week, off for one or two weeks. The international research scientists are in town only for a week or two. Thanks to the Internet, they do their data crunching back in their home offices. So our efforts were hit or miss. But we had fun. At nine thousand feet, you get kinda spacey from the lack of oxygen. I felt like we were on pot. We laughed a lot."

"Between our headaches," Ryan groaned.

"Yup, Boss, but we didn't discover one new clue. And if the murderer is part of the island's come-and-go workforce, he may already be off-island."

"I'm sorry. I thought surely you two would come up with some fresh evidence," I said.

"As they say, never assume. We met all sorts of people, from telescope engineers and project managers to construction guys. Nobody seems to know anything, and I mean *nada*. But that reminds me, the project manager on that giant HILT observatory we spoke to the other day, remember?"

Billy Bob interrupted, "Jürgen Bergen. I can always remember that guy's name because it rhymes."

Ryan chuckled. "Well, we saw him again and asked if he was sincere in his offer of a sunset tour of HILT."

"He said yes. So, we four can go see it!" Billy Bob said.

I was delighted to see the guys' mood lift. "HILT has been such a contentious project. I've seen photos online of the outer building. It looks like something out of the future. Very sci-fi. I'd love to see what it's like inside."

"Yes. Jürgen told me he's got plenty of room for five in his new Hummer. Said it'll go places other SUVs can't."

I was thrilled. "I've always wanted to see the sunset from Maunakea. They say it's a life-changer."

Ryan pulled a business card out of his wallet. "I'll set it up. We've worked hard lately, so I think we deserve a break." As he dialed, he walked out to the lanai where mobile phone reception was better.

Billy Bob gave me a curious look. "Things on the mend between you two now?"

"Sometimes I feel like the 'old' Ryan is back. On others, well, I wondered who I married. After he gets his law license, I hope we can put our troubles behind us. Just be Marie and Ryan, with him busy, happy, and in love again."

"It's the 'daily living' that gets in the way. Nat wants to get married, but from my experience, what happens next turns into knock-down drag-outs over who's going to unload the dishwasher or pick up my jockey shorts."

He shook his head cynically, a man with too many arguments with women I felt sorry for. Being married to Billy Bob would not be easy. Only a strong woman like Natalie could handle him.

"I guess that's why they call marriage 'a commitment.' But if the love is there, the shorts and dishwasher don't matter," I reminded both of us.

Billy Bob scoffed. "Nothing's easy."

Chapter Forty-Six

TWO OPPORTUNITIES

Marie Ingles

O
f all things to happen while Ryan awaited his bar results and our team resumed murder investigations, Maestro Devon Chua of Oahu Philharmonic called to say he wants me to play Saint-Saëns' *The Swan* in a concert three weeks from now. *Three weeks from now. Three weeks from now.*

Gads, my mind whirled when he asked, "When would you be available for a creative meeting?"

Later, when I told Ryan, he frowned in dismay because he thought he would have to travel with me to help with the cello.

"It's just a meeting. I don't need to take my cello. I can fly there, spend half a day, then fly back the same evening."

"If you think you'll be all right alone —"

"I will. You need to focus. After all, we're being paid."

"Okay, then I'll try to figure out which almost six-foot-tall guy with a narrow, arched nose could be our killer. Oh, and by the way, Jürgen Bergen from HILT texted me a date for our summit tour. Let's see what our calendar allows." Ryan checked his phone. "Yes, we'll do the Maunakea tour after you get back from your creative meeting."

Two days later, off I flew to Oahu, taking pride in myself as a solo artist. Perhaps this would be my chance to do more. Word gets around among orchestra creative directors. Who's good. Who's easy to work with. Maybe West Coast music directors would hear about me. Those trips would be easy enough from Hawai'i. But what if my solo career took off, and suddenly Chicago, New York, or even London wanted me? My hopes were soaring until I arrived at the creative meeting.

Maestro Chua quickly brought me down to earth. "Where's your cello?"

"Oh, I didn't realize...I thought we'd be reviewing arrangements."

"I handle the score and arrangements. I simply need you to play what I conduct."

I attempted a smile, although it probably appeared fearful. Naively, I'd thought Maestro Chua's invitation to a 'creative' meeting meant I would contribute ideas on how I'd like to play the solo. Silly me. "I'm sorry. I'll be sure to bring my cello in the future, Maestro Chua."

"Devon," he said. "I prefer a more collegial approach."

I nodded. "Devon."

He called in his assistant, and she went scurrying.

Thankfully, a cello of my preferred size was available in the off-site rehearsal hall, so I did my best to play the piece with passion. Although this cello lacked the deep, melodic tones of my own, Devon seemed pleased. Now and then, he stopped me to make notes on a section, and then he asked me to play it again with those tweaks.

After our session, we returned to Devon's office, where his assistant handed me copies of the revised score.

Devon also handed me a recording device. "We recorded your session. Please take this device home and listen to it before you practice. I think we're very near where I need you to be.

And I'm sure the energy on concert night will ignite your performance even further."

Very near. Ignite your performance. My mind whirled as I tucked the recorder in my purse and put the score inside a briefcase I'd brought to look more professional.

Devon interrupted my angst. "There are two formal rehearsals on Wednesday and Thursday evenings before the Friday night opening concert. So, you'll have to be here Wednesday through Sunday. You will receive emailed reminders. We'll be counting on you."

Again, I smiled as pleasantly as possible, although terror probably continued to prevail.

Three weeks.

I dreaded telling Ryan how many days I'd have to stay on Oahu. He'd feel compelled to be with me, and that would mean not doing FBI task force assignments.

Oh, gosh, why was all this happening now?

***

CHECKING MY WATCH, THERE WERE THREE HOURS BEFORE my return flight to the Big Island. Should I go to the airport, find an airline club, and have a drink to chill? The only people I knew on this island were Devon Chua and his assistant, or Mike Iona and the horrid Sonya, who had just made a huge pass at my husband by email.

Given my emotional state, I should have gone to the airport. Instead, I grabbed a salad and glass of chardonnay at a little cafe near the symphony office, then ordered a second glass of wine that fueled my decision to get a ride to the Iona Law Firm. My thought was to see if Big Mike was available, so I could ask for his advice. I told myself he deserved to know his associate was making a play for my husband, especially since

Ryan might partner with Mike's firm. But when I got there, the receptionist told me Mike was in court. Frustrated, I realized I'd have to leave without solving the problem, but just beyond the reception desk, I could see Sonya's ratty French twist angling down a hall.

Stupidly, I asked the receptionist if I could see Sonya.

I waited a while before her assistant innocently came out to get me and then took me back to Sonya's office.

Sonya didn't even look up when I walked in. "What can I help you with, sweetie?"

"Sweetie?" I replied sarcastically.

Sonya looked up and glared. "I'm busy, Marie. This isn't a good time."

As I stood across from her, I didn't even force my usual smile. Instead, I took a breath to control my anger, then reached inside my purse and turned on Devon's recording device.

That move may have been the first time I ever did something cagey.

"Sonya, I don't know if you are aware of my background, but my first husband was a pro quarterback. Handsome. Charming. Successful. Women swarmed over him like bees on honey. I don't know why women do this. Do they think a guy will suddenly tell his wife and kids he's leaving, and take up with some new woman? Or do they simply want to screw him? But even my philandering late husband wouldn't dump me for some tawdry groupie. I must give him credit for that. Then, after he was killed, I was lucky enough to find Ryan. We are in love like a husband and wife are supposed to be. We agree on most issues, we enjoy the same movies, and we even love the same classical music. But then comes someone like you, flirting disgustingly with my husband as though he's going to take up with grocery-store *poké* like you."

"Grocery store *pokē*, how dare you?"

"That's how Big Mike described you to me, anyway. But I'm here to let you and Big Mike know that the email you sent Ryan was unacceptable, to say the least. I feel sorry for you that you've developed a crush on him, but you had no right to threaten him with a complaint to the state bar if he told anyone about your advances."

Her overly made-up face turned blood red. "Why were you reading your husband's email? It was marked confidential. I can report your husband for violating his ethical commitments to this firm. If you recall, Iona Law has oversight of Ryan's bar status for any case in Hawai'i. He'll be in a lot of trouble if you tangle with me."

"Only until he passes the bar, Sonya, so your threats don't scare me. At dinner the other night, I chatted with Big Mike about your zealous flirting, and he was quite sympathetic. That's why I came here. To let him know about your advances, especially since you were threatening Ryan's bar status. No doubt, Mike would rather have my husband on his team than an untrustworthy person like you. And, by the way, I am recording this conversation, so if you pursue this matter beyond these office doors, I will file a complaint with the Hawai'i State Bar that you were threatening me and my husband."

With that, her face went white. Even her makeup could not hide her ghostly glare. But she dared me back. "In Hawai'i, it is illegal to record someone without their permission! You'll be the target of a civil lawsuit if you use that recording for any purpose."

"Then I guess we both have hit a wall. But if you make one more move toward my husband, I'll see you disbarred." I returned my most angry scowl and stormed out.

In the elevator, my knees shook with tremors. And after I got out and safely inside my rideshare to the airport, I sat silently in the back seat, feeling a terrible sense of dread. What would Ryan do when he finds out? Oh, gosh, I shouldn't have challenged her the way I did. Maybe I should've trusted Ryan to handle this on his own, but after a lifetime of groupies trying to take my man, I simply lost it.

I WAS SO FLUSTERED BY THE TIME I ARRIVED BACK AT OUR Big Island condo, I tried to ignore the fact that Ryan didn't smile or rise to hug me when I walked in. Instead, he sat at the kitchen table with a stack of mail and held up one letter.

"Signed, sealed, and delivered. For better or for worse, I passed the Hawai'i bar."

I rushed to hug him. "Congratulations, I knew you could do it. So now this means you are no longer under the oversight of Mike Iona's firm."

He shied away. "That's not the first thing that came to mind, but, yes, I am a solo practitioner, and I answer solely to the Hawai'i State Bar."

I faked my best delighted smile. "Shall we celebrate? Since there aren't many tourists on-island right now, I bet we could get in at Red's Beach Hut."

"We can give it a try," Ryan said, although not enthusiastically.

Oh, gads, he knew. Did Sonya email him or call? I didn't dare stoke the fire. As a dodge, I told myself maybe we could talk things over at dinner. So, I nervously opened a reservations app on my phone and got us in at Red's Beach Hut.

RYAN REMAINED QUIET ON OUR SHORT RIDE TO THE Kailani Hotel, where it takes many steps up, down, and then around the massive complex to reach the five-star Red's Beach Hut. But oh, it is worth the effort to get there. Sitting outside among tall palms and tiki torches, with a view of the ocean, is the Hawaiian dream come true for so many visitors. You wind up thinking, ah, if life were only this. During our honeymoon, Ryan and I fell under the spell, although it's not the reality of living here. Still, sometimes it's good for island residents to escape the quirky, dusty, backwater funkiness of day-to-day island life and reignite the dreams we once had of Hawai'i.

Over our entrées of tempura *ahi* for me and Kona *kampachi* for Ryan, I chattered about my trip. "I was supposed to bring my cello, not my creative ideas, or so I found out. But they found a cello for me. Devon was a bit perturbed at first, but after I played, he seemed pleased."

Ryan nodded silently.

"I have a recording of our session if you'd like to hear it," I ventured a bit too eagerly, then remembered that the device also recorded my threats to Sonya.

Luckily, Ryan waved off my offer to hear it right then, so I made a mental note to move or erase my interactions with Sonya. How to do that might take a YouTube video, but I certainly didn't want Ryan to hear it.

Again, he simply chewed his dinner and nodded. I could tell he had heard from Sonya, or even worse, Big Mike. Which one, I was dying to know but did not dare ask.

After our server delivered our mocha coffees and a shared pineapple *crème brûlée*, I decided I must bite the *kukui* nut. "Ryan, I can tell you're angry with me. And I know why."

He gave me a look that was far removed from love and admiration. "I wondered when you were going to confess."

I took a moment to gather my thoughts. I didn't want to

mess this up by blubbering. "Ryan, I kind of dove headfirst into the deep end today, but not like I did in the Seychelles, remember, when our team was celebrating our big win? One of my biggest faults in the past with Cole was not bringing up concerns I had. His usual response was brutish anger, so I avoided tough conversations. That's why we grew apart. I was afraid to confront him. Let him know how his behavior was damaging our marriage. But with you, I don't want to be that way. Shy away."

He stared at his coffee cup but said nothing.

"I went to Iona Law Firm to talk to Big Mike, but he wasn't there. Then I saw Sonya and asked to see her instead. I let her know I will not tolerate her efforts to seduce you. I knew you would hear about it and be angry with me. But I was very upset when I accidentally saw her email. I heard a ding on your laptop and thought maybe it was something you needed to see. But when I saw Sonya's name, you might say curiosity and my insecurities got the best of me."

"Marie, we've had our disagreements lately, and those concern me. It seems we're pulling opposite direction from who we were in Dallas. But I need you to trust me. I don't need a wife who snoops my email. Even Doreen didn't do that, but of course, nobody came on to me then. But now —" He shook his head as if confused.

"Women are coming out of the Koa woodwork?"

He glared, clearly appalled.

"Sorry. I guess I was trying to lighten the tone." I paused to think what else to say. "I apologize for snooping. That was wrong of me. But I'm not sorry I told Sonya to back off. I'm your wife, and her behavior was insulting to me. I needed to make that clear."

"Marie, I don't want a jealous wife who constantly questions my commitment. While we each try to find what and where we want to be, please decide who is the woman I married. The one who trusted me to get her out of a murder charge? Or the one who now questions every move I make?" He quietly tapped the table with his knuckles and got up. "I'm going to the restroom. You've got a credit card, don't you? If you can see your way to tally up the bill, I'll meet you out by the car."

Whoa. As Ryan turned on his heel and left me staring at our pineapple crème brûlée, I realized how deeply I had messed up. Not only did Ryan not verify my Marie-Needy feelings, but he was angered and appalled by them.

I didn't blame him. Maybe I'd rushed into a second marriage before I was rid of the mental damage from the first.

Chapter Forty-Seven

ZOOM, ZOOM, ZOOM

Marie Ingles

A gain that night, Ryan and I slept in separate rooms, but despite our personal dramas, we had an 8:00 a.m. Zoom session the next morning with the FBI task force. That didn't leave time to work through our concerns. Perhaps that was for the better, since his demeanor toward me during our ritual coffee-making in the kitchen was polite but detached.

I'd had a toss-and-turn night, disturbed by the realization of how badly I'd messed up. Yes, I was wrong to snoop. But I apologized. And so, instead of my groveling more desperate apologies, I used a tool I'd learned in one of my counseling sessions with Dr. Lockett in Dallas.

"If you've apologized, let it go. It's up to the other to forgive, not you," he said.

And so, I decided to maintain a "rise above" approach to anything connected with Sonya Pruitt. There would be no more flirtations with her, innocent or not. Now it was Ryan's turn to forgive, but heed my boundaries.

Dr. Lockett would be proud of me for actually setting some.

Just then, Billy Bob and Natalie tapped at our lanai door. When I opened it, Billy Bob said, "Our condo router is down. We need to sit in with y'all."

Oh, great. Now, Ryan and I had to pretend all was well. But to avoid video call echoes, Natalie and I shared a laptop at the breakfast table, while Ryan and Billy Bob took one of their laptops into the primary bedroom and closed the door.

Promptly at 8:00 a.m., Pua Akana appeared on our screens, along with Sheriff Bucky, Harold Koizumi, Nocona, Kekoa, assorted FBI analysts, and state investigators.

After a quick roundtable of updates, Ryan raised his Zoom hand to speak. "Pua, my team and I hoped to have more to share with you. But after re-interviewing about twenty workers up at the dorms, we are still empty-handed...although the project manager at HILT will take us on that sunset tour in a few days."

Harold Koizumi rolled his eyes and grumbled. "The state is not paying you thousands of dollars for taking a leisurely tour."

Uh-oh. Everybody got silent.

Pua spoke up softly. "I understand your resentment, Harold, but let's not take our frustrations out on our SMEs. This case is bigger than anything this island has ever faced. Whether or not we like it, tourism is this island's lifeblood. And even highly skilled investigators like yours have not uncovered much more."

Harold sighed. "Ryan, team, please accept my regrets for barking at you. I know you are trying. And perhaps this tour will bring some revelations."

"Sir, we are doing all we can, in terms of the interviews we were given to complete. If you want us to do more or do something differently, please say so. We are not in charge here," Ryan said with an edge.

"Now, team, let's not play the blame game. Leave that to 808 Insiders," Pua said.

Billy Bob interrupted. "Last night, I had an idea. Since standard investigative work hasn't produced results, how about we stir up the lava?" He paused and chuckled to himself. "Is that something y'all say? Hope it's not some *malihini* insult. Seems like any time I open my mouth, someone gets offended because I used the wrong word. But, anyway, what I suggest is the task force sends out a news release, saying the team is on the brink of a major discovery."

"But that's nowhere near the truth," Pua said in frustration.

"I hear you, but I tried something like this on a case in Dallas. It produced a bunch of tip line calls that helped us find the actual killer. You see, murderers like to read about themselves. But when they think someone's onto them, they panic. They'll try something new, do something different, or say something odd. And witnesses notice."

Pua interrupted. "But saying we're near to an arrest might backfire by getting activists up in arms for fear it's one of their members. Either way, Governor Loden would expect us to make an arrest quickly."

Billy Bob nodded. "I understand your concerns, but I think it's worth a gamble. Otherwise, we're sitting empty-handed and probably will be until this guy kills somebody else."

Pua sighed, clearly not on board. "This is definitely not FBI book procedure."

Harold Koizumi nodded but appeared to like the idea. "If this news release goes out under county letterhead, then FBI and state police are off the hook."

Everybody thought for a moment. Then Pua said, "If you do this, Harold, I'll need your officers to guard this station. I don't want two hundred activists outside threatening to kill me or our analysts because they think we're going to arrest one of them."

Harold nodded. "I am at the point of trying anything. County PR people can draft something that makes it appear we're close to resolving this case, but doesn't openly say so. We'll leave the FBI and state police out of it. Maybe quote Billy Bob and Ryan. Get them to shoulder the back-flak."

Sheriff Bucky said, "Ask your PR people to circulate the drafts to each of us for input. Then you can send it out, and we'll see if someone makes a move."

"And I'll keep an eye on 808 Insiders," Natalie said.

⁂

THREE DAYS LATER, AFTER BACK-AND-FORTH REWRITES, THE county police news release generated articles in print and online media and also made a statewide splash on TV news.

I watched alone since Ryan was working out. He'd managed to avoid me for three days.

PONO-TV's Michelle Kimura led with the story on her evening newscast. "Hawai'i County Police officials announced today that an investigative task force is on the verge of making an announcement related to the three murders of international astronomers and the attempted murder of a fourth. County police would not say what evidence had been gathered, as it might be used to convict potential perpetrators. However, Deputy Chief Harold Koizumi did say that Brazilian astronomer Flavia Valente was taken off the critical list and is expected to make a full recovery."

Next, Harold flashed on the screen. "Mrs. Valente is the only astronomer to survive these recent attacks. One astronomer was killed by a bow and arrow, one by poison that led to delirium, and one by a gunshot. Ms. Valente was also wounded by a gunshot. The cartridges from both gunshot deaths have been analyzed, so we know whether they came from the same gun."

I was happy to learn Mrs. Valente survived. I made a mental note to ask Nocona if he had interviewed her yet. I wished Ryan were there to talk it over, but suddenly I was surprised to see his face flash on TV with Billy Bob at his side. The titles under their names said, "Ballard / Ingles Investigative Consultants."

"Our team is re-interviewing all witnesses on behalf of the task force to discover if anyone knows the man in images we have from MPH security videos," Ryan said.

Billy Bob added, "We've got other images of the alleged killer from security cameras at Virgo Observatory offices. Although he's in elaborate native dress, someone might spot a familiar facial feature."

After that, Michelle Kimura said, "Here are those images."

On-screen came both shots. The first was the Kekoa impersonator, and then the next shot appeared to be a warrior activist in a headdress, black wig, and costume. The pictures were fuzzy, so it was difficult to tell one from the other.

Michelle Kimura closed with, "If you know anything about this man, contact the FBI Hawaii Task Force tip line at (808) 999-1111."

Uh-Oh. She mentioned the FBI and Pua. I could just see Pua cringing at being connected to what basically was a puff piece that said nothing. I also hoped she wouldn't get a herd of bullies at her office door.

I wanted to text Ryan to say I'd seen him on TV, but I thought better of that.

He needed to heal. As did I. Confronting Sonya was impulse behavior, fueled by two glasses of Chardonnay. Oh, I'd vented my frustrations and let Sonya have it. And I'd set my boundaries with Ryan. But deep in my gut, I knew he was right. I must stop splitting my focus, my marriage, and my emotions in so many directions. Especially since I'm the one who took all this on — the task force, my looming cello performance, battling Sonya, and now, Ryan's dismay.

I only hope I haven't lost his love.

Chapter Forty-Eight

MY SIDE OF THE MIRRORS

Jürgen Bergen / Zeno Kühn

O*h je!* A fuzzy close-up of my bronzed face was splashed all over the TV. Even though I'd made myself up with a different wig and costume, the screen image was a close-up. I fear someone might recognize me, especially these Ballard / Ingles *Klugscheißers*.

Dressed as Jürgen, I will take them on a sunset tour. I will show them HILT. Show them the shipping containers containing the priceless mirrors and instruments. And I will proudly demonstrate how Jürgen Bergen made all this happen on time and on budget.

Even the brilliant Ballard / Ingles investigators won't notice the explosives behind the shipping containers' castor wheels. After all, I've hidden the explosives inside wheel blocks with the words, "Hawai'i Island Large Telescope" branded on one side, and on the other, a warning, "Danger, Do Not Remove."

HILT's security guards think nothing of them. After all, Jürgen told the guards to put the wheel blocks there.

"We don't need a surprise earthquake jostling these containers into a roll down the mountain," Jürgen joked.

Since he hired these people, who would doubt him?

Once the tour of HILT is complete, I will put on my charming tour guide smile, take the four from Ballard / Ingles to the summit to see the glorious sunset, and then make sure they do not make it down the mountain alive.

I'll have to sacrifice the Hummer, but I've got other vehicles waiting. While people at the summit rush to save them, I'll steal my way back to HILT, don my Hawaiian costume, and make sure another "activist" appears on HILT's security cameras. That will give the FBI all they need to cast the blame. "Native Hawaiians did this. Anti-astronomy activists did this!" The mere accusations will cause chaos and disruption. And send American astronomy down the lava tube.

Of course, I'll have to avoid HILT security guards, but I know their routines. After Jürgen moves about the shipping containers and fiddles with the wheel blocks, getting himself filmed, I can make my way to my vehicle, then to Kona, where I've booked a room. There, I can scrub off the bronzers, bleach my hair back to its native blond, drive to the airport, and catch my flight as Zeno Kühn.

No one will be searching for him.

After I board my plane, I'll send text commands to the detonators, programmed to explode thirty minutes later. That will allow enough time for my plane to take off before the explosives end HILT's exalted reign as the world's largest land-based telescope to be.

Americans and their superiority complexes. Losing this equipment will be so devastating, HILT will never recover.

Oh, der Wahnsinn!

The FBI and police will pursue local activists. The various groups will dress up, pound drums, dance, and shout. "Racial profiling! The mauna was defiled. Stop the sacrilege. The summit should be cleared. The summit is sacred!"

I sincerely doubt the new Maunakea Authority will agree to HILT being rebuilt. But if they try, the Office of Hawaiian Affairs will sue. And nothing will get done. I've been here long enough to learn that's how it goes in this island state.

North American astronomy will be *der* toast.

I've planned. Prepared. Waited patiently. And now I look forward to Jürgen's grandest night before he vanishes in the thin Maunakea air.

Chapter Forty-Nine

OH, SCARY NIGHT
Marie Ingles

None of us remember the actual crash, but we each recall bits and pieces of what led to and followed it, enough to paste together most of what happened. Each of us was pretty banged up, Billy Bob worst of all. He'll be in Ali'i Community Hospital in Waimea for another week, while the rest of us were x-rayed, stitched, and bandaged, then released to our homes.

✦

I SHOULD PUT FIRST THINGS FIRST.

The afternoon before the crash, the HILT project manager, Jürgen Bergen, met us at our condo. He was handsome in an international way, with olive skin, dark brown hair and eyes, and an athletic physique.

Out front, his car was an amazingly equipped four-wheel-drive Hummer EV SUV.

Being the largest of our group, Billy Bob sat in the front passenger seat, while Ryan, Natalie, and I sat in the backseat, she in the middle. Ryan had remained so distant, it seemed silly for me to put myself so close to him when it was apparent he didn't want to be.

I'm not usually a car admirer, but this Hummer was awesome. First off, there was plenty of room for three in the backseat. Exceptional since Ryan is not a small guy. And up front, a huge display screen above the center console was as large as my kitchen TV.

Throughout the journey from Hōkele Kilohana to Old Saddle Road, Jürgen chatted energetically, and yet I couldn't understand why he was being so sociable. We'd just met the guy, but he was over the top, even a bit agitated. Like someone who's putting on a show.

Now, I know why.

Since he was from Zürich, I asked him how he got the position at HILT.

He told us, "The astronomy community is a world without boundaries. I'm trained as an astrophysicist, and yet I have experience guiding the construction of the giant AWE-T observatory in Chile. My goal here was to help astronomers from all nations compete in the new world of these enormous, land-based observatories. And I certainly wouldn't mind having the privilege of working with such a magnificent instrument in the future."

On Old Saddle Road, we stopped at a small ranch where Jürgen had prearranged an early picnic supper to help us acclimate to the rising elevation. The ranch was at about six thousand feet, so the air was jacket chilly. It was a pastoral property with cattle, horses, goats, sheep, chickens, pigs, turkeys, peafowl, and even some donkeys quietly grazing in fenced grassy areas.

As we four savored the bento boxes and beverages Jürgen had brought, I gave Ryan a hopeful glance. I was relieved to see him give me a conciliatory nod and flicker of a smile.

That warmed my soul.

We chatted with Jürgen about Zürich, his hometown in Switzerland, or so he said.

"I emigrated from Israel to England. My parents still live in Israel, but I wanted to study the stars. After many years studying in London — which is where this odd British accent comes from — a relationship took me to Zürich. It's still my home base, although I travel the world for my career."

"Zürich, huh? What's that like?" Billy Bob queried.

I glanced at Billy Bob, wondering why he would ask.

He gave me a quick wink, a sign he was slipping into investigator mode.

"Ah, Zürich…it's a mix of old and new. Historic buildings that date back centuries are set among modern skyscrapers, like any busy metropolis. Nothing like the slower pace here."

Ryan nodded. "Marie and I came here to escape the frenzy of Dallas. It's lovely living here, although a bit boring, as we're finding out. I may have retired too soon."

"Be careful what you wish for, Boss," Billy Bob said.

As we enjoyed our meal, we five grew silent, gazing at our pastoral surroundings. All around us were the contrasts of the Big Island. We'd left the beach and shore behind to drive six thousand feet up the slopes of the world's tallest volcano with an Israeli-born, UK-educated, Swiss project manager for an American astronomical observatory. For dinner, he'd brought us sushi and tempura shrimp bento boxes, and we four Texans did our best to navigate them with chopsticks as we enjoyed *kombucha* tea made in Hilo.

That thought made me smile, but Jürgen suddenly pulled me out of my reverie. "Well, we must get going or we will miss the sunset. We still have a mountain to climb."

As we piled back in the Hummer, Jürgen told us the next

stop would be the VIS. "You can use the restroom and buy a souvenir of our visit."

An hour later, after the Hummer climbed to nine thousand feet, we parked at the VIS and got out. The afternoon temperature was in the mid-forties, and it would be even colder at the summit.

Jürgen handed us each a puffy jacket and a pair of insulated mittens he'd brought in the back of the Hummer. "We have extras for when board members show up," he said.

After the gift shop and restroom, we five jumped back in the Hummer. Beyond the VIS and dorms, the road to the summit is unpaved and terribly bumpy. You must have a four-wheel-drive vehicle to make the journey. On the way, we passed the dormitories where some workers spend the night.

From the front seat, Billy Bob said, "It's amazing what's been built up here. The bunkhouses even have Wi-Fi."

As we bounced along, Jürgen scoffed. "Yes, much has been built upon the *mauna*, to the activists' dismay. 'Their sacred mountain,' they claim, although not all Hawaiians agree —"

Just then, we hit a major bump.

Jürgen sniggered. "Can you believe I drive to work on this crazy *autobahn*? They say the new Maunakea authority will pave it one of these days, but that would take a lot of state money. Besides, the activists would protest, an endless cycle."

He turned sharply around a hairpin turn as the rest of us grabbed whatever we could to keep us steady. During those turns, I couldn't help leaning into Natalie, and the two of us squealed, much to Billy Bob's dismay. But after a half-hour of jarring twists, turns, and jounces, we finally reached the HILT site, five hundred feet below the summit.

"Unlike the other observatories you will see later, HILT sits at a lower plateau to lessen its visual impact. This was done to appease activists, but there were some environmental considerations too. It's a more protected site than at the summit ridge," Jürgen explained.

When we parked and got out of the Hummer, the temperature was sub-freezing. The exterior of the HILT building was stunning, with a space-like architectural design. And its tall dome looked like a giant eye.

Jürgen greeted a security guard, who smiled and waved as if he knew Jürgen well. Then Jürgen used his passkey to unlock the front doors, where he motioned us inside. "Welcome to the future of astronomy."

I later understood. He was thinking about a different observatory, AWE-T.

Inside the dome area, I noticed Ryan's amazed expression.

"Why would anyone want to stop such a magnificent facility from being built?" he said.

"There are some who truly believe the mountain is sacred. Others claim the observatories are polluting the groundwater, but that is completely untrue. The bottom line is they think there's money to be had, or they simply want control. So, they use the excuse that their ancestors' beliefs are being disrespected by the observatories and the tourist operators."

Natalie hummed philosophically. "But when you look at fables from Judaism and Christianity, you'll find millions of people still believe those stories as well. So, why must Hawaiians stop believing their fables? Fairies leaping from mountain to mountain are no more preposterous concepts than someone turning water to wine or rising from the dead."

Jürgen shook his head. "From what I'm told, even Hawaiian royalty supported astronomy atop Maunakea. But over the past decades, some neo-natives demanded that everybody follow what they say are true Hawaiian ways. A rock pile became a religious site. Their twelve-alphabet language is so convoluted, one word can mean twenty things. Even so, the language is now required in schools. You should see what I go through typing reports, especially since I'm a German-speaking Swiss Jew who studied in England. There's a backward apostrophe, called the 'okina. You have to learn how to type that and another thing called the macron. It's that little bar above a vowel. I guess you've seen that on local street signs. It took me months to pronounce Anaeho'omalu Bay or Queen Ka'ahumanu Highway. I think some of these activists want to make life miserable for outsiders. Or else they want to go back in time."

"That's because they feel powerless," Natalie said firmly.

I could tell she didn't like Jürgen's obvious prejudices.

Ryan tried to steer Jürgen to less biased topics. "From what I've heard, removing the observatories would severely damage the island's economy."

Jürgen lifted his palms in a question. "Quaint little Waimea, where I live, would become a ghost town. To you, I may sound like some Nazi, but too many of these locals refuse to, what's that word used on Star Trek?"

"Assimilate," Billy Bob snickered.

Natalie spoke up more loudly this time. "But these are *their* islands. And they were stolen. Insisting on having their names, their language, their traditions—"

Ryan slipped into his mediator mode, trying to calm the rhetoric. "Good points, Natalie, as usual. There are truly two sides to the coin. And, standing atop this magnificent mountain, I for sure have no clue how to solve the problem." He chuckled a bit to lighten his tone.

I shrugged and fake-grinned at Natalie, who grimaced and sighed angrily.

Jürgen blew out a sigh too.

Politics, race, and religion. Maybe the thin air was having an effect, but I think we each felt dismayed and frustrated by what seemed insolvable — science and technology running headlong up against indigenous beliefs in fantastic fables and rocks that are alive.

As Jürgen resumed his tour through the interior of HILT, he showed us the telescope's massive support pillar and the seemingly endless mirror mounts, which looked like a gigantic spider web. Then he pointed out the side windows to the row of shipping containers covered with tarpaulins. "Those hold over eight hundred mirror segments that will become HILT's primary mirror, the world's largest at forty meters," he said with a bit of a scoff.

To me, his tone seemed biting in contrast to his earlier boasting. It was then that I glanced at his nose. It was arched and narrow, and that struck me: That was the shape the task force had been looking for. But as Billy Bob had mentioned before, Jürgen's skin was olive, not dark brown, and he was an astronomer himself, looking forward to doing research at HILT, so he couldn't possibly be the costumed activist who ran around murdering people. Or, so my mind justified to itself.

Some sleuth I am. It didn't dawn on me until too late, although Billy Bob later claimed he'd begun wondering back at the ranch.

After our tour, we got back in the Hummer, then drove another bumpy five hundred feet uphill and over a ridge near the summit of Maunakea, where the other observatories were arranged in a loop on orange-colored terrain. I was amazed at the height of the white or silver-domed buildings, some at least ten stories high.

When we got out of the Hummer again, Jürgen pointed out the Knight I and Knight II observatories. "In 2020, Andrea Ghez received the Nobel Prize in Physics for her work in proving the existence of a supermassive black hole at the center of the Milky Way galaxy. That's our own. Scary stuff to think that a black hole might gobble Earth up one day. She did her research using the Knight Observatories' lasers—advanced adaptive optics systems. They overcome the blurring effects of Earth's atmosphere and help obtain high-resolution images."

We four nodded stupidly as if we understood that.

Jürgen chuckled at our ignorance and then aimed us toward the blazing setting sun.

What a magnificent sight. At almost 14,000 feet, any clouds were far below our views of the sun setting on the blue horizon. Maybe it was the cold air or lack of oxygen, but when I gazed at that scene, I felt such a wave of nature's glory, tears overflowed my eyes. The view was so magical, I would've reached out to hug Ryan, but he had not given me even a brush of his mittened hand. I wondered if he felt as I did that our souls were beginning to part. With the recent dramas, I felt so confused and frustrated, I couldn't stifle my emotions. I worried my tears might turn to ice, so I kept brushing them away as the sun began glowing a piercing orange.

Just when I felt I might be losing him, Ryan walked up from behind and enveloped me with his arms. He nestled his chin into my neck and leaned to kiss me on my wet cheek.

"Why are you crying?"

"Just overwhelmed by the beauty."

In a soft voice, he whispered, "Don't ever doubt that I love you, Marie. I need you to know that. Know it in your beautiful body. Know it in your sweet, loving, passionate soul. You and I may disagree now and then. Heck, we may even fuss and fight. But we'll work things out. Just trust me. I'm not Cole."

I was so relieved to hear him say this, I started blubbering. "No, you aren't Cole. I must remember, the past is past."

Ryan turned me around, brushed away my tears with his mittens, and kissed me full on my wet lips to the point Billy Bob hooted at us.

"You two should stop off at the dorms on the way down."

Everyone laughed.

I gave Ryan another peck, then turned and nestled my head against his chest. It felt so good to have him hold me again. I felt the bulk of his body and the warmth of his love radiating through his puffy jacket.

To the side of us, Billy Bob and Natalie also stood in awe as the sun slipped toward the oceanic horizon.

I murmured, "No wonder the ancient people thought the mountain was alive."

"Well, it is. It's a volcano. The last eruption was about 4,500 years ago, but geologists say it will erupt again," Natalie said in her factoid voice.

"And we're standing on top of it?" Billy Bob shouted.

We giggled again, then went quiet, relishing such an extraordinary vision.

No matter what the lava was doing far beneath us, I got a feeling of otherworldliness. Part of it was the giddiness from less oxygen. Some of it was from Ryan's reassuring love. And the rest of it was simply that the sunset was so stunning.

Moments later, as the sky turned even deeper orange, Billy Bob suddenly made this scene more magical. Out of the blue, he made a big deal of standing before Natalie, dropping to one knee, taking her hand, and proposing. "Natalie Sherman, atop this totally enchanted and supposedly alive mountain, I'm asking you to be my wife."

Natalie yelped in surprise but managed to eke out a weepy, "Yes" in reply.

Billy Bob fumbled under his puffy jacket to his jeans pocket, where he pulled out a small black velvet box. He opened it and presented it to her.

Inside was a ring with a huge, pear-shaped diamond.

When he slid it on Natalie's finger, a crowd of tourists and tour guides applauded.

He stood and gave her a giant bear hug and a sweet kiss.

She had tears. That's the first time I'd ever seen Natalie emotional. She was always the rational one between us, and her tears were unexpected and moving.

A few moments later, Jürgen waved a hand for us to follow him. "I'm sorry to interrupt, but you must see this." He motioned us toward the other side of the astronomy plateau.

On the eastern side, Jürgen pointed us to Maunakea's true summit, a cinder cone blazing deeply orange in the remaining sunlight. On the summit's peak, a trail leads to two *heiau*, or rock formations, where Native Hawaiians practice their spiritual beliefs. And way beyond this orange cinder cone, out on Earth's blue and misty atmospheric layers, appeared the rising shadow of Maunakea. And above that, a rising golden moon.

In his tour guide voice, Jürgen explained, "They call this 'mountain shadow,' but it's an optical phenomenon caused by the interaction of sunlight with the Earth's atmosphere. You see, as the sun descends below the horizon, its light passes through the atmosphere at an angle. Dust, water vapor, and other particles scatter the sunlight, but the part of the atmosphere directly behind Maunakea is shielded by the mountain itself. This creates a distinct shadow that extends across the sky. It becomes more pronounced as the sun sets, making the shadow more discernible."

As Ryan held me close, he murmured, "Whatever the scientific reason, there could not be a more beautiful sight, other than you, Marie."

I giggled. "I need to deprive you of oxygen more often."

Still playing tour guide, Jürgen again interrupted our reverie to motion us back near his Hummer, but before we got inside, he held up a hand for us to wait.

As the sky turned from deep orange to dark burgundy and then into a midnight blue, some amazing sounds alerted us.

Several of the gigantic observatories started opening their domes for the night. *Buhhhrrrrroarrrrrrrrr* went these mechanisms, sounds so remarkable, we four looked upward to see what those huge telescopes might see — the brilliant display of stars and planets, so dense they were like glitter on velvet.

And just when we thought we could not be more impressed, off to our left, Jürgen pointed to the heavens as the Knight Observatories' twin lasers pierced the star-filled sky like two light sabers touching at the tips.

"Wow, what the —?" Billy Bob said.

"Those are the adaptive optics I mentioned."

"I had no idea all this was going on," Billy Bob murmured.

"Nighttime atop Maunakea is when real fairy tales come true," Jürgen said.

This was the sincere part of Jürgen, the man who took pride in being part of the world's astronomy community. Staring up at the heavens, he seemed lost in thought, but eventually motioned the four of us, high on our romantic notions, back into his vehicle.

And that's when the Hummer hit the fan.

MY MEMORY IS INCOMPLETE. BILLY BOB WAS IN THE front passenger seat. Natalie, Ryan, and I were in the back, again with Natalie in the middle. I would have sat by Ryan, but she said she was cold and needed two bodies to warm her up. I told her not to worry about pressing into me on the switchbacks, but she joked, "If you don't mind, I'd rather press into Ryan."

We giggled about that, and then I remember Jürgen getting in. He turned on the engine and the Hummer's running lights to keep light pollution at a minimum, then drove slowly downhill for a bit.

I remember he pulled over at a flat turnaround area. But that's when my memories go spotty.

At the emergency room in Ali'i Community Hospital in Waimea, Harold Koizumi of county police told us, "The Hummer went over the edge, but Jürgen Bergen wasn't inside the car. Do you know why?"

That spurred a fleeting series of recollections from Ryan, Natalie, and me.

"He told us he had to check a tire. So he pulled over, got out, and then the Hummer lurched. It was like he gave it a push," Ryan said.

"I remember someone screaming," I murmured.

Natalie said, "I remember *you* screaming, Marie."

"I guess that was me, but why would Jürgen push us over the edge?"

Ryan spouted, "That's what I want to know. After I got you two out, you and Natalie went over to help Billy Bob, so I looked uphill. It was dark, but with lights from the other cars, I could see Jürgen standing there, just watching. So I started climbing back up, but it was tough going in the dark. When I looked up again, he turned and ran. By the time I got to the top, I had no clue where that fucker went. I would have held him until police arrived."

Harold shook his head. "County, state, and FBI are on the hunt. But it's a huge mountain."

"Maybe he panicked, you know, ran away because he messed up," I said.

"That's a possibility. And once we find him, we'll know more. I'm just thankful you three in the back were wearing seat belts. And the Hummer had airbags," Harold said.

"I remember Ryan yelling at Billy Bob," Natalie said.

Harold nodded. "Billy Bob saved your lives. He managed to unlock his seatbelt and grab the steering wheel, but he couldn't move across the console to the driver's side."

Natalie fumed. "I remember Billy Bob shouting, 'Ryan, get the brakes!'"

Ryan seemed stunned. "Get the brakes? I'm embarrassed to say this, but I held onto Natalie as if she could save us all."

Harold laughed. "Billy Bob told me that you hollered, 'Nasty, how in the fuck do you expect me to do that?'"

Natalie grinned. "My hero would remember that."

AFTER ENDURING X-RAYS AND ALL SORTS OF PROBING, Ryan, Natalie, and I were released to go home, but first, we stopped by Billy Bob's hospital room, where the poor thing was bunged up with broken ribs, a concussion, and a full leg cast hoisted in a traction rig.

"This is what I get for proposing," he grunted.

Natalie gave him a light hug. "Don't blame me, mister. I'm the one who's gonna take care of you after you get out."

Poor guy was on so many pain meds, he detailed his heroism with delirious delight. "I couldn't get past that damn console, so I just kept trying to steer the Hummer straight. I couldn't reach the brake and thought maybe Ryan could jump over the seat. But I guess that was impossible. I wondered if maybe I should turn off the ignition."

Harold laughed. "You would have lost the power steering. Once you went over the edge, physics and gravity took over. But your ability to steer saved your spam *musubi*."

"Good to know, should there be a next time. Luckily, we hit a big rock. If that hadn't been there, we would have tumbled and rolled," Ryan said.

"It was a bunch of rocks. The Hawaiian heritage folks will claim it was a *heiau* and demand reparations, so Jürgen Berger's insurance will have to deal with them. And his lawyer will have to wrangle with state police. He could be imprisoned for the damage," Harold said with a sarcastic chuckle.

"He could be imprisoned for trying to kill us," Ryan said.

"You were lucky to survive, especially that a patch of spring snow was thick enough to cushion Billy Bob's fall," Harold said.

Billy Bob murmured through his medicated haze. "I knew something about that Jürgen guy was fishy, but I didn't know what. If not for the rocks and snow, we would have died."

That was Jürgen's plan. And even more.

Chapter Fifty

MY SIDE OF THE MIRRORS

Jürgen Bergen / Zeno Kühn

V*erdammt, verdammt, verdammt.* How could my plans go so awry? Everything was in place. All I needed to do while everybody stared at the Hummer crash site was make my way down to HILT, don my costume, get my activist persona video-recorded while security officers looked the other way, grab my luggage and burner phone, and then escape on the ATV I'd hidden back near the summit, behind Pleiades Observatory.

After I reached L.A., I would get a chuckle reading about the explosions.

Ach, but instead of the Hummer tumbling down the mountain, exploding in fire, and killing all aboard, the *verdammt* thing merely bent over the edge and careened straight downhill, bouncing and veering, but never rolling, until it slammed into a pile of rocks that have gotten a lot more holy over the past few decades.

When the front passenger door flew open, the fat private investigator sailed onto a patch of snow. He screamed so loudly, his voice echoed over the summit, alerting a herd of guides and tourists who scrambled downhill.

As I watched from above, I could tell from the Hummer's emergency lights that all four had survived.

My mind raced to calculate my next steps.

The first option was to head to my Kona hotel room to clean up, then take the red-eye flight I'd booked for Zeno Kühn. I'd return to Berlin as my true self. Jürgen would simply vanish. But HILT would not be destroyed.

The second option was to follow the crowd and rush downhill. Pretend this was all a terrible mistake. Exist as the contrite Jürgen for several days, then return to my summit office. Dress as a Native Hawaiian. Avoid security guards, get filmed, grab my gear and burner, then escape, leaving the island as Zeno Kühn, but blowing up HILT from the plane. That would accomplish all of my goals.

But my mind was a blur of fearful scenes. Police interviews, when Jürgen would present his phony papers. They're good: We paid dearly for them. But if police arrested Jürgen, his fingerprints would reveal our double identity. That would end the career of Zeno Kühn.

Despite my fears, I leaned toward the second option, hoping the police would accept Jürgen's apologetic pleas and not investigate further. But as I stared through the dusk at the flashing wreck a hundred meters below, I saw that hunk of an attorney, Ryan Ingles, kick his way out of a jammed door and stand to his full, bulky height. As the two women struggled to aid the fat investigator, Ingles turned and glared uphill directly at me. Even in the dim light, I could see the flash of anger in his atmospheric eyes. He knew this was no accident, and he began to run uphill after me like a — what do they call him — linebacker on a blitz.

The coward inside me turned and rushed toward the Pleiades Observatory. As I passed curious interlopers, I shouted, "Emergency, call 911, call 911!" and pointed back toward the scene, as if anyone who saw Jürgen Bergen would think he was trying to help.

Breathless at the Pleiades site, I peeked around its curved outer wall to see if Ryan Ingles had made it to the mountain's edge. Several minutes later, I saw the athletic hulk just clearing it. He stumbled but regained his footing, looking left and right to find me.

He didn't know where to look. But I'd planned ahead and knew where to hide.

I ran around the back curve of Pleiades, mounted my ATV, and then drove the back trail downhill to Parking Lot 3. There I'd parked my second escape vehicle, a four-wheel-drive SUV I'd rented from a local on Nextdoor. Kekoa Palakiko's IDs were still handy to use when people had no access to state ID data.

I started the SUV, yanked it into gear, then dodged foreign tourist groups who were like ants on a hill, busy with their star parties and oblivious to the wreck near the summit.

As I bumped and turned down the access road, one switchback at a time, the descent felt like it took hours. I could barely breathe. I constantly glanced in my rear-view mirror, fearful of seeing Ryan Ingles still running behind me.

Eventually, I reached Saddle Road, where I drove toward my Kona hotel. There, I would clean up, rest, eat, and later take my red-eye flight, boarding as Zeno Kühn. As the plane rolled down the runway, I'd send the code for HILT to be destroyed.

Jürgen would have to take the blame, not some angry activist. That in itself was disappointing. My plan was to prevent HILT's rebuild.

But as I parked in the motel lot and got out, I realized I had nothing with me. I'd been so focused on escaping, I did not have time to go back to HILT. Grab my luggage. Or, more importantly, the burner phone that could detonate the explosives. I'd left everything at the HILT office! All because that *gottverdammte* linebacker was coming after me.

Right there in the parking lot, anguish gushed from my vocal cords in such a loud growl, I feared someone might call the police, so I silenced myself and went inside my room, where I sat on the bed and sank into dismay. I even cried like a baby.

The purpose of my many months on Hawai'i Island, the destruction of HILT, was now an unreachable star. I'd let my panic defeat my plans to ensure that AWE-T would have no American competition built atop Maunakea.

Part of me considered going back. Being the apologetic Jürgen. But no. As my mind repeated my options, I had to accept that my mission had failed.

Also, I felt a horrible sense of regret. For *nichts*, I had killed three astrophysicists and shot a mother, although she thankfully survived.

Most tragically, I realized my career as Zeno Kühn was at an end. In its search for Jürgen, the FBI would find the burner phone and my fingerprints, then eventually match us up, all because Jürgen was too cowardly to face the linebacker, police, and the FBI.

Chapter Fifty-One

NOT OUR BEST LOOK

Marie Ingles

B ruised, bandaged, and staring at our pain-medicated images on separate screens, Natalie, Ryan, and I plugged into a Zoom meeting the morning after the wreck. We three looked and felt like hell. But we wanted to contribute as much as we could.

Pua Akana led off with concerns about our health, which was kind. Also expressing sympathy were Sheriff Bucky, Harold Koizumi, Nocona, and Kekoa, along with assorted FBI agents, state police, and county officers.

Ryan replied for our team. "We look like we just lost the war, but only Billy Bob had to stay in the hospital. I don't know what the rest of you have learned, but we're wondering why Jürgen Bergen wanted us dead."

Sheriff Bucky tossed up his hands. "Ryan, ladies, we wondered the same thing."

Pua fumbled with her keyboard. "One of our intelligence analysts on Oahu just texted me he has news. I hope he'll join us soon…oh, here he is. I'll let him in the meeting."

Our screens blipped with an image of "Intelligence Analyst

Amado Drummond," boyish-looking about thirty, with a surfer tan face and excited brown eyes. "Good morning, all. Our forensics team worked through the night and discovered some rather startling facts —"

Pua interrupted. "Team, especially you civilians, any information you hear is still confidential. There will be no leaks to the media or anyone. Do we still have your bond?"

We all agreed with serious affirmatives.

"In that case, Amado, please continue."

"Thank you, SSA Akana. Late last night, a German male named Zeno Kühn boarded a redeye flight out of Kona, bound for L.A. After he landed, Mr. Kühn changed his scheduled connecting flight from Berlin to Dubai in the UAE. This raised a red flag with TSA, so they questioned him but couldn't hold him. Unfortunately, TSA didn't get our BOLO until after his flight took off. But they sent us a screen-grab of Kühn. We compared it to a photo of Jürgen Bergen from the HILT website. Despite the differences in hair, eye, and skin colors, the two came up as a match."

Amado uploaded the photo. The Zeno Kühn fellow was blond, fair, green-eyed, and had an arched, narrow nose.

I thought to myself, "That's the same nose I noticed on Jürgen." I could have kicked myself for not anticipating what he did to us.

"So, Amado, your team says that Jürgen Bergen is actually a German named Zeno Kühn?"

"Yes. And to verify the facial recognition software, we got an emergency warrant this morning to search Bergen's apartment in Waimea. We ran fingerprints there against Interpol's database. The two individuals have the same prints."

On-screen, our collective expressions appeared dumbfounded.

Amado Drummond continued, "Jürgen Bergen is definitely Zeno Kühn."

"And so, who is this Zeno Kühn, since he's not the Israeli-Swiss guy we thought he was?" Natalie asked.

Nocona Parker interrupted, "I've heard of him. He's from Berlin and was a project manager for AWE-T, Europe's giant observatory in Chile."

"You're right, Mr. Parker. Kühn served as assistant project manager there but has been on a year's leave of absence. However, according to his social media page, which has another photo we used to identify him, he recently came to the Big Island. At first, he was staying at the hotel inside Volcanoes National Park. The hotel has security video of him checking in. This image also matched Jürgen Bergen," Amado said.

Pua shook her head as if she could clear the fog. "So, this Zeno Kühn fellow spent how many months here, masquerading as Jürgen Bergen, project manager for HILT. But if he was our killer, what was his motive?"

Amado cocked his head as if he was spinning a tale. "Well, again, we've unearthed fresh evidence. In addition to searching Mr. Bergen/Kühn's apartment, we searched his office at the HILT site. That was where we found a Native Hawaiian costume, skin bronzers, and luggage. We also found a burner phone with one number programmed in it."

I asked, "Did you call it?"

Amado smiled sarcastically. "Unlike what you see on TV's FBI show, we didn't dare call that number to test it. But we thoroughly searched HILT, inside and out. Over by the shipping containers, we found a bunch of sandbags tucked under the container wheels. You know, like wheel blocks. But these had explosives inside, along with receiving devices and detonators. Our tech guys matched those receivers with the number in the burner phone."

"You're saying this guy was going to blow up HILT?" Harold asked.

"It appears so. But — well, we don't know — maybe in the frenzy of escaping, he forgot his phone?"

"Oh, my God," Harold said. "Can you imagine the destruction, the injuries, and the chaos?"

Everyone went silent for a while, thinking about what could have happened.

Eventually, Nocona perked up. "Huh! In a weird, winding way, this is making sense. AWE-T is in Chile, but HILT will be one meter wider. And it will sit higher in clearer skies. So, it would be superior and enable North American astronomers to achieve greater discoveries. To have HILT destroyed would be devastating. For decades, who knows how long, AWE-T would remain the world's largest land-based telescope, and Americans would not have access to it."

Amado Drummond continued, "And there's more. We found traditional native clothing, wigs, headdresses, hair dye, brown contact lenses, and bronzing cosmetics in Mr. Bergen/Kühn's apartment, so it's clear he was the one masquerading as the activists who would be blamed."

Sheriff Bucky slammed his fist with a bang. "So, you're saying this Zeno Kühn pretended to be a local *brah* who killed three astronomers and shot another. Then, posing as Jürgen Bergen, he tried to kill our four SMEs, all so — what — he could blow up HILT?"

"That seems to have been his plan," Amado said with a sardonic grin.

"Why not just blow up HILT?" Pua asked.

Amado shook his head. "Might have been too simple a plan for a mad scientist. We can't say for sure, but his efforts may have had socio-political layers. If a Native Hawaiian were convicted *unfairly* for these murders, well, you experienced what happened when Mr. Palakiko was jailed. Demonstrations erupted. Perhaps Kühn hoped for violence and chaos. And after he blew up HILT, maybe he thought the state might prevent its reconstruction or ban all observatories atop Maunakea."

Nocona chimed in. "Kühn is a planetary astronomer, one of those hell-bent on discovering Earth's twin planet. Maybe he saw this as his only way to compete."

Natalie's stunned expression blipped on the screen. "But to kill three people, try to kill another, try to kill us, and then try to destroy—."

Pua sighed, "He must be nuts."

Nocona nodded. "Maybe he got lost in an evil quest for fame. A Carl Sagan wannabe gone awry."

"Well said, Nocona. His efforts to kill the Ballard / Ingles team gave him a chaotic diversion. While everyone was focused on helping them after the wreck, he could have dialed the number to detonate his explosives and head home to Berlin as Zeno Kühn."

"But he forgot his phone," Amado replied wryly.

"If he succeeded, we'd probably be chasing another activist, and all hell would break loose," Harold said.

Amado nodded. "Unfortunately, we did not connect the dots before his flight left for Dubai. It's still in the air. We've notified Interpol and requested an investigation, of course, but since he hasn't been charged with a crime, he'll walk."

"He'll have to hide in the shadows, pretend he doesn't exist, and send anonymous emails to old friends," I murmured, thinking about Lena Verano.

"Or change his identity," Natalie said.

With that, the rest of us stared at each other's screen images with expressions I'd call stunned and dismayed.

Chapter Fifty-Two

DUBAI? DÉJÀ VU

Marie Ingles

The next morning, before Ryan and I had a chance to read the day's news, Pua Akana telephoned. "The FBI has officially requested extradition, but you know the UAE. Little cooperation unless they get triple back in return."

"Oh, no. The families of those who died should see this nut brought to justice," I said.

Pua replied, "We can hope that one of these days you will see Mr. Kühn returned for trial."

"I hope so too. The loss of those three brilliant researchers tears my heart."

"We feel the same. Perhaps more so, since it was our duty to stop this creep. But I also want to thank you and Ryan for the tremendous effort you gave our task force. If you ever need a job, we would love to enroll you at Quantico."

Ryan winked at me. "Many thanks, Pua, but our investigative work on the Big Island is kaput, and I don't mean *Kapu*." He chuckled.

"Gosh, Ryan, that was your first Hawaiian-style joke," I laughed.

"You should be proud of me for learning enough local words to make one."

"At least you two try," Pua said.

"Thanks for giving us credit for trying. But as it turns out, we are also trying to figure out our next career steps. Our lease is up, so it's decision time."

"I would hate to think this is *aloha*," she said, and her wistful smile told me she was sincere.

Again, this reminded me of the kind and sincere people who live on these islands, not the angry protestors or grifters with their hands out, but everyday working people who are truly blessed with the *aloha* spirit.

Ryan glanced at me with those eyes, oh, those eyes. "Not quite yet, until we figure out what we both want."

With that, we signed off our laptops, then blew out simultaneous sighs, probably feeling the same sense of futility.

"Dubai again? I'm feeling *déjà vu* Lena Verano."

"Seems where criminals easily escape justice." Ryan checked his watch and realized the time. "My gosh, we've got to get moving. Billy Bob and those crutches…I've got to help him with the luggage."

With that, we rushed next door.

BILLY BOB'S HEAD WAS STILL BANDAGED, AND HIS SPARE tire and chest were wrapped with a rib support. Poor thing hobbled out to our SUV on crutches. Natalie had to squeeze in the tailgate with the luggage, so Billy Bob could stretch out his leg cast. I offered to stay behind, but she didn't want that.

At the airport, Ryan and Natalie rolled the suitcases to the check-in area, where the airline put Billy Bob in a wheelchair. It was way too narrow for him, so he looked like a crumpled giant. At least Colleen Ballard had approved first-class fares, since Billy Bob needed to straighten out that leg cast.

Ryan pushed the wheelchair as far as security. At that point, we had to give them each a hug and tell them goodbye.

Natalie's dark eyes appeared wistful. "Of course, you'll come to the wedding, as soon as we figure out when and where."

Billy Bob gave her a deadpan expression. "Wedding? What wedding? My concussion…"

Natalie laughed. "If you weren't so banged up, I'd…" She raised a fist as if to fake-punch him.

Ryan reached out to shake his buddy's hand. "I'm sorry this mess landed you in the hospital. As the Hawaiians say, *mahalo* for all your *kokua*. I'm sure Colleen will send the state of Hawai'i the bills."

We wistfully waved goodbye and walked back to our car, each of us feeling gloomy that our friends were leaving. I consoled myself by remembering my friendship with Ailani Moreau. And Ryan has gotten to know Gilles better. I didn't feel we were friendless on this Big Island. And yet, when we returned to our condo, I told Ryan that I felt untethered.

"Maybe because we haven't been here long enough and joined in as much as we should, but after living here almost six months, I don't feel as drawn to the Big Island as I used to be when you and I visited here."

"I know the feeling. Maybe we made a mistake trying to live our favorite vacation."

"Big Mike said island life either pulls you in or pushes you away. No matter how much we love the wondrous things about this island, I don't think it's the right place for either of us to resume our careers."

Ryan ventured, "There's still the Oahu idea. We could live the Hawai'i dream there."

"But it's so crowded, especially with tourists. And with the demographics of Oahu, we might feel even more foreign. I don't want to live somewhere I'm out of place or somehow 'less than' because I'm not from the 'right' demographic group. We were naïve to move here."

"Decisions, decisions. Hopefully, the right one will appear. As for now, I'm going to take my battered body for a hot tub. Maybe a steamy soak will get the brain juices flowing. Or at least heal our crash wounds. Wanna come?"

"I just hope my bruises will heal before my solo next week. At least I have that to look forward to."

Ryan grinned. "That and a lot of very thick make-up."

We both chuckled at that one. Still, as we sank our sore bodies in the steamy waters, surrounded by the garden-like bliss of tall palms, Hong Kong orchid trees, red, yellow, and white hibiscus flowers, and blooming white plumeria trees, I couldn't let go of my sadness for the people who had died at the hands of a deranged man. Such a terrible loss of brilliant researchers. And, of course, the senseless and tragic losses to their families.

Clearly, Zeno Kühn was a sociopath, not unlike my former bestie. To have Kühn also wind up in Dubai was a piercing reminder of all Lena Verano had put me through.

Chapter Fifty-Three

ANOTHER MOUNTAINSIDE

Zeno Kühn

As I feared, police questioned me at the Dubai airport, but what did they have but a request that I return to the United States to be questioned about a crime I may have committed. I'd done enough legal research to know the UAE wouldn't send me back. So I made it off that *Gottverdammt* island. But where in the *Hölle* am I?

All plans awry, I've spent a week hiding in a bed and board I found in Dubai's old town. The place is small, clean, family-owned, and not a chain. No computers. No credit cards. Just *dirhams* for a bed, access to a bath, and three meals delivered to your room each day.

Sequestering here has given me time to think. I know UAE leaders strive to make their country as successful as Western nations in terms of facilities, tourism, and science. So, although I was fearful about going out, I went to an Internet cafe.

Online, I read about the Al Thuraya Astronomy Center. The website said it was, "...established in 2018 to serve the education and tourism sector, while promoting the Arabic heritage and culture of astronomy. It will provide scientific awareness to the community and enrich it with astronomical activities and events."

The site also said they wanted to establish an astronomy and space research center.

Aha! Perhaps the UAE might like to have a new astrophysicist. But since I can no longer exist as Zeno Kühn, I'll need a new name. Definitely a new face. Fingerprints. New credentials. Those can be had if you have plenty of funds.

Luckily for me, nonprofit observatories are easy targets for an insider who knows which budgets to steal from. Over the years, I've pilfered a good five million euros, invested offshore, of course. And since eighty-five percent of Dubai residents came here from another nation, I should be able to find some helpful people to establish the new me. But I must network carefully.

Who knows? With proper planning and patience, I might become the UAE's star astronomer, even one who can contact HILT or AWE-T with proposals for their very large telescopes.

No one needs to know I helped build both of them. I can silently take pride in that.

Chapter Fifty-Four

MY SIDE OF THE STORY

Lena Verano

Gads. The freaky Dubai Gestapo caught Terry surfing a gay social app, where he stupidly sexted pics of his erect body part to an undercover sting operation. One of the cops set a time to meet Terry at a gay bar but didn't show. So, Terry picked up a different gay guy, another American.

Little did Terry know, but the undercover cop and his buddies would follow the pair and bust in while they were doing the nasty.

Both were arrested, but the other guy was released.

By phone from jail, Terry blubbered, "Since I'm American, being gay isn't a crime for me, so I had no clue the cops would work a sting. The other guy is American too, so the fuckers let us both off on the gay charge. They deported him but charged me with using a VPN to commit a crime. Ain't that splitting hairs?"

Now, I would have had sympathy for Terry — after all, he's my official husband — but he left off a few facts. Police did a background check and found the FBI's extradition requests for the murder of Luca Scarlatti. Terry told them I did it, not him.

Thank you, Terrance. Not only that, but he told them we were in an open marriage. Both things sent the Dubai Gestapo looking for me.

So, while Terry sat in jail, spilling his guts for mercy, police tracked me to my lover Wahid's apartment. They must have used listening devices from outside because they bashed in the door of his apartment while Wahid and I were also doing the dirty.

I screamed, "What the fuck," grabbed the white sheets and sat like a cloud with my stormy hair and black eyes sticking out the top.

One fuming officer with medals on the breast of his beige uniform shook his finger and shouted a bunch of stuff in Arabic, as if I could understand a word of what he said.

Still naked and standing there with a semi-hard, Wahid hollered, "You didn't tell me you were married!"

"I'm sorry, Wahid. My husband is impotent...with me, anyway."

He grabbed a towel in disgust and wrapped it over his black hairy crotch.

Next, an officer with a dark green beret yelled at me in English, "You must not see one another again." Then he and the other officers walked out to the living room.

"They're letting us go?"

Wahid nodded silently. "Apparently."

But dumb me, I didn't get what else was going on.

As Terry said, Dubai is considered lax on *Sharia* law, but the police are hair-splitters. Two unmarried people having consensual sex is okay, but a Muslim man having sex with a married woman is a crime, with a one- or two-year jail sentence. Police could have arrested Wahid that night, and they could have deported me for adultery, but they only gave the two of us warnings. Why? They had other plans for Wahid.

He was so angry, he gave me the silent treatment.

I scrambled out of bed and scurried to the bathroom to dress. When I came out, Wahid was in the living room. Again, he was pouting and refused to look my way. So, I went beside him, stroked his shoulder, and told him, "I couldn't live a life without sex. And you are such a wonderful lover."

Again, he didn't say a word. I grabbed my stuff but couldn't resist a parting shot. "Ya know, your beloved country is a fucking snake pit of preposterous laws and people who pretend to be so righteous and pure but do whatever in the fuck they want as long as they're discreet."

Maybe I shouldn't have said that, but I didn't suspect police would use Wahid later to gain extradition leverage.

The next day at my apartment, a courier delivered a passionate letter from Wahid. "My darling, I'm sorry for the way I treated you. I forgive you for not telling me you are married. I understand why your marriage was an open one. I could be put in jail for this, but I love you and want you to be my wife. I am making arrangements and will contact you in a few days. Do not call, text, or email me until you hear more. If your answer is yes, please rip up this letter and flush it down the toilet. Be patient. I will be planning for our future together."

My God, I stupidly took the bait. I so desperately wanted out. An out of my marriage to Terry and an out of Dubai. Even though this plan did seem a bit easy, I fell for the trap.

Several days later, a courier delivered another letter. "Pack only one bag and bring your papers to the charter aviation terminal at Dubai Airport, 2:00 p.m. I'll have a plane ready. We will be together forever, my darling. I have arranged to keep you safe. Now, tear this and flush."

I threw as many clothes as I could in a carry-on bag, put my IDs and important papers in my purse, then dropped my apartment keys in the drop box by the management office.

They'd figure out Terry and I were gone when the rent didn't get paid.

Outside, I went to an ATM, flagged a taxi, and paid cash. I didn't dare use a credit card. When I got to the general aviation terminal, I went inside, found a seat, and waited.

And waited until an hour had passed. So I got up and checked with a gate attendant, who entered my name on a computer to see if there was a plane reserved for me. As soon as she did, it seemed like the time it takes lightning to strike before six UAE Ministry of the Interior officers swarmed in, cuffed me, and escorted me to a black van, where they slammed me in the back.

Inside, it was so dark I could not see my knees. Talk about panicked. If I could have cried, I would have, but sociopaths don't cry. Do they?

Jostling inside my dark trap, I wondered if I'd just become bait for a prisoner swap. I thought about Marie Donovan, oh hell, the remarried Mrs. Ingles. How pleased she'd be to see me captured.

Dear Marie, always so needy. Hell, she should be grateful I knocked off her arrogant first husband, although I will never know how she could marry that lunk, Ryan Ingles, of all people. The fucker is good-looking, I'll admit, but I'd never allow a penis that has been inside his ex-wife Doreen into any of my orifices.

Gads.

I wonder if Marie or Ryan has noticed that 808 Insiders has gone silent. Terry was the computer guru and brains behind that group page, but we both had laughs stirring angst with our anti-Ballard / Ingles quips.

Chapter Fifty-Five

MISSING: 808 INSIDERS

Marie Ingles

S everal days after Billy Bob and Natalie left, she called to say she'd noticed the 808 Insiders page hadn't posted anything new for quite some time.

"Absolutely zero posts about Jürgen Bergen or Zeno Kühn. But the group members have been posting and asking the admin what he thinks. All to no reply. Very odd."

"Why are you still working on that case, Natalie?"

"You know me. No loose ends. Oh, and I noticed the profile for that snarky AstroExplorer also vanished from MakeFriends."

"That's odd. Do you think 808 Insiders and AstroExplorer were both Zeno Kühn?"

"I don't know. All I can do is send my data to Pua. FBI profilers can take it from there. They have a lot more access than we mere PIs do."

"Definitely. Oh, and how's Billy Bob?"

"A handful. Headaches. Rib pain. And his leg itches. I made him a coat-hanger scratcher to reach inside the cast."

"Oh, bless his heart. Hope the itches stop soon. Please give him our best."

"Will do. And tell Ryan hello for us."

"Natalie, before you go, I want you and Billy Bob to be the first to know. Ryan and I have been talking. We hate to give up on what we call 'our Hawai'i dream,' but with his hope to stay active in law and my hope to be a solo cellist, we've taken a hard look at staying on the Big Island or moving to Oahu. After a lot of thought, we decided to return to the mainland after my solo performance this weekend."

"Are you coming back to Dallas?"

"Sorry, but no. Ryan and I both want another adventure. Living in Hawai'i has been a fantasy come true, except for this horrid Kühn character. But we're not wanted here. We're the dreaded mainlanders that islanders love to hate."

"Keep going, and I'll get on my soapbox about being a Black woman in America."

"Touché. At least I now have a better understanding. From my experiences of being yelled at for crossing a parking lot to being glared at for going to a public park or being glared at by foreign tourists who don't belong here, either, I get your drift. I just wish Hawai'i would find a better way for its melting pot to live together. Setting one race above the others doesn't work, even if their ancestors were the first to arrive. Before we moved here, I thought to myself, we are all Americans."

"But who are Americans but a bunch of immigrants? That's what bothers me as a Black American. I am just as American as someone who got here from France or Italy."

"Natalie, I hear you, louder and clearer than before."

"They say travel is educational."

We both hissed a giggle at that platitude.

"Do you know where you'll go? Make it sexy, so Billy Bob and I will want to visit you."

"Sexy, huh? How about San Francisco? Of course, it's expensive there, but Ryan and I both love the city's vibe of the arts, bay views, and interesting things to do. Ryan can practice big city law while I could audition for the San Francisco Symphony. I'll have my Oahu solo on my resume by then."

"We are sorry to miss your concert, but break a leg, or whatever you say to cellists. Let us know how it goes."

"Thanks. And please send us that wedding date."

"Billy Bob's waffling. But I'll get him corralled. You and Ryan will be the first to know."

Chapter Fifty-Six

TAKING ANOTHER BOW

Marie Ingles

My plans to travel to Oahu alone for my cello solo seemed silly after so much had happened. Even more ridiculous was my expectation to practice daily before the concert. With so much else to do, I didn't dare tell Devon Chua or even Ryan that I hadn't done so. All I could do was hope my training and cello would carry the day.

Ryan was so dutiful about my gig, he traveled with me to Honolulu and even attended both rehearsals. I kept encouraging him to stay at the Halekulani Hotel to get some beach time, but he would hear none of that. Maybe he felt guilty for our recent troubles, or maybe he was simply trying harder. I didn't know which, but it was comforting to have him with me, rather than eyeing Sonya Pruitt's cleavage or listening to Big Mike's pleas to join the Iona Law Firm.

By the time the performance hour arrived at the beautifully appointed Hawai'i Theatre Center, Devon Chua had grilled me with his expectations for the piece.

"As you well know, 'The Swan' is the penultimate movement to *The Carnival of the Animals*, and the only one Saint-Saëns allowed to be performed during his lifetime. We're using it as our opening piece to set the tone for the entire concert. That's why I need you to be superb."

Only just superb?

I certainly felt the pressure, but luckily, Devon was not one of those minor-league conductors who declare that the traditional way of playing a piece wasn't what the composer had in mind. Rarely does this philosophy work for the musicians or the audience, so that's why conductors like those remain in the minor leagues.

Turns out the energetic and handsome Devon had quite a bit of flair, even during rehearsals. His animated and emotional style brought out the best in the orchestra, even the second violins, which provide harmony or texture to the violins, but normally slide by unnoticed. And on the Friday night opener, as I awaited my entry from the wings, Devon strode onto the stage with a self-assured gait.

There was only a smattering of applause, which concerned me, but after he took the podium, he turned to the audience. Speaking in English, he referred the audience to their programs' printed translations of his remarks in *ʻōlelo* Hawaiʻi, Japanese, and Chinese, and described what the audience should expect.

"You've heard this piece at weddings. You've heard it at funerals. You've heard it when Olympic skaters glide. But perhaps you didn't know its name. 'The Swan' is the thirteenth movement of a suite called *The Carnival of the Animals* by Camille Saint-Saëns. The entire work was meant to be light-hearted, even humorous, but 'The Swan' grew legs of its own. The movement was originally scored for one cello accompanied by two pianos, but we have one piano tonight. I predict you will hear 'The Swan' played better this evening than you may ever hear it again, with piano by our resident pianist, Tanaka Akiraku, and cello by

Marie Ingles. Her Guarneri del Gesù cello is the perfect instrument for conveying the work's deep and melodic tones. And now, from the Big Island, please welcome Marie Ingles."

Ryan told me later that the applause was enthusiastic, but I was so nervous when I walked on stage, I didn't hear it. As I sat and arranged my cello between my knees in the ungainly position they must be, I hoped my long, flowing black gown would hide any bruises still present after the Hummer crash.

Once settled, I glanced over at Akiraku and back at Devon, then ventured a smile.

Devon's eyes twinkled, he nodded back, then turned and raised his baton.

I heard the piano intro, then easily drifted into my long-remembered zone. *The Swan* was the first piece my Oregon teacher, Eric LeBeau, and I worked on together. To soothe my nerves, I thought of Eric, not romantically, but how grateful I was to have him care enough to bring out the best in my playing. As I remembered his encouragement and his gentle touch, I became enraptured in the movement. It's a piece that can remind you of a sad love affair or the loss of a friend. But it can also sound like a new love beginning. And with Ryan's and my adventures ahead, I found myself playing the piece slightly toward "hopeful." To me, the swan wasn't dying but slowly paddling toward fresh waters.

As Akiraku and I ended the piece *en même temps*, Devon put his arms to his side, and there was a frightening silence. Had I played it like a 'ditty' and not an emotional movement?

I turned back to see Devon. To my surprise, he had tears in his eyes. He stepped off his podium, took my hand, helped me rise, and then the applause began.

"Thundering," as the islands' arts reviews would describe it the next day.

Take that, Terrance Nichols, with your frequent jabs at me in your column, *Out and In*.

As I nervously took my bows, I wondered if my legs had the stability to carry me off-stage. But when I looked over to the wings, there was my blue-eyed, brown-haired, hunk of a middle linebacker, ready and waiting with open arms to guide me to my dressing room.

Inside, it was bursting with floral bouquets from Ryan, Devon, Billy Bob and Natalie, Ailani and Gilles. The last card I opened from a bouquet of hibiscus and plumeria was signed "With Aloha, Big Mike."

"How kind of him," I said to Ryan. "People like Big Mike make me wonder if we really should leave. He seems to be the true Hawaiian. Earnest, wise, and kindhearted. I wish we could meet more people like him and fewer who want to run us off the islands."

"Mike was here tonight, he and Sonya both. He gave me a *shaka* from the third row."

"And Sonya?"

"I avoided eye contact with her. Didn't want to stir things up. But I am very glad she heard you play. Now she knows why Big Mike thinks you're toro, and she's grocery-store *poke*."

I laughed. "I never thought I'd be happy to be the underbelly of a bluefin tuna."

THAT NIGHT, WE MADE LOVE TO THE CRASHING OCEAN waves outside our open slider door. I didn't even wear a nightie because Ryan didn't want me to.

"I want you straight out of the shower, no makeup, no hairpins, no anything to hide your true self," he said.

That scared me. I've always used my up-do and makeup as a

protective costume that keeps me in control. But after I tucked myself beside him, what developed was a slow, natural lovemaking session, his eyes on me most of the way. We were passionate, yes, but not strained by the fretting and fuming we've had since our move to the Big Island.

No longer a humuhumunukunukuāpuaʻa out of water, Ryan was himself again, athletic, strong, and very male, moving with his waves of pleasure to satisfy his needs as well as his woman's.

Emotionally, I yielded in a way I had not before with Ryan, fully freeing my body and soul for him to do whatever he wanted. At last, I knew I could trust him.

Chapter Fifty-Seven

JUSTICE AND A HUI HOU

Marie Ingles

O
ne very rushed week later, Ryan and I packed up to vacate our Hōkele Kilohana condo. I felt gloomy about leaving our nest. We'd lived on the island for only six months. Were we being too hasty to leave?

As Ryan closed and locked the door, he gave me an empathetic tilt of his head. He may have felt as I did. That we'd lost the game. Played poorly somehow.

I murmured, "Big Mike and Ailani told us the islands either pull you in or push you away. I guess we got pushed."

"The islands taught us what we needed to know. Escaping our high-pressure life in Dallas had tremendous appeal, but the limitations of island life weren't right for us, either."

I took his hand as we walked to the car. "But Hawai'i is such a beautiful place, let's promise to return. I don't want to think our Hawai'i dream is over."

He gave me a sweet peck and smiled. "Next time, we won't be the *haole* transplants. Just the dreaded resort tourists. Maybe for Dallas snobs like us, that's where we belong."

I laughed. "But we now have friends to visit. I plan to stay in touch with Ailani. And Pua Akana too."

"And I'll keep my relationship alive with Big Mike."

My mind quickly wondered if that would open the door to more worry about Sonya. But I coached myself. *I trust Ryan.* So, I told him, "Seems a waste not to use your Hawai'i bar license."

He gave me a knowing look and a sweet smile.

After we got in the car and headed out of the resort entrance, Ryan reached out to pat my hand. "I was going to tell you this after we got on the plane, but I got an email last night from Big Mike. He asked his IT guy to send him Sonya's email—the one you read. After Mike saw how she threatened my bar license and, well, came on to me, Mike told her to find another firm."

"I can't say that makes me sad."

"Me neither. And it leaves things open for casework here. You can ride shotgun as my paralegal."

"Another promotion? Now I feel better about leaving. We don't have to say a sad '*aloha oe*,' Ryan. Instead, we'll say '*a hui hou*.' That means, 'until we see each other again.'"

Ryan did an Arnold Schwarzenegger impression. "Kind of like 'hasta la vista, baby'?"

"Well, not that sarcastic. '*A hui hou*' is more hopeful."

"You and your Hawaiian lingo."

"A Hawaiian is a person of Native Hawaiian descent."

He shook his head and grinned. "I stand corrected. Again."

❁

It took us forty-five minutes to reach the airport and turn in the rental car. After check-in and security, we went to our favorite spot and ordered a sentimental pair of Mai Tais. All around us were travelers from many nations, a rainbow of skin colors and facial shapes. That was what I loved about Hawai'i. The mix. The melting pot. The variety.

Just as we took our first sips, who should tap Ryan on the shoulder but Big Mike Iona.

"Aloha, you two. Or should I say, '*a hui hou*'?"

Ryan and I swiveled our barstools to face him. "All these phrases ... I need to take a class. Maybe when we come back for a case, *Brah*. Is that how I should say it?"

Big Mike chuckled. "Dat right, *Brah*. I just finished a case here, so I'm heading back to Honolulu. After you get settled, I hope we can work together again. You got that license, so let's use it. You handled Nocona and Kekoa's cases so well. And Marie, I hope to see you perform again. Your cello solo, well, I admit I got a few tears."

"Mahalo, Big Mike. You and our friends Ailani and Pua are just some of the people we met who have the true aloha spirit. I wish we'd had time to meet more like you, not the angry people who resented our being here."

"The activists who want to take Hawai'i backward are my state's worst enemy. Please understand. They do not speak for the majority. Most of us, especially on Oahu, want to move beyond the hocus pocus fantasies. Even though you two were *malihini*, you shared your talents here. I hated seeing you mistreated by these nuts on social media."

"This morning, Marie and I felt as if we'd somehow failed."

"Naw, *Brah*. You managed to stop Xeno Kühn from blowing up America's best shot in astronomy. And your team helped prevent huge losses to the islands' economy."

Ryan nodded and grinned. "I guess we did, but Zeno Kuhn's motive was maniacal ambition. As for the anti-astronomy activists, I still don't understand why they're attacking a beneficial science."

"Astronomy was a weak target."

"But the island's restaurants, shops, jobs, and education would suffer if astronomy goes away. All in the name of what? Ancient beliefs that one mountain is, what's the word, *kapu*? Those observatories discover magical things every night, knowledge to protect our planet and understand our place in the universe. This whole mess reminds me of sci-fi movies when the locals refuse to believe the scientists' dire warnings."

Ryan was ranting a bit by the end of his remarks, so I touched his arm to calm him down. "But you've always seen both sides before."

"Before, I was trying to be diplomatic. Trying to fit in here. But more people, especially locals like Big Mike, ought to say what's right and true for today's Hawai'i, instead of bowing and scraping to people who want to take these islands backward. There's plenty of room on Maunakea for all practices. Scientific. And religious."

"Oh, but remember, we have to call it a 'cultural practice,' not a religion, so it doesn't violate the state and U.S. constitutions," Big Mike winked.

Just then, over the loudspeakers, he heard his flight to Honolulu called. "That's me. Better run." He gave Ryan the *braddah* handshake. And then he looked at me and held his muscular arms wide. "May I?"

I slipped off my stool and gave him a warm hug. "Thank you for your aloha spirit, Mike. Please plan a trip to San Francisco. We'd love to host you, wherever we wind up."

"Now, there's a plan. I wish you both *pōmaika'i* — that means 'good fortune.' And a fond *a hui hou*."

"*A hui hou*," Ryan repeated as Big Mike gathered his bag and headed to catch his flight. Then Ryan grinned. "You see, I'm learning to speak ... what did you call it?"

"'Ōlelo Hawai'i, dear."

After we turned our stools back to the bar, a news report flashed across a TV screen above us. The headlines read, "FBI extradites Most Wanted Fugitive. Alleged Dallas murderer arrives from Dubai."

That got our attention. Both of us watched a team of FBI agents escort a handcuffed and chained Lena off a private jet. Camera lights flashed. There was a close-up of Lena's face. She looked haggard. No bright lipstick. No energetic smile. As reporters shouted questions, the agents silently ushered Lena into a black van that sped off. Following that came photos of Luca Scarlatti and Cole, with captions saying Lena "allegedly" had murdered both.

"Allegedly, hah!" I murmured, as relieved tears flooded my eyes. "Justice, finally, not only for killing Luca but my boys' father too."

Although I had mixed feelings after Cole's death, from shock to anger and bitter relief, I will always remember the passion I once felt for him when I was a much younger woman.

Ryan gave me a light hug. "Feeling better now?"

"I feel liberated, but sad that there's so much evil. Lena Verano. Zeno Kühn."

Ryan shrugged somewhat glibly. "Evil keeps defense lawyers like me and Big Mike in business."

I was taken aback. "But where there's murder and death, someone is grieving. Luca Scarlatti was a lecherous jerk, but his family in Italy mourned him. And even though Cole and I weren't happy, I still grieved his loss. We were together for twenty years."

And there I went, sniffing and blubbering into my napkin.

Ryan took my teary face in his hands. "I'm sorry if my remark seemed shallow. I know you loved Cole. Maybe I'm jealous of that. Maybe I don't want you to still love him, still yearn for him. I'm just sorry that I ever caused you to worry."

My answers tumbled out in teary chuckles. "Thank you, Ryan. I'm a far better woman now and with you. And I shouldn't drink Mai Tais during stressful moments."

After we shared a soggy, joyous kiss, the bartender and travel crowd burst into cheers and applause. Someone shouted, "Save it for the mile-high club!" And everybody clapped again.

That embarrassed us. We'd been too inside our shared emotional bubble and unaware we'd made a scene.

Ryan grinned and raised his Mai Tai glass to the crowd. "My wife and I have been privileged to live on this island for six months. We'd like to toast the Hawaiian people. Mahalo for allowing us to enjoy your beautiful home. *A hui* — how did you say that, Marie?"

I choked out, "*A hui hou.*"

All around us, people shouted toasts and cheered.

After the noise settled down, we heard our San Francisco flight call. Ryan leaned over and whispered. "Now, let's get to our next beautiful place, where hopefully, the two of us can kick some ass."

"Spare me the football player lingo! As that old saying goes, 'Ball players never grow old. They just lose their b— '"

Ryan held up a hand. "Don't you dare finish that."

"I was gonna say 'bounce.'"

Ryan grinned. "Billy Bob tells that joke a whole different way."

"And that's why you still call him Nasty."

ACKNOWLEDGMENTS

For this novel especially, the author and publisher are grateful for the input from the following beta readers and fact-checkers:

Laura Aquino — Hawai'i Island
Reed Livingston Bates — Las Vegas, Nevada
Christopher Erickson — Observatory Engineer, Engineering Technical Advisor, Summit Kinetics, Hawai'i Island. (Great input, thanks.)
Jayne Daytor Freeman — Hawai'i Island
Toni Knight — Denver, Colorado
Donna Konie — Hawai'i Island
Jill McElroy — Hawai'i Island
Amy Montanaro — Hawai'i Island
Larry O'Brien — Hawai'i Island (Larry did a stalwart editing job, for which the author is grateful.)
Pam Boyd Roberts — Arlington, Texas (Pam designed the cover for *Ice and Fire*.)
Donald Rudny — Hawai'i Island
Linda Thomas — Santa Fe, New Mexico
Jean Toyama — Honolulu, Hawai'i

GLOSSARY OF TERMS

To give the novel flavor, the author sprinkled non-English-language terms within the story. The author and editors at A.M. Chai literary have done their best to use and define the terms correctly. To submit corrections, please contact the publisher at AMChaiLiterary@gmail.com. We regret any misuse or errors.

French
au naturel — (as used in this story) nude
en même temps — at the same time

German
Ach du liebe zeit — Good heavens!
Ach je — Oh dear; Oh, no!
Autobahn — expressway, highway
Doppelrolle — double or twin
ein Clusterfehler — a cluster fuck
eine ganze Menge — a whole lot
Freunde — friends
Glücklicher umstand — lucky circumstance or break
Gottverdammt — goddamned
Heimatstern — home star
Hölle — Hell
ja sicher — for sure, surely
Kinder — children
Klugscheißers — smart asses, know it all's

Mein Glück — What luck!

Mein Gott — Oh, my God!

Mein Güte — My goodness!

natürlich — naturally

Oh, der Wahnsinn! — Oh, the insanity!

Riesenstein — giant rock

Schweineschnitzel — pork cutlet

Sie sind darauf reingefallen. — They actually fell for it.

Spaetzle — dumplings

verdammt — damn

Verflixt — Darn it!

Waltzer — waltz

Was in aller Welt — What in the world?

Wir hatten glück — We were lucky.

Wundervoll — Wonderful!

ʻŌlelo Hawaiʻi and Hawaiian Pidgin Terms

a hui hou — see you next time

chee-hoo — cheer

dey — Pidgin for "they"

hammajang — all messed up

haole — foreigner

hauʻoli — happy

hoʻohiki — promise

huhū — angry, offended, indignant

ʻāina — land

kahuna — big wig

kamaʻāina — child of the land; local resident

Kiaʻi — a name for the "promise keepers" of Maunakea

kōkua — help

kūpuna — elderly people

lotsʻa kālā — lots of money

mahalo — thank you

makahiki — year

malasadas — donut-like pastries that originated in Portugal

malihini — newcomer

mauna — mountain

mōkākī — mess, chaos, disorder

'Ōlelo Hawai'i — the language of Hawai'i

pōmaika'i — good fortune

rajah — Pidgin for "right" or "got it"

shaka — official Hawai'i state hand gesture, made by extending the thumb and pinky finger while curling the middle three fingers. It represents friendship, understanding, compassion, and solidarity. It can also mean "hang loose," "right on," "thank you," "things are great," or "take it easy."

wahi kapu — sacred place

Portuguese

Preciso de ajuda agora — I need help now

ABOUT THE AUTHOR

Pat Dunlap Evans was born in Michigan but at age two, her family moved to San Antonio and later to Dallas, where she was an age-group swimming champ. At South Oak Cliff High School, Pat was an officer in the renowned Golden Debs drill team and was co-editor of the school newspaper. She won a scholarship to attend Southern Methodist University.

Early marriage and the birth of three children plunged Pat into the world of motherhood until the kids were mature enough for her to complete her bachelor's and master's degrees in English at the University of Missouri, Kansas City. The master's degree program offered an emphasis in creative writing. Pat quickly fell in love with the craft of creating characters, predicaments, and plot twists.

Pat's first husband was a quarterback with the Super Bowl IV-winning Kansas City Chiefs. After the 17-year-long marriage ended, Pat stressed her way as a single mom through a career in advertising, PR, and marketing in Dallas and Austin. A second marriage to Dr. Bill Evans enabled Pat to focus on writing novels. She used her NFL experiences as background in the novel *Out and In*: a mystery-thriller, the first book in the Curious Cellist Series.

Pat and Bill lived on the Big Island of Hawai'i for three years, but the pair eventually returned to the Mainland.

If you enjoyed this novel, Pat requests your ratings on your favorite retail site. No book report is needed. Simply leave as many stars as you like.

To contact the author:
AMChaiLiterary@gmail.com
patdunlapevans.com

A CONVERSATION WITH THE AUTHOR

1. Where did you get the idea for this novel?

My first published novel was an emotional family story, *To Leave a Memory*. After writing it, I wanted to try a page-turner mystery with a female sleuth. I also wanted to use my long-ago experiences as an NFL wife as a fictional backdrop. So, I wrote *Out and In: a mystery-thriller*. The story's ending begged for a sequel. After my husband and I moved to the Big Island in December 2019, I decided to set the sequel there. Months later, the Hawai'i legislature wrangled with activist attempts to remove all astronomical observatories from Maunakea. This would ruin America's leading role in astronomy and damage the island's economy. That's why *Ice and Fire* has astronomy as a backdrop. The issues remain hot buttons. For example, the Thirty Meter Telescope has faced activist opposition that may prevent its completion on Hawai'i Island. This is a great loss, economically and scientifically. Some readers may resent what certain characters say in *Ice and Fire*, but I've tried to present both sides through the characters' voices.

2. Did you always want to become an author?

Not really, although they say you should do the first thing you try to do as a child. For me, that was writing a neighborhood newsletter, but I couldn't type very well at age six. I also tried writing a musical, but again, the typing. Later on, I thought I might be a hairstylist. I was known for cutting a great bob in my dorm at Southern Methodist University.

3. Did you major in creative writing?

My first interests at S.M.U. were Spanish and math. Years later, I majored in P.E. at the University of Missouri, Kansas City. I thought I might coach high school swimming and teach English classes. A freshman comp teacher convinced me to look at an English major, so I signed up for American Literature and Creative Writing. That's where I met Professor James C. McKinley. He was bright, articulate, and funny as hell. I was enthralled by his ability to express every thought I'd ever had. Jim's classes and the friends I made in the English department became my escape from the win-or-lose world of professional football.

4. Was *To Leave a Memory* your first novel?

No. After I got my degrees, I tried to publish an amateurish work based on my years as the wife of a pro football quarterback. Probably because of the commercial aspect, it was almost published. "Almost" was the keyword. After a painful divorce, I had three children to support. I went into public relations and advertising for twenty years and sidelined my creative writing for far too long.

5. What is *To Leave a Memory* about?

It's a poignant tale about a family struggling to move beyond grief. That sounds terribly sad, but there are joyous moments. In fact, there is more humor in *To Leave a Memory* than in *Out and In* or *Ice and Fire*. The elderly hero's grandchildren added many opportunities for humor, and the main characters are intellectuals, so their wit was easier to incorporate. It's difficult to have a lot of humor in suspenseful tales, although I always try to give readers a smile.

ALSO BY THIS AUTHOR

OUT AND IN

The first novel in the Curious Cellist Series, *Out and In* is an emotionally charged mystery in which a lovely quarterback's widow and her legal team battle a psycho murderer, a meddling maven, and a corrupt offshore banker. A good dose of romance and a shocker ending make this an engaging page-turner.

TO LEAVE A MEMORY

If you enjoy "good-cry" films like *On Golden Pond*, check out *To Leave a Memory* — a heartwarming, weepy, and witty novel about a Georgia family that learns to forgive and love again, after a long-ago tragedy.

BACKSTORY

Backstory: Behind the Scenes of a Famous Film-Thriller is an edgy, funny, scary portrait of a Texas single mom's quest to find new love and Hollywood fame as a screenwriter, unaware that a murderer is stalking her and her daughter. Told as "the true story" behind a 1990s award-winning film, the novel weaves a patchwork of emotions, quirky characters, laugh-out-loud scenes, touching relationships, and a shocker ending for readers to unravel with a wry smile.

NOTES

www.ingramcontent.com/pod-product-compliance
Lightning Source LLC
Chambersburg PA
CBHW070546260626
47161CB00002B/520